DECEPTION IN PARADISE

PARADISE SERIES

BOOK 2

DEBORAH BROWN

DECEPTION IN PARADISE
All Rights Reserved
Copyright © 2012 Deborah Brown

ISBN-13: 978-1475013269
Cover: Natasha Brown

PRINTED IN THE UNITED STATES OF AMERICA

DECEPTION IN PARADISE

Chapter One

With my heart in my throat, I pulled to the side of the road, threw open my car door, and reached for my cell phone to call 911. Moments before, a beat-up red Pinto had raced around my Tahoe on the passenger side, almost clipping my front bumper. The car sped into the intersection, weaving and skidding out of control, and smashed into a light pole, where the front end folded like an accordion. The Pinto ricocheted back into the intersection. One of the tires had flipped into the air, landing on the windshield, of the Pinto shattering the glass.

Sitting with cell phone in hand, I breathed a sigh of relief when the door of the Pinto opened; the crazy driver must be okay since he was climbing out. I watched with open-mouthed, wide-eyed shock as Joseph got out of the car, clearly drunk. He weaved back and forth, hunched over, threw up several times, stood up, looked around, and stumbled off. I wondered whose car he'd been driving. His last two or three cars had been impounded, and the court had revoked his driver's license months ago.

Looking around, I realized I was the only

eyewitness. The traffic light and the cars driving by barely looked at the car abandoned in the middle of the street. I ran across the road, looked in the wreckage for other passengers, and breathed a sigh of relief that it was empty. I took a deep breath. No one was paying any attention, as I walked back to my SUV. The police could investigate without my help. If asked, I wouldn't lie for Joseph. I'd learned a long time ago that lying to cops was a good way to end up in jail.

When I first arrived in Tarpon Cove, I didn't know my way around. It didn't take long for me to become the go-to girl for free rides to those with no transportation. In addition to the jail, I'd made several trips to the probation office and managed to get a couple of people to their court hearings on time. Most of them were my tenants. The irony here is that Joseph would call me for a ride home from the jail. My biggest problem was saying no.

* * *

Fall in South Florida is one of the reasons a person lives here year-round. The weather's perfect, warm days with baby blue skies, white fluffy clouds, and cool evenings. An added benefit for me, my shoulder-length red hair isn't the curly, frizzy mess it usually is. In fact, in the fall, it is almost straight, unlike the humid days of summer.

I loved driving through the streets of The Cove, windows down, fresh air in my face. Weekends were a good excuse to take the long way and drive along the Gulf with its white beaches and clear blue water. The Overseas Highway was always stacked going north, with tourists driving back from Key West to Miami and beyond.

I turned the corner onto Cove Road and was surprised to see my gate standing open. A sleek, black two-seater Thunderbird Roadster sat in my driveway. Fab had once again traded for a new sports car. She changed cars like she changed shoes. I parked next to her and pulled my workout bag out of the backseat. As I walked up to the front door, I saw her through the kitchen window, feeding my cat Jazz on the counter.

"Madison, let me explain," Fab said.

I threw my bag on the floor. "What have you done now?"

Fab had become my first friend in The Cove. Jake at the local bar described her as his favorite kind of trouble. Sexy and hard-bodied, she was the kind of woman every man wanted until they discovered that she packed a gun in the front of her bra.

"I took on a small side job," Fab said. "I need your help."

"My help?" Afraid to ask, I put my purse and keys on a bench in the entry and pointed to the man in my living room. "Who's he?"

The stranger sat tied to one of my chairs, a piece of tape across his mouth.

"Calm down. Now, about your help."

I walked into the kitchen. "I'm not helping you with kidnapping. Why can't you ask for favors that are legal?"

"I didn't kidnap him." Fab's blue eyes flashed with annoyance. "He skipped on his bond. He had a court hearing this morning and was a no-show. Brick posted the bail, and he gets his money back if he's in court tomorrow morning."

"I thought you handcuffed people."

"He *is* handcuffed. He jerked around on the chair so much, I thought he'd tip it over and break something. The tape was necessary. He wouldn't stop whining, and I couldn't take it anymore. It was either that or kill him."

"Okay, Fab, I get the part about you doing investigation work for Brick. Why's this man in my house?"

"It's shift change at the sheriff's station. I have another pickup to do. If I take him in now, I'll have to sit there for at least an hour. I thought I'd leave him here, come back and get him, and turn him in before the next shift change."

"What was he arrested for?"

"Dickie was arrested on a sex charge."

"Dickie?" I turned and looked at the man again. "Fab," I said in a loud whisper. "That's Dickie Vanderbilt. He owns Tropical Slumber Funeral Home." Dickie was nice enough, but he had the creepy factor going for him. Maybe because I knew he hung out with dead people all day. "Sex charge? As in sex offender? I don't believe that."

"That's what he was whining about, saying it was all a misunderstanding. They all say the same thing. He should've shown up in court and told his story to the judge. Plus, you don't use Brick for bail money and then skip."

"Where was he when you found him?"

"Slumped over his desk, drunk, at the funeral home."

"Doesn't seem like he skipped anywhere to me. I'm taking off the tape." I walked over to Dickie and started to pull the tape off slowly, while he squirmed around like a two-year-old.

Fab came up behind me. "Stop." She stepped in front of me and ripped the tape off his mouth.

Dickie screamed.

"I know it hurt, but faster is better. Now you two can sit here and talk all you want." Fab grabbed her keys off the counter. "You going to be okay with me leaving him here for a couple of hours?"

The space between my eyes started throbbing, announcing a whale of a headache. "Dickie, I don't know if you remember me, but I'm Madison Westin. We had the funeral for my Aunt Elizabeth at your place."

"Yes, I remember." He sniffed. "The best turnout I ever had."

"Gee, sorry I missed that." Fab rolled her eyes. "So, he can stay?"

"Dickie, can you behave yourself?"

"Yes," he said, tears in his eyes.

"He can stay," I told Fab. "Untie him. Cuff one of his arms to the chair if you have to."

"What if he tries to get away?"

"Then I'll shoot him."

I'd never seen such a big smile on Fab's face. In addition to her hotness, I had no doubt she was crazy.

"I have a Glock in the car," Fab offered.

"Thanks, but I have my own Glock." My brother Brad had given me another gun when I told him I passed an advanced gun safety course. He increased my arsenal to three guns. I was now the proud owner of a Beretta and two Glocks.

"Don't worry; he'll be here when you get back." I turned to Dickie. "Promise me you're not going anywhere."

"I promise. You won't have to shoot me," Dickie said.

"So what's your plan?" I asked Fab.

"I'll be back in a couple of hours to take him off your hands. I want to beat the night shift rush, when they bring in the street girls and dime dealers."

"Can I ask where you're going?"

"No." She hesitated, her eyes fixed on me. "I've got another job from Brick." Brick Famosa owned several high-end car rental businesses in South Florida. In addition, he'd just opened a bail bond business not far from the courthouse. He'd gotten his start with a hole-in-the-wall pawnshop that he turned into a string of locations throughout Florida. If it had to do with cash, high interest rates, and the possibility of getting your ass kicked if you screwed him, then he owned it.

"Another kidnapping?"

She shook her head. "Something different."

"Good thing. Your latest ride only holds one other person, in case you forgot."

"I get my cars from Brick, so when he calls, I have to respond. Besides, the jobs are easy, and it's all about the perks." As a private investigator with dubious clients, Fab rarely separated the line between legal and illegal; in fact, she pushed the line wherever it served her purpose.

I walked Fab to the front door. When I opened it and saw my mother standing there, the blood must have drained from my face. "I wasn't expecting you."

"Really, Madison, you don't look happy to see me. Do you want me to leave?"

"Fab has something to tell you," I blurted.

"Hi, Fab honey. How are you?" Mother asked.

"I'm good. Love your shoes." She pointed to Mother's bright red peep-toe pumps. "I'll let Madison explain. I'm late for a job." She pushed past us and ran out the door.

"Fabiana Merceau!" I yelled. "Get back here!"

Fab waved as she got in her car and peeled out of the driveway.

Chapter Two

"Where's the fire?" Mother asked.

Mother looked good for her sixty years. She wore her short blond hair in a way that framed her face, and could pull the perfect outfit out of her closet in a minute. Mother was trim and tan, dressed in white capri pants and a red sweater set. She looked younger than all her friends. I tried clothes on and changed them until I had a pile on my bed before making a decision.

"I need to explain."

"Really, Madison. Do you plan on making me stand outside?"

"Come in. I'm happy to see you." I hugged her. "You look great."

Mother walked into the kitchen and pulled a bottle of water from the refrigerator. "I know that look. You've done something and you don't want me to find out. I thought we weren't keeping secrets."

"Just remember, this isn't my fault." Whininess must've been contagious because I sounded like Dickie.

Mother walked into the living room. "Hello, Mr. Vanderbilt." She looked at me. "Did someone pass away?"

"Call me Dickie, Mrs. Westin. I prefer Richard, but no one seems to be able to remember."

Mother pointed at Dickie and then glared at me. "Why is he handcuffed to your chair?"

"I'm going to let Dickie tell you."

"I want to hear it from you," she demanded. "Uncuff him. You can't do this."

"I didn't. Fab did. I walked in from my self-defense class, and he was taped and tied up."

"Fab?"

I told Mother everything Fab had told me…well, almost everything. I hit the highlights, making it sound like the complete story.

"What was he arrested for?"

I pointed to Dickie. "You tell her."

"Sex in public," he whispered. Fear written all over his face; the little color he had turned his skin the same color as non-fat milk.

Mother made a snorting noise that I knew was choked-back laughter. She looked at me and raised her eyebrows.

"If convicted, he'll have to register as a sex offender," I said.

Dickie started to cry.

"You're a respected businessman," Mother scolded him. "Why would you do that?"

"You don't understand." He wiped his nose with his long skinny fingers, and then rubbed them on his shirt.

I tossed him the Kleenex box and made a mental note to disinfect anything he touched.

"Raul had broken up with me. I got drunk at Benzo's party. You know Benzo. Someone gets arrested at every one of his parties, but I didn't think it would be me. I was sitting out by his pool, feeling sorry for myself, and before I knew it, my pants were down around my ankles, and honestly, I didn't know the neighbor was watching." He started to cry again.

I stared at my feet and bit my lip. I would not laugh. This was worse than anything my brother Brad or I ever confessed to.

"She called the police," he continued. "I never thought I could get arrested for…well…honestly, I never thought about it."

Mother was a champion in a crisis; she never blinked. "Do you have a lawyer?"

"Tucker Davis."

"You need a better lawyer," I told him. I'd had unpleasant dealings with Tucker in the past and barely survived.

"He's the only lawyer I know. Raul can't find out about any of this, or there won't be any chance that he'll take me back."

"Explain that you were drunk and distraught over the break-up," Mother suggested.

"Would you accept that lame excuse, Mother?"

"Madison, you're not helping." She turned back to Dickie. "Do you mind me asking why you broke up?"

"I'm a sex addict. Raul thinks I haven't taken therapy seriously, and that's why I cheat."

I stared at him. "*A what?*"

"Shh, Madison. It's none of our business."

Now she decides it's none of our business. Did she forget she's the one who asked the question?

"Last week, Raul forgot something at the office. When he walked in, he caught us drunk and bouncing on the desk."

"That's a relationship killer. Trust me. I know," I said.

"Did Dickhead cheat on you?" Mother asked.

Dickhead was a nickname my family gave my ex-husband. Mother never knew half of the insanity of the train wreck that was my marriage. Since moving to Florida, I had moved on, and it felt great.

"Mother, that was a long time ago." I looked at Dickie. "You need to get your sorry act together if you want Raul back."

"I'm sorry, Madison," Dickie said. "I love Raul, and I'm trying to convince him I'll do whatever it takes."

"I'm not the one you need to convince."

"Honey, you should have told me. I would've been there for you." Mother hugged me.

I held up my hand. "Stop, Mother. Good luck, Dickie. If Raul forgives you, he's truly an incredible man." I felt bad for a man I hadn't met. That was a lot of forgiveness to ask of a person.

"This seems bad right now," Mother told Dickie. "But with a good lawyer, I'm sure the charges can be plea bargained. The sex offender thing seems excessive."

"The district attorney is running for office next year. He's taking a hard stance on crime," Dickie said.

"What does Tucker say about your case?" I asked.

"He didn't seem very optimistic."

"You should think about getting someone else," I said.

"I don't know anyone else. Tucker scares me," Dickie admitted. "Can you recommend anyone?"

"I'll call Cruz Campion," I offered. "He's a top criminal lawyer. If anybody can help you, it would be him." I couldn't resist the opportunity to stick it to Tucker Davis.

"What about Tucker?" Dickie asked with a look of fear.

"Trust me, you're better off without Tucker," I said. "Just because he's well known around here doesn't mean anyone would retain his services. Most of his clients are hardcore criminals."

"If you think Mr. Campion's a better lawyer, then I would appreciate you calling him," Dickie said. "Raul and I have worked hard to build our business, and if I ruin it, he'd never forgive me. I finally get that I have to stop being so stupid."

I picked up my cell phone. Cruz told me once that having a good criminal lawyer on speed dial would come in handy; I thought he was arrogant, but it turned out to be a good tip. "This is Madison Westin. If Mr. Campion's not busy, may I speak with him?" I waited on hold only a minute or two.

"What can I do for you, Madison Westin?"

"I have a new client for you. Dickie Vanderbilt, the owner of Tropical Slumber Funeral Home, is in desperate need of a good lawyer. You told me yourself you're the best."

"Yes, I am." He laughed. "Gossip was rampant at the courthouse this morning when he was a no show."

"He's here at my house now. Fab's coming back to turn him into the jail. His current lawyer is Tucker Davis, but I convinced him you're the superstar."

"Put him on the phone."

I handed Dickie the phone. "Here, Cruz wants to talk to you."

I walked into the kitchen, opened a drawer, and helped myself to two aspirin. "Would you like some?" I asked my mother.

"I find Jack cures even my worst headache." She reached in the cupboard for her favorite whiskey. "Madison, did you think about telling Fab, 'No'?"

I shrugged. "Mother, when do I say no?"

Dickie yelled from the living room, "Mr. Campion wants to talk to you, Madison."

"What's the update?" I asked Cruz.

"I'd like him to stay overnight with you," Cruz said. "In the morning, I'll meet him at the courthouse, and he can turn himself in."

"Did Dickie explain why he's at my house?"

"Tell Fab there's a slight change in plans. Tell her to do it for old time's sake, and I'd consider it a personal favor."

"Don't worry. He'll be there."

"I'll fax Tucker and let him know he's out and I'm in." Cruz laughed. "I wish I could be there to see the look on his face when he reads the memo."

Dickie sleeping in my house was my punishment for one-upsmanship of Tucker, but probably the only way to appease Fab. "I'll see you in the morning," I told Cruz. "Okay, Dickie, you can stay tonight. Just know that if you even think of leaving, Fab or I will shoot you."

"I won't be a problem," Dickie promised. "What about Miss Merceau? Do you think she'll agree?"

"I'll take care of Fab," I said with more confidence than I felt.

"You'll take care of Fab how?" she asked, walking in through the French doors from the back patio.

"Did you knock?"

Fab shook her head. "Well?"

"There's been a change of plans. Cruz represents Dickie now. He wants him to stay here overnight and turn himself in in the morning."

"Are you out of your mind?" Fab huffed. "What about Brick?"

"Cruz told me to tell you to do it for old time's sake. I want to hear about that later."

She gave me a slight smile. "I'll have to call Brick." Fab took her cell phone out of her pocket and went out to the patio.

"Tonight or tomorrow, he's turning himself in," I called after her. I turned to Dickie. "Seriously, you can't run. There are too many people sticking their necks out for you."

"Don't worry. He's not going anywhere," Mother said. "I'm spending the night, and you better not even look at the door." She stared Dickie down until he looked away. "I know how to use a gun, too."

Dickie stood and took a step back, bumping into the wall. "All of you are crazy."

Fab returned from the patio. "Brick said you owe him, Madison. I'm staying overnight, so that's three women and three guns," she said to Dickie. "These two would just think about shooting you; I'll do it and think about it later. Tomorrow, you'll be in court if I have to tie you up and drag you."

"Can I lie down?" Dickie asked. "I feel nauseous."

"Upstairs, first door on the right. I hope you feel better."

"I'll be sleeping on the couch in case you get any ideas," Fab yelled.

Chapter Three

Mother lay next to me against a mountain of pillows on my king size bed, staring out the window. My bedroom window gave a great view of the swimming pool and colorful pots of tropical flowers.

"Did you get any sleep?" she asked.

"I tossed and turned mostly. I waited for Dickie to make a run for it and shots to ring out."

"She wouldn't have killed him." Mother patted my leg. "This isn't one of those cases where you can drag him in dead."

"Thanks for making me laugh." She was the kind of mother you wanted in your foxhole.

"Don't get me wrong. While lying here, I thought, 'I'm glad I'm not Fab's mother.' I could see where one of her would be equal to four, maybe five, children. When you and Brad got into trouble, it was for stupid stuff, like throwing Mr. Simm's rock garden in the street."

I gave her my best innocent look. "As I recall, neither one of us copped to that."

"I'm not sure when you two decided I was the town idiot. Honestly, I chose to ignore that the two of you lied. I was embarrassed. We would've had to move. I couldn't have looked at him every day after that."

"Is that why you made us pick up all the rocks?"

"I was happy it turned out to be a hot day, and it took you a few hours to clean up the mess, and proud when you stayed and helped him rearrange the ugly things."

"Trust me, we never thought about touching Mr. Simm's rocks again. Besides, after the rock caper, he crept around always looking out his windows, so we started going the long way around the block to avoid going by his house." We laughed.

"What are your plans for today?" Mother asked.

"I'm going to meet Fab and Dickie at the courthouse and introduce Dickie to Cruz. Cruz was much more confident about the resolution of the case than Tucker."

"I don't want you mixing it up with Tucker," Mother said. "Leave that sleeping dog alone, lest you wake him and he mauls you."

"Good point. After that, I'm going to The Cottages to check on my regulars. I need to make sure nothing happened I don't know about."

"I'm going home. Poker girls are coming to my house tonight. You're always welcome, just bring money." Mother winked. "If you need anything, Coral Gables isn't the end of the earth."

"I'm happy you stayed." I kissed her cheek.

I was surprised and relieved when I went downstairs to find Fab and Dickie had already left, leaving a note on the counter.

* * *

First thing in the morning wasn't the ideal time to find metered parking at the courthouse. The parking lot was my only option, and I got one of the two spaces left on the roof. I raced up the stairs to Superior Court, happy to see that the line for the metal detector was short. I hurried to the elevator and took it to the third floor. When I stepped off, Cruz and Dickie sat on a bench, outside of the courtroom. I breathed a huge sigh of relief.

Fab appeared out of nowhere. "That was nice of you, calling Cruz for him."

"I did it to screw Tucker. Just because his plan to screw me out of The Cottages for his ugly-ass shopping mall failed doesn't mean I've forgotten." I changed the subject. "Were you and Cruz involved?"

"Back when."

I'd have to pry the information out of her. She wasn't one to volunteer. I turned to look at Cruz, admiring the view. He wore slick like a badge of honor. His expensive suit didn't do him the same justice as the well-worn pair of jeans I'd once seen him wear. "Is he as good looking with his clothes off as on?"

"Better."

I forced myself to stop staring. "Nice."

"It's always hot with the high intensity ones." Fab looked Cruz up and down. "It's all fun and games when we're banging out the animal sex. Then, when we're out of bed, fully dressed, it's blah, blah, blah about how I'm a handful."

"And Marco?" Marco was Fab's latest boyfriend, but I hadn't met him yet.

"We haven't tried on a real relationship yet. We live together, but undercover work doesn't leave a lot of at-home time. So far, we haven't had the 'honey, you need to lose the crazy' talk."

"When do I get to meet him?" The subject of Marco had always been off limits.

"When he retires. That's the part about his job I hate. It's dangerous to have friends."

"I had a girlfriend back in South Carolina whose sister worked for the CIA and, by mandate, never discussed her job. I knew it worried her family."

Dickie rushed over. "Thank you, Madison." He threw out his arms in an attempt to hug me.

I jumped back. "Oh." I don't do handshakes or hugs.

Dickie didn't seem to notice that I had stepped away from him. "Cruz was great," he gushed.

"You're not behind bars?" Fab asked.

"Cruz convinced the judge it was all a mix-up due to the lawyer change; my bail got reinstated. Cruz's going to try to get the charges dropped or reduced. He's pretty confident, not like Tucker, who had me doing prison time."

"If Raul doesn't know about any of this, you need to be the one to tell him," I reminded him. "Don't let him hear about it from someone else."

"If you ever need my services, I'll do something special." Dickie waved as he walked away.

Fab and I looked at one another and laughed.

"Are you going to play matchmaker and get Raul and him back together?" Fab smirked.

"It was good advice."

"Did you meet Raul at your aunt's funeral?" Fab asked.

"No, I didn't. I wonder what he's like."

"The whole dead people thing creeps me out." Fab looked at her watch. "I have to go. I'm working another case and have a meeting in an hour."

"Another bail jumper?"

"No, the less I do of those, the better. A friend had a shipment of knock-off purses stolen off a delivery truck."

"Be careful. And if you're paid in purses, I want one."

"Don't worry. If I need backup, I'll call you."

"I wish you wouldn't."

"You so owe me." Fab smiled, tossed her long brown hair, and walked to the stairwell.

I left the courthouse and started down the steps. The fresh air felt good. I was happy I wasn't the one entangled in the legal system. I'd had a couple of brushes with the law since moving to South Florida and found it to be nerve-racking. Just as I reached the top of the stairs, someone grabbed my arm and jerked me around.

"You bitch," Tucker Davis hissed in my face.

He had me trapped on the concrete steps, and I was sure he was going to push me down them.

"You stay out of my business." He tightened his grip. "Vanderbilt was my case, until you stuck your nose in."

I tried not to show fear. "Let me go."

He shook me hard before loosening his grip. "If there weren't so many people around, I'd push your ass down these stairs and be done with you."

I stepped back. "Leave me alone." So much for self-defense class. I was conscious of the steps behind me and afraid that any sudden movement toward him might backfire and have me tumbling backward.

"Just remember this: I get what I want." He turned and walked toward the courthouse doors.

The ferocity of his final statement had me more afraid than angry. He'd never forget or forgive that I'd stood in the way of his development project. I gripped the railing and walked down the stairs.

Chapter Four

I sighed with relief when I turned onto the Overseas Highway, where traffic was light. I needed to go to The Cottages and talk to Joseph. I loved going to the Miami area for shopping and restaurant hopping, but driving was like navigating land mines. There were nothing but nut jobs on the road, honking, cutting off other cars, and waving with their middle finger.

After inheriting The Cottages from Aunt Elizabeth, I took over day-to-day management and my top priority became a makeover of each unit. At first, I did it to keep busy, then I found out I was good at painting, decorating, and searching flea markets for fun pieces. I turned the corner and was pleased to see the palms and tropical flowers planted. I had gone to every nursery in town, tracking down hibiscuses in every color. My initial plan was to do all the planting myself, until reality set in. When I planted my first sago palm, I knew I was in over my head.

A young girl had ridden by on her bicycle. "You don't know what you're doing," she declared.

"Anyone can dig a hole," I shot back, not letting on that the work was harder than I imagined.

"That's a terrible location for that ficus tree. Do you even have a plan?"

"Let me guess. You're the expert." I pointed to her T-shirt, which read "Gardener Girl." She also had a pair of gloves hanging out of her short shorts.

"Without a plan, you're not going to be happy with the overall effect. My name is Jami."

Jami was outspoken and full of energy, and I liked her immediately. I was an easy sell. I had her finish the planting, and then hired her for regular maintenance. She listened to what I wanted in tropical plants and annuals, and I was happy with the finished project.

I swung into a guest parking space. Everything looked quiet. There were five cottages on each side of the driveway and a pool at the opposite end, which overlooked the beach. The new manager Mac was sitting on a bench outside the office, her face upturned as she enjoyed the sunshine.

I remembered the day she tracked me down by the pool. I'd been trying to understand the directions in the new water test kit.

"I heard you're looking for a manager." She picked up the box, took out the vials, and put the chemicals in each one before handing them back to me.

"You have a pool?" I asked.

"No, but I know enough about more than a few things to make me useful and dangerous."

I'd only voiced the thought once or twice about getting a manager, but word that I was hiring had spread through the neighborhood like wildfire. Was I ready to surrender control? The job required someone to be in the office every day. I was a poor choice; I lacked the necessary patience for sitting behind a desk.

Mac and I had sat by the pool and talked. I found her to be direct, a little off center, and someone I'd bet heavily on in a bar fight. She was the opposite of whom I thought I'd hire, but she charmed me, and it turned out she was good with the guests and the regulars. She had a nose for trouble and knew not to rent to the riff-raff. When they came to visit, she kicked them to the curb and made it clear it wouldn't be in their best interest to come back. Kevin Cory, one of the sheriffs who regularly patrolled the neighborhood, had stopped complaining about all the nuisance calls.

I took off my heels, threw them in the back of the car, and traded them for a pair of flip-flops.

Mac Lane was tall, heavy at the hip, and on the high side of forty. She had a look that said she didn't tolerate any shenanigans. She showed off her body in a tight hot-pink top and painted-on jeans; on her feet a pair of lime-green fuzzy slippers with big eyes and a smiley face embroidered on the top. I thought they only existed under her desk; I didn't know she wore them outside.

When I hired her, I found out Mac was short for Macklin and she'd been named after her grandfather.

"Hey, Mac!" I called out. "How are you?"

"You know I'm fine," she said, opening her eyes. "I stopped complaining when I was at the drugstore last night and walked by the lice and wart section. I thought to myself, I don't have either one of those, so it's all good."

I was lice and wart-free, too, so by that standard, it was a great day. "Is Joseph around?"

"His probation officer picked him up this morning."

"Did he leave in cuffs?" I asked.

"No cuffs. All seemed good. He left early, and I don't think he's come back. He tries to sneak around like Creole, but he's terrible at it."

"I'm still annoyed at Creole, moving out and then back in without asking," I said. "It didn't occur to him to find out if he was still welcome? He just left rent money under the office door."

"That one is a tall, cool drink of water," Mac purred.

Creole, lean and lethal, had skin color the same as my caramel latte and kept his dark hair pulled into a ponytail. I knew he carried a gun; I noticed the familiar bulge in the waistband of his well-fitting jeans. Too bad he didn't stay around long enough to exchange a word of conversation. "Yes, I noticed. Have you learned anything about him?"

"As far as I can tell, no one knows anything about him. He's the ideal tenant. He's not around much. Pays on time and never any trouble," Mac said. "All's quiet with the regulars. We're booked on the overnight cottages, starting this weekend and going out a couple of weeks. Word is getting out, and we're getting good feedback."

"Happy to hear that. Seems quiet around here today. How's Miss January?" Miss January was one of my aunt's first tenants.

"She looks like walking death, but I'm beginning to think she'll outlive us all."

Miss January was a bony, frail-looking woman in her forties that looked twice her age. Two years ago, her doctors had told her that her life was over, and she'd be dead any day. She'd given them the figurative finger and lived her days inside of a vodka bottle, taking an occasional break to smoke a cigarette.

"I've had about enough of that cat of hers," Mac said. "I told her yesterday Kitty was dead and needed to be buried."

"No, you didn't," I gasped. I wasn't sure how long Kitty had been dead, but it was long before I took over.

"Oh my lord, girl, she started howling. The most pitiful noise I've ever heard. I couldn't have felt worse. I told her she misunderstood me and the cat was fine just so she'd stop with the noise."

"I don't like that she has a dead cat for a pet, either, but we're going to have to ignore it. I thought about getting her another cat, and then decided I didn't think she could take care of one that was alive. At least Kitty doesn't smell." I looked over at Miss January's cottage; she must have still been asleep because her door was closed. "I don't know who did the stuffing, but they sure as heck didn't do a good job because Kitty's lumpy."

Mac stared at me. "To look at you, you'd never guess the weird people you attract. Anyone else would give them the boot but, oh no, not you."

I stood up. "Don't tell Joseph I want to talk to him. I'd like to surprise him."

"Uh oh, what did he do now?"

I shook my head. "You know I keep my peeps' secrets."

"That's not right. How am I supposed to stay on top of everything?"

"Talk to you later." I waved and started toward my SUV.

"Liam!" I called when I saw him sitting in the barbecue area. I walked over and sat down next to him. "I haven't seen you in a while. How have you been?"

"My mom has a new boyfriend. He's in the *I want to impress you* stage."

"Do you like him?"

"I liked him better when he was married to my aunt," he said, looking down.

"Are you okay?" I brushed his blond hair out of his face. *Married to his aunt*?

"Just downloaded a new game on my phone."

"Who's that?" I nodded toward the sharp-featured wiry man with a pencil-thin mustache, shuffling across the driveway. I'd have been afraid if I ran into him at night.

"Uncle Daddy."

I laughed. "Who?"

"My mom's new boyfriend. That's what he wants me to call him."

"What'd you say?"

"I asked him if he was drunk."

"Bet he didn't like that."

"My mom doesn't make good choices when it comes to men. She's too nice. Her sister kicked him to the curb. I thought when he was coming around, we should be nice to him because he was getting a divorce. I knew it was serious when he and my mom showed up together at my grandmother's house. He's got to go and soon. I'm working on a plan."

"If you need help with that plan, I know someone who can drop-kick his butt into the next state."

"I'll let you know."

"Do you have my number in that fancy phone of yours? Nice, by the way." I fumbled in my purse and pulled out my cell phone. "Here, use my phone to call yourself, and then we'll have each other's numbers."

"You have a cool phone, too." He checked out my programs before handing it back.

"What about Kevin?" Kevin Cory was his uncle and a local sheriff. He could be overprotective, but it was because he loved his sister and nephew.

"I can't do that to my mom. Kev would come over and blow everything out of proportion, and I'd have to go stay with him until my mom got rid of Uncle Daddy. I hate going there for more than a day. Kevin treats me like a baby. The first thing he'd do is take away my phone."

"Why?"

"He thinks twelve is too young for a phone. I think it's because I have a better phone than he does. Besides, my mom needs me; I watch her back. Kev is by the book. All he thinks about is his job and catching criminals."

"If you ever need anything, you can call me anytime, twenty-four hours. This guy I know is big and scary, and no one messes with him."

"Thanks. You're cool."

"You're not bad yourself. Just remember, you've got my number."

"Thanks."

I couldn't resist asking, "So, have you called him Uncle Daddy?"

He rolled his eyes. "Are you kidding?"

"How do you get around it?"

"He's a dumbass. I don't talk to him, but if I have to say something, I look his way and start talking."

I laughed again. I loved that kid.

Chapter Five

I dropped my keys and purse on the bench in the entryway, kicked the front door shut, and walked into the kitchen. Opening the refrigerator, I was happy to see there was still some iced tea. I poured myself a glass, added ice, and started for the living room.

I screamed when I saw a man sitting on my couch. "What in the hell are you doing here?" Jackson Devereaux lounged against the couch cushions, Jazz in his lap and the remote in his hand.

"Honey girl, is that any way to talk to your husband?" he drawled.

"*Ex*-husband. How did you get in here?" I had to admit he looked good. He had on white shorts, showing his long tan legs and bare feet. His usual brown hair was much lighter, evidence he'd been spending a lot of time in the sun. Apparently, he brought his own beer. Anyone walking in would think he lived here.

"I walked in." He smiled, looking me up and down.

I picked up his shoes and threw them at him. "You're a long way from home." He was born and raised in South Carolina with a family that went back several generations. I was sad that his family had become a casualty of the divorce.

He threw his shoes back on the floor. "Maybe not." He picked up his beer and finished it off.

"Are you drunk? You're not making any sense." He looked healthy. Gone was the twitchy, street-junkie look and, along with it, the gray pallor and sunken eyes. He looked more like the man I'd married.

"I'm sober. I've been drug and cigarette-free for a year now. I'm here to check out a business opportunity."

He had a self-assured look on his face that worried me. "Care to elaborate?"

"Real estate deal, like the old days."

"I liked those days," I said. "The first few years were fun ones. We were a successful team then. The market has changed a lot."

Someone pounded on the front door, and it sounded a lot like a cop knock. "Hi, Kevin," I said, opening the door. In or out of his uniform, there was no doubt Kevin Cory was a cop, filling the doorway, official looking. "What's up?"

"We got a report there was a prowler in the neighborhood. I thought I'd stop by, check on you." Kevin walked in and immediately saw Jax. His eyes flashed with annoyance. "Your name, sir?"

"Jackson Devereaux. My friends call me Jax." He used his friendly, good-old-boy smile.

"Kevin, what's going on?" I asked.

Kevin turned and looked at me. "He fits the description of the prowler. I'd like to see some identification," he said to Jax.

"This is my ex-husband. He's a lot of things, but he's not a prowler." Someone in the neighborhood must have seen him, probably my neighbor Mr. Wicker.

Jax picked up the briefcase sitting next to him on the floor, pulled out his driver's license, and handed it to Kevin.

Kevin looked at the license. "I didn't realize that the two of you had gotten back together," he said to me.

"What are you talking about?" I asked.

Kevin handed me the license.

"This isn't possible," I said. The address read 3 Cove Road. "This is a fake."

"I looked it over carefully, Madison, and it doesn't appear to be fake," Kevin informed me.

"It's a crime to give a fraudulent address to get your license. I can arrest you here and now," Kevin told Jax with authority.

"This is my house," Jax said. "I have no intention of going anywhere."

"Jax, what are you up to?" I asked. Kevin had been to my house before, but never on official business. He knew Jax was lying.

"Do you have any proof to back up your claim?" Kevin demanded.

"As a matter of fact, I do." Jax winked at me.

"That's not possible," I mumbled.

I could see Jax's response surprised Kevin as much as it did me. "I want to see the proof now, and if you're wasting my time, I'm arresting you."

Jax handed Kevin a file folder. He looked through the papers and passed them to me. There was legal correspondence from a law firm, his car registration, and voter card, all of it addressed to Jax at my address.

Kevin turned to me. "Madison, if you want him out, there's nothing I can do to help you. He went to a lot of work to get all of the right paperwork to establish that he lives here, and now it's a matter for a judge. You'll have to take him to court and go through a formal eviction."

"I can handle this," I said.

"Watch yourself," Kevin said to Jax. "You so much as jaywalk in this town, and I'll arrest you and lose the paperwork." Kevin motioned toward me. "I want to talk to you in the kitchen."

Out of the corner of my eye, I saw Jax smile and give Kevin the finger.

"Thanks for not arresting him. I don't know what's going on, but I can work it out with him."

"The bottom line is you can't throw him out. It's now a civil case, and a judge has to decide. How long it takes depends on what he wants and how hard he wants to fight. He's a slick bastard, I'll give him that."

"Thanks for the info."

"One more thing, if this doesn't turn out to be as easy as you think, it wouldn't be good for you if he got the shit kicked out of him, or worse, disappeared altogether. You make it clear to your friend Spoon and any of your other questionable friends that he's off limits."

Spoon ran a local auto body repair shop, among other things. Those other things never got discussed. He'd scared me when I first met him, but I soon found out there were two sides to him: the hardened one from his years in prison and the charming one, the one that flirted with my mother. She assured me they only shared an occasional cigar. I knew without a doubt that if I asked Spoon, Jax would disappear, no trace.

"Thanks, Kev. It's not going to come to anything rash. I'm glad you drew the short straw on the prowler call."

"I volunteered when the call came over the radio." He laughed. "Never a dull moment in this neighborhood. Case closed. It looks like our prowler is only going to be a pain in your behind."

"I've been forgetting to ask you, have you heard of a Luc Baptiste? My aunt left an envelope for him, and no one seems to have known him, and I need a forward."

He paused for a beat before answering. "I can ask around, and if I hear anything, I'll let you know."

I was anxious when Kevin walked out with

Jax still sitting on my couch. What was he up to? How much trouble could he be in? I already knew from past experience: a lot.

"What the hell have you done now?"

"You've been a naughty girl." He smirked.

"Just give me a straight answer and tell me what you're up to."

"I wondered where the slot machine went." He pointed to where it sat in the corner, shaking his finger at me.

"All was fine when you thought your worthless cousin stole and pawned the damn thing. You're evading my questions. I want to make something clear right now. This is a new day. What's mine is not yours."

Jax stood and went to the kitchen to get another bottle of beer. "You need to sit down and keep an open mind until I finish."

I put my hands over my face and moaned. "I can't promise."

"It's going to seem worse than it really is," Jax started.

I sighed. "Just blurt it out."

"I got into some trouble in South Carolina, and I needed a lawyer to straighten everything out."

"What kind of trouble?"

"I was on probation for a DUI and violated it by not being at home when my probation officer came by for bed check."

"Okay. How did you manage to involve me?"

"A lawyer contacted me and told me he would

represent me for free, and all I had to do was sue you for half of this house."

"You bastard!"

"I know it sounds bad."

"Really? You think it sounds bad that you're going to help someone take my house. On what grounds?"

"Calm down. I had this idea of how I could get the good lawyer and you keep your house. I promise I'm not going to sue you."

"This sounds like bad news to me," I said.

"Oh, stop. I still love you. I'm not the one who wanted the divorce. You left me." He reached out to touch me.

I pulled away. "Why would a lawyer in South Carolina want half my house? What do you do with that?" I shook my head. "That's if you can jump the hurdle of not ever being on the title."

"Lloyd Samuels, a well-known criminal attorney, offered to make all my problems go away. He assured me he could get my case settled without jail time. I'd like to be able to go home and visit my family without fear of arrest."

"I don't even know Lloyd Samuels. Did he say why he wanted my property?"

"He told me flat out I couldn't ask any questions. It was a take-it-or-leave-it deal."

"Did he at least tell you why he thinks he has a case?"

"According to Samuels, half of this is mine." Jax threw out his arm, encompassing the room.

"He says it's because you didn't disclose this house in the divorce."

"How could I disclose this house in the divorce when I didn't own it?"

"You were on the title long before Elizabeth died and while we were still married."

That caught me by surprise. "Cut to the chase and tell me how you plan to screw your lawyer, who, by your own admission, is a good one, and somehow not end up screwing me."

"I told him I wasn't signing anything until I had proof that my case was closed and I could breathe when I walked by a cop and not expect to get arrested."

I stared at him. "Was this your real estate deal?"

"I was working my way around to giving you the details."

"This is nothing like the old days. We were honest and aboveboard. We got screwed a couple of times, but we didn't do it back." I wanted to help him, and I wanted him gone all in the same emotion.

"Honey girl, I love you. I know you remember how great we were together. We had good times. We could be happy again if you'd give us another chance. Come over here. I'll show you." He held out his arms.

"Don't even suggest that we sleep together. Not going to happen. Mr. Samuels took your word that you'd file suit against me?"

"Once he's negotiated a plea in my case, I'll have to ink his deal before my own."

"Do I get a vote?" I asked.

"This deal is going to work. He can't do anything without me, and I'm not signing a lawsuit."

His reassurance did nothing to calm the foot that had gotten inside my stomach and begun kicking me.

"Come on, Madison. Let's start over."

"No, and don't suggest it again. Do you have keys to my house?"

"You left the French doors unlocked. I need to stay a few days to make it look like I'm doing my part because I know Samuels is keeping tabs on me."

"I want to help you, but it feels like this is going to cost me." I picked up Jazz and started up the stairs. "I'm calling my lawyer in the morning."

"If you change your mind, I put my suitcase in the other bedroom," Jax called.

I stopped on the stairs. "This is not permanent. Don't get too comfortable. I'd hate to have to shoot you, so don't come near my bedroom."

He laughed. "Sweet dreams, honey."

Chapter Six

I lay staring at the ceiling, Jazz snoring next to me, when I heard the doorknob jiggle.

I couldn't believe Jax was trying to get into my bedroom. Scaring him was going to be fun. I slid open the drawer of my nightstand and pulled out a 9-millimeter baby Glock. A birthday gift from Brad.

When I heard a pick inserted into the lock, I knew it wasn't Jax. Besides not knowing how to pick a lock, Jax was too lazy, especially when he could put his foot to the door. The door opened and closed quietly. I snapped on the light and aimed my Glock at the intruder.

"That's not the greeting I was expecting," he said, taking a step forward.

"Stop right there."

"Okay, don't get excited." He watched me intently. "Is the safety on?"

"No. Take off your clothes."

"I don't like this kind of foreplay." He took off his shirt and tossed it on the chair.

"I've had a crappy day, and I'm the one with the gun. Hurry up, or I'll shoot you in the knee so you'll limp the rest of your life."

"You'd go to jail." He kicked off his shoes, then unzipped his pants and let them fall to the floor.

"I don't think so. I have friends." Watching him undress turned me on. I loved everything about him. I pulled my T-shirt over my head and threw it at him. "Come on." I crooked my finger.

He stood silently, all muscle, rock-hard abs and ass. "The gun is a hindrance to hot sex."

"Stop with the excuses." I put my Glock back in the drawer.

He walked to the end of the bed, pulled my leg, and stretched me out underneath him. "I know you've missed me." He took my face in his hands, his lips pressed hard against mine, and he slipped his tongue in my mouth, eager and hungry. He pulled away slightly, studying my face.

"Yes, Zach Lazarro, I've missed you," I whispered. I tried to kiss him, but he wouldn't let me. When I first moved to The Cove, Zach had become my boyfriend to help me keep my more unstable suitors at bay.

He grabbed both my arms and held them against the bed, kissing me unmercifully. He lifted his head, moving down, and his tongue expertly found my left nipple. I groaned and wrapped my legs around his middle to bring him closer.

Zach pulled me up, and I straddled his lap. He entered me quickly, filling me completely. I was aware of nothing but incredible feelings ripping through my body.

Afterward, I rolled off him, and we lay next to each other on the bed. Zach and I had an undefined relationship. We were exclusive, he always came to my rescue, and I returned the favor.

"Is that Dickhead downstairs?" he asked.

"That would be him." Zach always knew what was going on with me. On the occasions I slipped off the radar, he got bossy and protective.

"Kev called and told me about Dickhead being reported as a prowler. Kevin couldn't figure out how he managed to get legitimate paperwork making it look like this was his primary residence and no one found out. He told me he'd have to arrest me if I killed the asshole."

"I got the same warning, but it's not going to come to violence. Jax had some help from a South Carolina lawyer. The paperwork was from his lawyer's law firm and you know anyone can get a driver's license over the counter."

Zach nibbled on my neck. "What does he want?"

"He's in trouble and needs my help." I related everything Jax had told to me.

"Throw him out. Let him figure out his own problems."

"I'm going to get some legal advice of my own in the morning."

"I wonder which one of the neighbors noticed

him lurking around?" Zach asked. "How long has he been in town?"

"No idea. People come and go a lot around here." I rolled on top of him. "Enough about Jax. Our time together is too short. Tell me you're staying."

"I thought we'd have breakfast in the morning."

"We need to take it to the Bakery Café. I don't want any confrontations until I have a plan." I kissed his chest.

"I'm a phone call away if you need me."

"What about want?" I tried to sound sexy, not whiny about how little time we had together.

"I'm a terrible boyfriend. Every waking moment, I concentrate on business. I don't have a lot of time left to be romancing my girl."

"Is the bandage on your leg work-related?"

"One of my clients had a break-in the other night, and Slice and I chased the thief onto the roof. We had him cornered, and I fell over a pipe and took a tumble across the gravel."

"Did he get away?"

"Nobody gets past Slice." He laughed.

Slice was a two-hundred-fifty-pound solid wall of muscle. The scar that ran from his forehead to his collarbone made him look even more menacing. I had watched him pick up Zach's brother Dario with one hand and practically shake his teeth out of his head.

"Isn't the owner of a security company

supposed to take the easy jobs?" I asked. "Not be jumping rooftops in the dark."

"I like the action. Otherwise, my days would consist of ass-kissing the clients."

"At least the guy didn't shoot you."

"That hasn't happened in a while."

"You need to be careful. I have a handful of your IOUs," I reminded him. "It's impossible to collect if you're dead."

"The felons and newly paroled stop asking you out?" he laughed.

"Everyone in town thinks you're my boyfriend, which benefits me."

"Make sure your *ex*-husband knows that. You're good for me. When we're together, I forget what an S.O.B I am."

"We don't have to define our relationship tonight. I'm fine with I save your life, you save mine, and we have sex." I liked what we had, although I wanted more time. "We'll see where it takes us."

"How modern of you." He wrapped his fingers in my red curls and played with my hair.

"Not so much. When I'm done with you, I may shoot you. I've never been good at sharing. What's mine is mine, even if I don't want it anymore." I rubbed against him.

"It's just that little bit of crazy that turns me on." He pulled me on top of him and kissed me hard.

* * *

I opened my eyes, and Zach lay stretched out, his dark blue eyes staring into mine.

"Did you get any sleep?" I asked.

"I didn't come here to sleep." He kissed me. "Dickhead has been up for a while, roaming around. You need to lock up anything valuable. Let's shower, and then I'll go out the back, you out the front, and we'll meet for breakfast."

"Sounds good." That was the way I liked to start a day.

He picked me up and carried me into the shower. "I ran into Cruz yesterday. He told me some bullshit story about you, Fab, and that weirdo Vanderbilt from the funeral home."

"What about client confidentiality?" I glared at him.

"I tried to get the details, and he laughed in my face. You need to stop hanging with Fab, or I'm going to call your mother and convince her Fab isn't a good influence."

I gathered up my hair and put in a clip. "What are you, my father?"

"She's going to get you in trouble with one of her so-called jobs." He pulled me to him, soaping my back. "You're too nice to tell her, 'No'."

"The same way I've been too nice to tell you, 'No'?" Now it was my turn to wash his back.

"Just be careful. You know I like Fab, but she's wild card crazy."

I stepped out of the shower and tossed him a towel. "So noted. I do have a backup plan. If I get in over my head, I'll call you."

He groaned. "I wish I believed that." He tossed his towel on the floor. "I think you'd call Spoon first. Is he still eyeing your mother like a cat does cream?"

"Stop. She says it's all about the cigars. He has a connection to those pencil-thin Cubans she likes."

"I saw Spoon the other day, and he had a stupid smile on his face," he called from the bedroom. "My money says they're banging boots."

I went into the bedroom to rummage through my closet. "That's my mother you're talking about. She doesn't bang boots. Why aren't you warning her about Spoon?"

"Are you kidding?" He arched his eyebrows. "She scares me. Sic your brother on that situation."

"Brad still hasn't gotten over the fact that when he got back from salmon fishing, you and our mother were best buds." Brad would like Zach better if Zach weren't sleeping with his sister, but he was coming around.

"You distract dumb dick, and he won't hear me going down the back stairs. Meet you in ten at the café." Zach kissed me.

Chapter Seven

I pulled into the only parking space in front of the Bakery Café, a restaurant that had quickly become a favorite of mine. You could choose to sit inside or at one of the tables along the sidewalk. In addition to the soups, salads, and sandwiches, it had a dessert bar that I never passed by without a purchase. I always sat outside; it was my favorite place to people watch.

A caramel latte waited for me on the table, a great way to start the day. I slid into a chair next to Zach. I leaned over to give him a kiss. "My favorite," I told him, running my finger through the whipped cream and licking it off.

"Did Dickhead have anything to say?"

"We really didn't talk. I fed Jazz and left." I didn't tell him Jax had wanted to spend the day with me.

"What are you going to do about him?" He wiped the corner of my mouth with his finger.

"I need a lawyer referral. I'll call Whit and see if he has time to see me." Ernest Whitman III was my CPA and one of my Aunt Elizabeth's best friends. "Knowing him, he'll want to meet and get details."

"I know you like him, but give me a day or two. I can get you a name of someone. Besides, he talks too much," Zach said.

"The last thing I want to do is hire a lawyer, but I need to know my legal rights."

The server put omelettes and fresh fruit in front of us. The food looked good, but I would've ordered a cinnamon roll.

"What's on your agenda?" Zach asked.

"I need to swing by The Cottages and chat with Joseph."

Zach shook his head. "What's he done now?"

"He's the master of chaos, and I'm exhausted from it all," I sighed.

"I'll send a couple of boys over, and they'll move him out."

"I want to work it out with him, if I can." Elizabeth had inherited him as a tenant when she bought the place. "What about you?"

"I have a proposal sitting on my desk, waiting for finishing comments before my meeting this afternoon. A potential new client; it would be a large account. Business is good right now and, getting better."

I smiled at him. "Congrats. Lots of new clients lately."

"FYI, Anoui's going to run a check on one Jackson Devereaux. I'm sure you'd like to know what he's really been up to. I know I would."

"Would you ask her to run a check on a Luc Baptiste? I'm trying to track him down. I have an envelope Elizabeth left for him. It's odd that no one knows him."

We stood up. "I'll call you later." He pulled me to him, kissing me hard on the lips. "I like sneaking around," he whispered. He walked me to my SUV and kissed me again before he turned and went to his black Escalade.

"See you later." I waved.

* * *

I took the shortcut down Old Beach Road, and then cut through the alley to Gulf Boulevard, which ran along the Gulf of Mexico. I drove with the windows down, so I could smell the beach air and listen to the waves crash against the sugar-white sand. I loved going that way, even though it was busy with more lights, cars, and pedestrian traffic. I called Whit's office and left a message with his assistant Helena.

I turned the corner to The Cottages. The "No Vacancy" sign glowed bright. The locals had been skeptical it would be nothing more than an over-decorated flophouse, but the renovations had paid off. The outside had also been given a lift with a fresh coat of paint, each unit painted a different color. In addition to the landscaping, I had updated the pool area, turning it into a tropical oasis overlooking the beach once I removed the ugly cedar fence. In the barbeque area, I put in a grill that actually worked and a large concrete table with chairs and benches. With creative advertising, we had a waiting list.

Mac sat outside, talking on her cell. She never missed a chance to catch some sun, and she had on the biggest red and pink bedazzled sunglasses I'd ever seen. Instead of her green slippers, she had on orange flip-flops with matching flowers that almost covered the tops of her feet.

"Hi, Mac."

She finished her call and closed her phone. "Hey, girl. What brings you here? It doesn't start shaking until the afternoon."

"New hair style? You've got yourself a big bouffant." She looked like Dolly Parton. The girls looked in pain, stuffed inside a top a couple of sizes too small.

"You know your hair needs to be as big, if not bigger, than your can," she said straight-faced. "That's just a general rule of thumb. Big up here, big down there." She pointed to her butt.

"I didn't know that." I had learned a lot of interesting things since hiring her. She had the requisite amount of crazy to fit in, plus a generous heart, and she made me laugh.

"I'm here to see Joseph. Is he around?"

"You've got that look in your eye, girl. He's in trouble, isn't he?"

"Joseph and I need to get a few things straight between us." I made it a rule not to gossip about my tenants.

"He's been acting weirder than usual." Mac

glanced at his door. "I think he's hiding out. I heard at Custer's he's in for an ass kickin'!"

"Custer's? You drink at that rat hole?" The one time I had gone there, they had prominently displayed their C-rating sign from the health department that someone had changed to an F.

"Hell, the beer's cheap, and if I have to pee, I go outside."

"That surprises me about Joseph." He loved to start fights between people, then sit back and watch the fireworks. His own participation was not part of his game. "Anything else going on?"

"I made up a survey for our guests. I tell them if they fill it out, I put their name in a bowl, and they could win a prize. They always ask what the prize is, and I make up something different every time."

"The survey's a great idea. How often do you have your non-existent drawing?"

"Once a month," she said with pride.

"We should think of a real prize to be awarded. Restaurant certificate, something extra for return guests. We'll discuss it at our next business meeting."

Her eyebrows went up. "When are we going to start having those?"

I could see she liked my idea. "When we stop our impromptu meetings in the driveway. Then, we'd have more to talk about."

Her smile went away. "I'm not giving up the driveway chats for a meeting where we're stuffed in the office."

"What if I said the meeting would be out by the pool, feet in the water mandatory?"

She nodded. "Now that I like."

I stood up. "I just saw Joseph open his blinds and then close them again. I need to hurry before he sneaks off." I ran over to his door and beat on it with my best cop knock.

"Cut that crap out," he yelled when he opened the door. "You know I hate it when you knock like that. I knew it was you, and it scared me anyway."

"Expecting the cops?" I walked past him and inspected the chair before I sat down. The last time I was there, I sat in something wet, and it made me want to throw my skirt in the garbage. He'd made attempts at cleaning, but he didn't correlate that if you cleaned more, the cockroaches wouldn't fight to get in. He made the exterminator happy.

"No," he grumbled. "Want a beer?"

"It's not even noon."

"I guess that's a 'no'." He walked to the refrigerator, his stoop more pronounced, and pulled out a can of beer. "What's up?" He sat down, kicking up his feet. He had several days of facial hair growth and looked as if he'd been rolling on the ground. It made me wonder if he'd just gotten out of jail again.

"I like you, Joseph."

"But what?" He gripped his beer.

"I'm over the driving drunk thing. I was in the intersection when you crashed. I watched you get out and stumble off."

He refused to make eye contact. "I don't know what you're talking about."

"Don't lie to my face. You're not going to live here, drive drunk, use this place as a stolen car lot, and bring the police and other problems. The place looks great now. We're getting advance reservations, and you're not going to interfere in any way."

"You're overreacting."

"And I look the other way on your use of herbal relief."

"That is prescribed to me for pain."

I didn't have to be a Mensa member to see he was sick. "I don't care if you drink. But don't freakin' drive. It's not your right." I took a breath and calmed down. "I didn't call the police on you last week because no one was hurt. If anyone found out, they'd haul me in, and I'd be charged with a crime. That was my one and only freebie. Get your act together now, or I'll have your stuff moved out."

"That's illegal."

"I dare you to call the cops." I stared him down.

"I like living here. Elizabeth told me I'd always have a place to live."

"Stop whining. I'm immune to the Elizabeth card. It's not like I'm asking you to give up drinking and smoking cigarettes and pot. Stop committing felonies. You need to remember, just because I don't actually see it happen only means that five minutes later my phone will ring with the news."

"Okay, okay, no more driving."

"Why is one ankle more swollen than the other? I thought you were getting better with the new medication." He looked as if he was beating down Death's door. I was used to his skin always being different colors and none of them attractive. His face was an ash-gray at the moment, and that couldn't be good.

"The medications helped a lot." He lifted his pant leg. "Do you like my new jewelry?"

"When were you fitted with an ankle monitor?"

"A couple of days ago. My probation officer showed up, just like you did, tired of my bullshit."

"More like tired of you jerking him around, reminding him of your veteran connection."

"That damn accident. The only reason I'm not in jail is because he couldn't prove I was behind the wheel. Thank heaven, the camera at the intersection has never worked." He sucked down half his beer; his hand shook. "They ran the plates. The car was registered to Billy Kyle. He told the cops I stole it. He knew I ran out of my meds and used his car to score an ounce. He got scared, didn't want them to think he crashed the car. He's a felon, too, and it's my word against his. I think the cops believed Billy, but they can't prove a case against me."

"Where humans failed, the anklet will keep you in line. I'm surprised you both didn't get arrested."

"I had a choice: wear this or go to jail. I'm on a short leash. I have to call the monitor service if I leave the property."

"Stop looking so hangdog. What about the damage to Billy's car?"

"He reported it stolen so the insurance company would pay."

"You and your friend Billy are skating on illegal thin ice. I'll be sad if you end up in jail again."

"I've always told you, you're way too nice for your own good." He burped.

I stood and headed to the door. "See you later."

"Has that hot friend of yours gotten rid of her boyfriend?" He smiled, showing smoke-stained and missing teeth.

"Fab?"

"She's smokin'."

That was suicidal nonsense on his part. "She's still with the same boyfriend. You'd better be careful. She'll kick your ass, and if she's having a bad day, she might shoot you."

"It might be worth it."

"Trust me. It won't be." I closed his door. I

wondered what he'd say if I told him Fab thought he was a sneaky, repulsive liar.

As I walked down the driveway, my cell phone rang.

"Madison, it's Whit. What's up?"

"I need a referral for an attorney who can tell me what my rights are before a civil lawsuit is filed."

"Against you?" He sounded more interested than surprised.

"Yes. Can you recommend someone?"

* * *

I walked into the offices of Ernest Whitman and headed straight for the snack bowl. I pulled out a one-hundred-calorie bag of Oreos, which meant there were only a few cookies. Instead of taking two bags, I chose a miniature candy bar. Holding the sugar in my hand made me feel less anxious. I grabbed a bottle of water and headed to his office. He'd told me that everyone had left for the day and to come on back.

"Have a seat, Miss Madison, and tell me what you've gotten yourself into this time." Whit laughed.

I told him all about Jax's scam-plan and didn't leave out any details.

"He's got a pair. I'll give him that. You're sure he hasn't signed anything?" Whit asked.

"He says he hasn't. How do I protect myself?"

"I'll call Chet Mitchell, a real estate lawyer, when he gets back to town. Right now, there's nothing that you can do because no suit's been filed. I'm almost certain there's an end run you can play on the lawyer. Jax will end up scamming the lawyer twice, and it will leave you out of it all together. He ends up holding the bag and reaping the wrath." Whit slapped his hand on the desk. "I like that."

"What does this entail?" I didn't share in the humor.

"Chet needs to be involved; he's the one with the expertise. I'm certain this situation can be handled as long as you're getting the inside information, and you stay one-step ahead. I honestly don't think Jax has a valid claim, and without him, the shyster lawyer certainly doesn't have one."

"I don't like any of this, but at least I know what's coming."

"Don't worry. Just make sure that if there's any movement in this case, you're the first to know. I'll get with Chet the day he gets back, and he'll have definitive answers for you," Whit promised.

I smiled. "I'll take you to dinner when this is all over."

Chapter Eight

Aunt Elizabeth's house is a comfortable, white two-story Key West style, with a wraparound porch on the second story. It is located on the outskirts of Tarpon Cove, on an unmarked side road off the main highway. The street sign had been stolen several times, and the city stopped replacing it years ago. My brother and I had spent all of our summers with Elizabeth. While Brad spent every second swimming in the Gulf, my aunt and I had spent our time planting every tropical variety of hibiscus that we could find. My idea had been to use seashells as mulch. I'd loved my aunt's house as a child, and with my personal stamp on it, it had become my haven. Elizabeth would have been very pleased.

I pulled my SUV next to Fab's Thunderbird. I peeked in the kitchen window and saw Fab sitting at the counter with paperwork in front of her. There was no sign of Jax.

"Honey, I'm home," I called, opening the front door. As long as Jax was there, I didn't dare leave my purse and keys in their usual place on the bench in the entryway. I was afraid he'd take my keys and drive off in my SUV.

Once when we were married, he loaned my Tahoe out to repay a drug bill. No amount of threats was enough to get it back from the girl. One week later, it just showed up in the driveway. It turned out she was a single mother who lived with her mother, and they supplemented their income by dealing. I heard later that she used the money to take her kids and mother to Disney World. The only reason I could come up with for not calling the police was that I wasn't sure I wouldn't end up in jail along with everyone else. I had been in over my head. I didn't know anything about enabling and addictions.

"I'm here in the living room," Jax yelled.

I walked into the kitchen. "I wasn't talking to you. I meant Fab."

"Is that why you've been acting so weird? You've gone lesbian? I didn't think a divorce would have you jumping sides. Mr. Sir misses you."

"Mr. Sir?" Fab whispered.

"He named his…you know," I told her.

She snickered.

I pointed at Jazz. "If he pukes up all that chicken you're feeding him, I'm going to save it for you to clean up."

"Bad day, huh?"

I gestured toward where Jax sat in the living room. "I'm worried how this is going to turn out."

"I can hear you," he yelled.

"Then, don't listen," I yelled back. "I have every right to be worried about this scheme of yours."

"I'm going out. Get in a better mood by the time I get back." He slammed the door.

"You didn't tell me he's cute."

"When he's sober and not using, he's funny, hard-working, and generally great to be around. But when the drugs and alcohol took over, each day just got worse."

"He told me about his half-owner scheme. Seemed sure of himself," Fab related.

"I need to speak with a lawyer, get answers to some questions, and find out if this lawyer of his has a legitimate case. Whit doesn't think so, and I hope he's right."

"If you want him out, just say the word." Fab flexed her arm muscle.

"It's only for a few days, and I need to remind him of that. I need to be in the loop of any new information, not the last to know. What's up with you?"

"Brick wasn't happy with the way things went down with Dickie. He calmed down when I assured him there'd be no more no-shows. So he's fine with everything."

"I'm hungry." I opened the refrigerator. "How about dinner?"

"We don't have time for that."

"What?"

"I need you to be backup."

"Is it illegal?" I wanted a margarita on the rocks and some Mexican food.

"Do I have to remind you that you owe me from even before Dickie?"

"Just tell me what you want."

"My friend Gracee designs jewelry and sells her pieces to high-end boutiques. Her work appears in fashion magazines and on the catwalks in fashion shows. Three weeks ago, at a photo shoot, a blue diamond necklace that was on loan went missing. Zoe was the model at the shoot, and two days ago, Gracee saw a picture of her in a tabloid wearing guess what around her neck at an opening."

I gasped. "Zoe stole the necklace?"

"Get this. Gracee called and asked her to return the necklace, and she said it belonged to another designer. I'm going to go and retrieve it. I just need you to sit in the lobby of her condo and call me if she shows up."

"You're going to break in and steal the necklace?"

Fab narrowed her eyes. "I'm only returning it to its rightful owner."

"Why doesn't Gracee call the police?"

"Zoe's a train wreck, and Gracee doesn't want the negative publicity. Contrary to what you hear, some publicity is just bad all around. If the police become involved, they'll keep the necklace until it goes to trial, which could be months. Who knows what condition it'll come back in?"

"If we get caught, we'll be arrested," I pointed out.

"You're such a worrier. If Zoe comes back, you call me and then leave. I'll call you when I exit the building, and you pick me up."

I shook my head. "When are we leaving?"

"Now. We have to drive up to Miami. I'll stop and get you a hamburger on the way."

"I'll change." I started for the stairs.

"No need. Great dress. You'll totally fit in with the South Beach crowd."

"It would be terrible if I didn't fit in," I grumbled. I slammed the front door behind us, a childish gesture, but I didn't care.

"This is my first ride in the Thunderbird," I said, opening the car door. "Nice. You've never said exactly what you do for Brick."

"This and that."

What the hell kind of answer was that? My guess was that it was her nice way of saying, "Mind your own business."

"Joseph asked about you today," I said.

"Where did you see him?"

"Where do you think? The Cottages."

"You seem to like being a property owner," Fab said.

"I love it. I'm there every day. Between The Cottages and the house, I've got a full-time job."

"What do you want to eat?"

"Nothing. You're driving so fast, I'm afraid I

might get sick." My fingers gripped the armrest so hard my knuckles hurt.

"Oh, for heaven's sake, I'm only twenty miles over the speed limit."

"Anyway, Joseph's still interested. He's waiting for you and Marco to break up."

"You can tell him that if he and I were stranded on a deserted island, I'd kill him."

"He's in love."

"Stop laughing. I'd almost rather date Dickie, and that's not going to happen, either."

Fab exited the freeway and flew down Collins Avenue, weaving in and out of traffic. There was no moon out, and the ocean was pitch black, but I could hear the water lapping the shore.

"Where does Zoe live?" I asked.

"She lives a few blocks down in a penthouse on the water."

High-rise million dollar condominium complexes lined the beach, each with its own spectacular view.

"She can afford to live in this neighborhood and steals jewelry? What's up with that?"

"Zoe takes what Zoe wants. She has a bad reputation. If you want your clothes, jewelry, and etcetera back after a shoot or an appearance with her, you'd better send a bodyguard. Once she leaves with your stuff, you don't get it back. She's immune to threats." Fab looked over at me. "You've got that look on your face. What?"

"Zach can't find out about this. We have so

little time together; I don't want to waste it having to listen to a lecture about you."

"He just worries about you. He's right about one thing, though. I'm not a good influence."

"He threatened to tell my mother. Does he really need to be reminded I'm a grown woman, and I'll pick and choose my friends, thank you?"

"If anyone asks, I didn't tell you this…"

I sighed. "What did he say to you?"

"Not him, your mother. She told me if I ever got you into trouble with my *shenanigans*, she would hunt me down and kick my ass. She added if you ever got hurt, she'd have to kill me."

"Wow."

"The way she looked at me, I admit I stepped back."

"Okay, so we don't tell her anything, either. But if we ever get caught, we'll need her for bail."

"I'd call Arlo the bookie before your mother," Fab said. "The drawback there is he wants repayment in sex."

"What's he look like?"

"He's a cross between Dickie and Joseph."

I conjured up that image and laughed. "You're better off calling my mother. I'll protect you."

"Don't get me wrong. I like Madeline, but quite frankly, she scares me." Fab pulled into a parking space in front of a towering glass condominium that sat steps from the white sands of Miami Beach.

"So this is where the fabulous Zoe lives?" I thought the condos were a blight on the shoreline, no matter how expensive they were.

"This is it." Fab tossed me the keys. "If Zoe comes back, you call me. If the police show up, call me. I see your name on my screen, and I'm out of there. Once I'm outside, I'll call you and tell you where to pick me up."

Fab slid her lock pick out of the pocket of her black pants as we approached the building. She popped open the lobby door in less than ten seconds. "I'll meet you here in the lobby if nothing goes wrong. Pretend you're on the phone, and no one will bother you. In these places, the only time you see someone is if they're coming or going."

"I'll be fine. Hurry up and be careful." I sat on one of the couches, running my hand over the soft white leather and keeping one eye on the driveway.

I walked over to the floor to ceiling windows and looked out at the pool area. The water was inviting, Caribbean blue with a dozen floating lights, and running lights in the trees. The state-of-the-art gym had a view of the beach to inspire one's workout. I was all nerves and fidgety; sitting was out of the question. I paced back and forth.

When I heard the elevator bell, I jumped into the nearest chair and quickly put my phone to my ear.

A security guard stepped out and looked my way. "Do you live here?" His nametag read "Al."

I tried to stay calm. "I'm waiting for someone."

"Guests can't hang out in the lobby. Which resident are you visiting?"

The elevator bell rang again. I jumped up to distract Al from looking toward the door. "Salvatore Luciana." He was a notorious badass who constantly made the gossip columns. I caught a glimpse of Fab's back disappearing in the opposite direction.

The name caught Al by surprise. "He lives in the pink and green monstrosity about a block down." Al shook his head.

"No wonder he's late. I knew I should've written down the address."

"How did you get in here?"

"Someone was leaving, and they held the door for me." I smiled.

"That's trespassing, but I'll let it go this time," he said, staring at my cleavage. "Be careful."

I breathed a sigh of relief and walked calmly toward the car.

"Let's get out of here," Fab said. "What did the rental guard want?"

"Just weeding out the riff-raff." I closed the car door. "Did you get it?"

She unzipped her jacket and pulled out a black velvet necklace box. "She had it sitting out on her dresser, lid open." Fab snapped open her phone and punched in a number. "Gracee, I got it." Fab was smiling at the phone. "I'm with my friend Madison. We should be there in about an hour, depending on traffic." She snapped her phone closed. "I should've asked you before committing to going to Gracee's."

"I bill by the hour," I said.

"Gracee started crying when I told her. She had money and time invested in this piece, and she wasn't sure she'd ever get it back."

"I'm excited to meet her. I've made a few pieces of jewelry myself. I haven't had any time since I moved here, but I still have my tools and boxes of supplies. I found a great table at the flea market last weekend that I'm planning to refinish and put in my office. I'll use it for future projects."

"You never cease to amaze me. You're going to have to show me something you've done."

* * *

We pulled up to a small 1920s bungalow house, painted white, window boxes filled with red, white, and pink annuals. A vintage pink glider rocker sat on the porch, along with two mismatched white metal chairs.

Gracee opened the front door as we walked up

the steps. She threw her arms around Fab. "You're so fab-ulous." Gracee was small and delicate, with her thick brown curly hair tied back in a ponytail. She was barefoot and had the arms and legs of her oversized sweats rolled up.

Fab held out the necklace box and snapped open the lid; it was a show-stopping piece. The focal stone was a large blue diamond with three strands of blue and white diamonds up each side, the intricate gold clasp, a detailed, one-of-a-kind creation.

"I want you to meet Madison. She was my lookout."

"Come in," Gracee said, pulling Fab inside. "Thank you both. Zoe never intended to return the necklace. She said as much the last time I talked to her. I told her I would never again loan any of my pieces to a shoot or anything else she was a part of."

"What did she say?" Fab asked.

"She laughed at me."

"Bitch. I'm glad I could help out," Fab said.

"Hi, there," I said to a four-foot-tall white dog who walked up beside me. The dog would easily tip the scales at one hundred pounds. "Is he a Great Dane?" He nudged my hand when I stopped petting him.

"That's Beck. He's a Pit Bull-Great Dane mix and the sweetest dog ever. I rescued him as a puppy from a guy down the street. One day, I watched Beck's owner put a cigarette out on his back, and I decided he'd never spend another night with that bastard. That night, I coaxed Beck out of the yard, and he had burn marks all over him, underfed, and dehydrated. I kept him inside and nursed his wounds. His old owner never seemed to notice. Then about a month later, the guy moved, one step ahead of the police who showed up looking for him."

I walked over to a sideboard that held several of Gracee's pieces on pedestals. She was truly an artist, and I could see why her jewelry was in high demand. I had to force myself not to touch anything. I really wanted to try on the blue-green pearl necklace with the abalone focal piece so I could brag I'd once worn a Gracee design.

"Those pieces were just delivered back to me from the Palm Beach magazine shoot," Gracee said.

"They're beautiful." A beach collection, each piece used shells, pearls, and mother-of-pearl.

"I have an early morning pickup at the airport." Fab hugged Gracee. "I'm body-guarding Israel, the newest Latin singing sensation, for the next couple of days."

"Thank you both again. If there's anything I can do for either of you, just let me know." Gracee hugged me.

"That's what I like to hear," Fab said. "You owe me."

We laughed.

"Nice to meet you," I told Gracee.

We left and got into the Thunderbird, where I pulled my seatbelt tight. Most of the way home, Fab drove as if she were in the final NASCAR race of the season at Homestead. I was an avid fan and loved watching fast cars turn left, but I wanted nothing to do with riding in them.

"What are you going to do about Jax?" Fab asked.

"I want to help him, but not at my expense. I'm not losing my house for him or anyone else. I don't like his chances of coming out on the winning end of screwing a lawyer."

"What happened between you two? If you don't mind me asking."

"Alcohol and drugs. The breakup still feels like one of my biggest failures. I didn't see it happening, maybe because I had no experience and never knew what to look for."

"He traded down, in my opinion," Fab said.

"Eventually, he drank more than he worked. He brought home equally drunken friends, who soothed his tortured soul and helped stave off his self-doubt. I had much less lofty opinions of them than he did. Frankly, most of them scared me. The fun and the romance became non-existent. Our lifestyle turned downright seedy."

Fab finally stopped tailgating the car in front of us and pulled around. "What was the final straw?"

"One day I came home and caught him in a drunken sex frenzy with an unwashed, alcoholic woman he kept around to boost his flagging self-confidence. She was a more *sympathetic muse*, he insisted."

"Oh, brother."

"But of course, he was adamant that he was the wronged party. If I'd been more supportive, not so demanding, not so critical…you get the drift. It was a relief when I made the decision to pack my things and run as far away as I could get. Whenever I think back on those days, I can't place myself in that situation. It's so alien to my life now; it seems a terrible nightmare that someone else dreamed."

"I don't know what to say." Fab reached over and patted my shoulder.

"Thank you for listening to all of that. You're the first person I've confided in about the disintegration of my marriage. I didn't know anything about addiction or my part in it all."

"If I can be of any help, just ask."

"Back atcha. You being someone I trust is the best gift of all. We've come a long way since you told me you didn't have girlfriends and didn't want any."

"It's worked out better than I thought it would," Fab laughed.

"I know it was all about my knock-off shoe connection."

"I love that store. There's nothing a new pair of shoes can't cure."

The house was dark when we pulled up. I

hadn't seen Jax since he walked out saying he'd be right back. "Thanks, Fab." I got out of the car. "Let's do this again. Come by when you finish up with Israel."

"I'll go in with you."

"Not necessary." I waved at her and walked inside the house.

Chapter Nine

The phone rang in the middle of the night, which was never good news. That sickening sensation hit me before I even knew who was on the other end. I didn't recognize the number, but it was local.

"Hello," I said my voice thick with sleep.

Jazz meowed in my face, telling me, "It's not time to get up. It's still dark outside."

"Madison Westin? This is Captain Burton from the Coast Guard. I'm calling to inform you that your boat was in an accident tonight."

"My boat? Is my brother okay?"

"He said he was your husband, Jackson Devereaux."

"Is he okay?" How had Jax gotten the keys to our boat? A better question, how had he found out I had one?

"No, ma'am. We have a man overboard, Pavel Klaus, and we're searching the water now. Your husband's on his way to the county jail to be booked for suspicion of BUI."

"Is there anything I can do?"

"This is a notification call. We'll release your

boat once the investigation is finished. Call my office, and we'll let you know when you can pick it up."

I hung up the phone, taking small breaths to calm the tight knot in my stomach. Jax hadn't been around in a few days; I figured he'd found new friends to bother. A missing man? If Jax was drunk, what would that mean?

"What am I going to do, Jazz? Jax just dropped a bomb into the middle of my life." I held Jazz until he meowed to let me know he'd had enough.

I called the jail. After a long wait, a woman answered in booking. She politely informed me that Jax was in custody until a bond could be posted. Shell-shocked, I wondered what to do next. I realized I'd drifted off when my phone rang again.

"You're receiving a collect call from an inmate at the county jail. Will you accept the charges?" an anonymous voice asked. I accepted the call at three dollars a minute.

"Madison, please help me," Jax said. "I'll be out of jail in about an hour. Can you come pick me up? I don't have anyone but you."

"What in the hell happened?"

"I can explain it all to you when I see you." His desperation came through loud and clear.

"I go along with some hair-brained scheme, and now this!" I yelled. Jax had been to jail before and, as much as he hated it, he was back to doing the same thing he went to jail for the last time.

"Please, you know I don't have anyone else to call."

I sighed. "All right."

"Thank you."

* * *

My previous trips to the jail had consisted of me making pickups in the front. It was my first time behind the twelve-foot chain link fence. I found it intimidating to park and walk inside the barbed-wire fenced compound. There were several tall cement buildings with postage-sized windows at regular intervals. After the guard searched me for weapons, he pointed to the left. When I walked into the lobby, I was surprised at how many people filled the chairs at a time when even the bars had closed.

The receptionist barely looked at me as she directed me to a plastic chair.

"How long until he's released?" I asked.

"When you see him walk out of that door over there." She pointed. "You'll know."

I sat in an uncomfortable plastic chair, trying to stay calm and disengaged from my surroundings. The minutes slowly ticked into two hours. I sat staring at the door opening and closing, men and women walking out, free at last, for the moment anyway. I noticed a long delay between releases, which had me wondering if one person worked the busy night shift. Finally, the door opened, and Jax walked out. He looked hung-over, his clothes dirty as if he'd been wearing them for days.

He threw his arms around me and hugged me. "Thank you, Madison." He started to cry.

"Oh, shut up. I want to hear what happened." I'd decided a long time ago that his crying was pure manipulation.

"I'll tell you everything after we get out of here."

He held my hand tightly as we walked in silence back to my SUV. The morning was chilly, the first rays of light beginning to show in the sky. I breathed easier as we passed the guard shack and the end of the barbed-wire fence, saying a silent thank you that I wasn't forced to stay. I wanted to go home and shower off the effects of that dreary place.

"Start talking," I demanded when I pulled out of the parking lot.

"We were out on the water having a great time when one of the girls screamed that Pavel was no longer on the boat. I immediately turned the boat around, and we got out the spotlight and searched the water. I radioed the Coast Guard and continued to search."

"Who's Pavel?"

"I don't know. I met him for the first time a few hours ago. He was a friend of a friend."

"How did you find out I had a boat? What gave you the right to take the boat in the first place? Start from the beginning, with how you found the keys and then the boat."

"I found the keys hanging on the key rack in the kitchen."

"Why is it that you think if you find something, it's yours?"

"I don't want to fight. I'm worried about Pavel."

"Back to the keys."

"I saw the plastic buoy key ring; I knew they were boat keys. I know you keep notes in your phone book, so I found the number for the storage place and called them to let them know I would be taking out the boat."

"We had it in dry storage. They just gave it to you?"

"Well, they gave it to Brad."

"You used Brad's name? You'd better be long gone when he finds out." Jax and Brad had been friends during the good years of our marriage. When things started to crumble, it created distance between my family and me. Being a supportive brother, Brad blamed everything on Jax. Being married to someone my family didn't like was difficult, and Jax gave them good reason to feel that way.

"I had the boat out on the water all day, drinking beer and getting some sun. I cruised through the channels and took it out into open water, then went over to one of the islands and did some swimming."

"The Coast Guard guy said you were drunk."

"I had a few beers," Jax said. "Besides what does he know? I didn't blow."

"Who was with you?"

"A couple of friends."

"You have friends here?" How long had he been lurking around, managing to stay out of sight?

"You know how I am. I've been hanging at the Jumpin' Croc. The beer's cheap; the locals drink there. I made some friends at Causeway Beach. People like me. Everyone wants to hang with the Jax Man."

I knew the kind of people he liked to hang out with. He could go anywhere and ferret out the bottom feeders; stranger and best friend were synonymous with him.

"Who exactly was on the boat?" I demanded.

He hesitated. "Pavel and his girlfriend and another couple."

"Who in the hell are these people?"

"Do you want to know what happened?"

I shook my head. "Go ahead."

"I was getting ready to put the boat away for the day, and one of the girls who'd been on it earlier called me."

"Does she have a name?"

"Mary or something like that."

"Let's call her something," I said with disgust.

He never forgot names. What was he hiding?

Anger flashed across his face, a familiar look. "*Mary* had a couple of friends, Pavel and Kym, that she thought could use a boat ride. I swung by the dock and picked up the three of them and Mary's boyfriend."

"When was this?"

"It was almost dark."

"If it was that late, what were you going to do with the boat?" I asked. "Key Marina is closed."

"I've been sleeping on it."

"What?" I shrieked, wanting to slap him.

"Do you want to hear what happened or not?"

I glared at him.

"The two girls and Pavel sat on top of the back seat. All of a sudden, Kym, Pavel's girlfriend, yelled 'Where's Pavel?' I turned around, and he was gone. I searched the water, called the Coast Guard, and reported Pavel overboard. The Coast Guard, Fish and Wildlife, and Sheriff boats showed up in about ten minutes. They had me show them where we noticed him missing and then backtrack." Jax took a long drink from my bottled water. "Then, the Coast Guard had me follow them back to their dock. They separated the five of us and took our stories. They asked me how much I had to drink. I told them I only had a few beers. I refused to blow, and they arrested me for BUI."

"Three people sitting on the back bench, one goes overboard, and the other two don't know what happened? What about Mary's boyfriend?"

"He was up front with me. The girls said they didn't see anything."

"How's that possible?" I shook my head in disbelief.

"They were busy."

"Doing what?"

"Kissing," he mumbled.

"I thought Kym was Pavel's girlfriend."

"You know how it is."

I noticed he had stopped looking at me. "No, actually, I don't."

"I heard Kym tell the Coast Guard that she and Pavel had been at the beach all day drinking and fighting."

"So what you're telling me is that she wanted to piss off her already angry boyfriend by kissing a chick?"

"I also heard Kym say that Pavel had jumped off a couple of other people's boats, swam to shore, and stayed out of sight to prank them."

"What a jackass."

"Don't worry. He'll show up. I'm going to turn this town upside down tomorrow. I'll go to every bar in town."

I was happy to be home. "I want to know if you hear anything about Pavel, and I mean the *second* you hear."

He opened the door of the SUV. "I'm going to get a shower and wash the jail stench off me. Hopefully, get some sleep and then start asking around about him." He slammed the door.

"You better hope he turns up in one of those dingy bars you like!" I yelled.

Chapter Ten

I inherited the art of being great in a crisis from my mother. After Jax and I got back from the jail, I went to my bedroom for a nap, but instead, I lay there and made a mental to-do list. Triple-starred at the top of the list was finding Pavel as quickly as possible and, most importantly, alive. My connections in The Cove outmatched Jax's any day of the week. I needed to make a few calls and, if Pavel was alive, he'd be found.

I took a long shower, using up all the hot water. I stepped into a jean skirt, pulled on a long-sleeved white tee, pulled my hair into a ponytail, and slipped on some denim boat shoes. When I walked by Jax's bedroom, I was happy to see that he had already left and surprised that he'd fed Jazz. He left a note on the kitchen counter, 'I really am sorry.'

One of my first calls had to be to my mother. She'd kill me if she heard about Jax, the boat, and a missing man from someone else. I hoped she'd offer to tell Brad that the Coast Guard had impounded the boat that he and Moron had spent months restoring. Angelo Marone, whose nickname of "Moron" from high school had stuck with him into adulthood, was a master at boat repair; a regular boat whisperer. Elizabeth had long ago stopped using the boat. It had gone into disrepair and become a labor of love for Brad, and he and Moron had spent the summer making all the repairs. Furious wouldn't cover his response when he found out Jax was involved. Mother could defuse a situation like no other. She had a way of downplaying the worst of facts.

I picked up my phone. "It's your favorite daughter."

"It's early for you. Is everything okay?"

"How about lunch?" I tried to sound casual. "I have a couple of ideas I'd like to bounce off you."

"I'd like that. I can't today, though. Is tomorrow okay?"

I was disappointed. I needed to talk to her, and in person, not over the phone. "What are you doing?"

"Spoon is taking me to Islamorada on his boat for lunch."

"Spoon?"

Her voice turned defensive. "It's a beautiful day to be out on the water. We're sharing cigars, a bottle of Jack, and enjoying the ride."

"Can we meet tomorrow at the Crab Shack? I can reserve us a window table."

"Great! See you tomorrow. Thanks, honey." Mother was definitely excited.

"Have fun."

Mother and Spoon had definitely gotten closer if they were sharing a boat ride down the Keys. That was a romantic way to spend the afternoon. Brad would flip out, and there'd be no talking him down. When our father died, Brad had stepped into the role of protector, and he took it seriously. He hated Dickhead because he broke my heart, and he only tolerated Zach. He'd kill Spoon.

Spoon was not my idea of a stepfather, much less my mother's lover. He had done time in prison, but had since become a successful businessman. However, I wasn't entirely convinced that his auto body place was totally legitimate. In addition, there was an age difference, which made my mother a cougar.

I had so much on my mind I almost missed my turn. For a moment, I wanted to pull over, walk out on the white sandy beach, and watch the waves break onto the shore to clear my head. Instead, I pulled into a parking space marked "Office" at The Cottages, jumped out, and went straight to Joseph's. His door stood wide open, and he sat in his favorite chair, drinking a beer and watching a soap opera.

I walked in and pushed some newspapers aside to sit on the couch.

"You could knock," he said.

I reached over and knocked on his coffee table. "Anyone home?"

"Want something to drink?"

"No, I came for information, and you need to keep it quiet. You can brag you knew all along when it hits the fan. I would like to think you wouldn't gossip about me at all, but I know that's too much to hope for."

"What's in it for me?" His lips, riddled with sores from his medication, parted in a rusty smile.

"That's nervy, even for you. I'm cashing in one of the thousand IOUs I have with your name on it."

"You can't blame me for asking."

"There was a boating incident last night, and a guy named Pavel Klaus went overboard. I want you to find out everything you can about him, and if anyone has seen him around today."

"You're light on the info, girl. How about some details?"

"I hit the highlights. My money's on the fact that when I hear from you next, you'll know more than I do right now."

"Where did he go over?" Joseph asked.

"Right where you hit the open water, just past 33rd Avenue." I stood up.

"If he was a floater, he should've surfaced by now. Is he local?"

"I believe so. Call me as soon as you hear anything." I walked to the front door. "The emphasis on *as soon as* you hear."

"I'll know something in a couple of hours. I'll put my shoes on and head down to the Jumpin'

Croc. Somebody there will be talking. Nothing but locals and the fishermen crowd drink there."

"Thanks, Joseph."

* * *

I drove to 33rd Avenue and circled the block a few times. Everything was quiet. Seeing into the canal from the street was impossible, and I wasn't getting out of my SUV. The last thing I wanted was for someone to see me snooping. I could call Zach, but what would I say? "Hey Zach, can you help with my ex-husband?" Awkward.

I turned my SUV around to head home, taking the back streets that ran along the water; never discovering a single dead body. The reality was that I couldn't have picked Pavel out of a lineup as I didn't even know what he looked like. I wanted Jax to stay away from my house, but I feared if I took my eyes off him, he'd disappear, leaving behind a new set of problems.

Not having eaten all day, I pulled into Roscoe's drive-thru, a run-down, dumpy dive that made the best burgers in the Keys. I once asked Roscoe why he had big outside tables, but no chairs.

"I provide great food. Go eat it somewhere else. I don't want no trouble," he had responded.

What did he care? He always had a line waiting. I ordered my usual hamburger; no "meat surprise" with Roscoe, he used only first-quality ingredients. I sat in my driveway, turned on the radio, took the hamburger out of the bag, tossed half the bun back in the bag, and devoured it. I wasn't in the mood to share with Jazz or anyone else.

Everything was quiet. I sucked down the last of my lemonade and went inside. I was relieved I had the house to myself. Calling and asking for Spoon's help was out of the question since he was with my mother. She couldn't find out until I told her.

My phone rang. "It's Joseph," I told Jazz. "I hope he has something good."

"I got your information."

"That was fast."

"Pavel hasn't surfaced. He's the talk in every bar in town. Pavel worked for Sid Byce on the docks, unloading fish off the boats for his restaurants and seafood store. Byce owns several restaurants up and down The Keys. He's a big deal in this town, owns a lot of real estate, knows everyone, used to be on city council, and family connections that go back to his great-grandfather."

"Doesn't he own The Wharf restaurant?"

"That's one of his. Good food, overpriced, attracts the hip and mindless. Byce has a friend on the Coast Guard, so he also got a call last night that Pavel went missing."

"What's the talk?"

"Did you know Pavel jumped before?" Joseph asked. "It's assumed he'll show up in a day or two."

"Who jumps off boats in the dark?"

"Drunks." Joseph laughed. "Pavel and his girlfriend live in those apartments behind the biker bar on Second Street."

"Isn't that down by the docks?"

"It's also across the alley from where he works. Here's a weird one for you. Pavel's girlfriend and another girl have been walking up and down Gulf Boulevard, drunk, looking for him in every bar they can find. The guys in a couple of those bars must have thought it was their lucky day, as women never go in those, not even the skanky ones."

"Is that it?" Where could Pavel be hiding? If he were still alive…

"You could've told me trouble came to town."

"I need more info, as you like to say," I said.

"Seems your husband and his friends were drunk, attracting attention, racing around the canals in no-wake zones. The Coast Guard found a half-dozen empty half-gallon liquor bottles and a shit load of empty beer cans."

I knew Jax's story had holes in it big enough to drive through. "Do you know who was on the boat?"

"A couple of newly relocated friends of your husband."

I had a bad feeling about his so-called

anonymous friends. Jax didn't do alone; he hated to be by himself. It made sense he brought hangers-on with him. "If you hear anything, please call me. If there's a sighting of Pavel, call me. I don't care what time it is."

"Don't worry. He'll turn up laughing it up in some bar, probably the Croc."

"I hope you're right." I hung up, wanting to throw my phone across the room.

Chapter Eleven

I heard the bedroom doorknob turning. I held my breath for a second, and then heard the familiar sound of a pick inserted into the lock. I smiled, wanting to run naked to the door and throw it open, but I needed margarita courage to do that.

"That was a little slow," I said.

"If you knew I was here, why didn't you open the door? Playing hard to get?"

"As a matter of fact..." I pulled my T-shirt over my head and threw it at him.

He kicked off his shoes, unzipped his pants, and let them fall to the floor. "You like watching me undress?"

"Try not to dawdle."

He laughed. "What's been going on?"

I crooked my finger. "Come over here, and I'll tell you about my day."

He crawled into bed next to me, wrapped me in his arms, and kissed me. "No wonder your family calls him Dickhead."

"That's not foreplay talk." I rolled on top of him, my face against his chest, and ran my hands through his thick black hair. I pulled his face to mine and inhaled his earthy, male scent. "Did you sign your new client?"

"I signed two."

"I know how we should celebrate." I lowered my mouth to his in a hungry kiss. His body responded to mine. I loved the feel of our naked bodies; we fit together in all the right places.

* * *

I woke up with my head on Zach's chest, our legs tangled together. "Why are you playing with my nipples?"

He chuckled. "I thought it was a nicer way to wake you up than shaking you."

"It's still dark out." I loved waking up next to him, and I wanted to prolong the moment.

"I've got back-to-back meetings today. We need to talk, and I'm hungry."

"I'll cook while you shower," I offered.

"That's funny."

"I'll put the frozen waffles in the toaster for you."

"Your mother told me you were an amazing cook. She says you did all of the holiday cooking for family and friends. How do you go from a gourmet cook to take-out and microwave food?"

"Jax happened." I sighed. "He liked his own cooking over mine. Mine wasn't southern enough. The last dinner I cooked was on

Christmas, three years ago. He was several hours late and walked in drunk. He asked where the macaroni and cheese was, then left." Jax hated Christmas; his father had died on Christmas day.

"He's going to jail. How much time he spends there will depend on whether Pavel's found dead or alive."

"Did you run the report on Jax?" I hated asking for help with my ex-husband.

"Anoui was supposed to have run that check. I did tell her there was no hurry, but that's changed now. You know Anoui; if Jax has lint in his shorts, she'll find it. I'll ask her to rush the reports and get them to you by this afternoon or tomorrow. Then we'll know what he's been doing and who he's been doing it with."

"I've asked Joseph to ask around about Pavel," I said. "I told him to call immediately if he finds him. Can Anoui run a check on Pavel, too? I'd at least like to know what he looks like. A picture would be nice."

"Where's Jax now?"

"He's out looking for Pavel. He wasn't around for several days before the accident, and I haven't seen him since."

"I'll help in any way I can. I'd rather you call and tell me these things than hearing from Big Louie on the docks."

I wrapped my fingers in his hair, pulled his face to mine, and kissed him. "Thank you."

"You know, if we shower together, we can

take care of two things at once."

I rolled over and jumped off the bed. "I'll race you to the bathroom."

* * *

Zach and I came down the stairs together, and I could smell the coffee and hear Fab talking to Jazz. I was surprised she could work the coffee machine.

"I thought we had a talk about you feeding Jazz on the counter," I said.

"He's old, and he likes it up here. Besides, as his Auntie Fab, it's my right to spoil him."

"Auntie Fab." Zach snorted and shook his head.

"I'm cooking," I told Fab.

She raised her eyebrows. "You are? What are you cooking?"

"Frozen waffles," Zach said.

"I'm fine with coffee," Fab said.

"Me, too," Zach added.

"We could all go to the Bakery Café," I suggested.

"In that case, I'll have an artichoke soufflé, fresh squeezed orange juice, and a latte." Fab smiled.

"And you?" I asked Zach.

"I'll have the new French toast thing with the egg and bacon in it, orange juice, and coffee."

"Both of you are turning down my home

cooking for all that yummy food. You're both spoiled."

"What about you?" Fab asked.

"I'll make up my mind before we get there. Separate cars and we'll meet there?"

"Ride with me," Fab said. "I'll bring you back."

* * *

"They forgot the kibble for your yogurt," Zach pointed out.

"They're bringing me my granola," I said. "I'm having lunch with my mother later; I need to save room. When Anoui runs the check on Jax, have her find out the issue date on his driver's license."

"It would be better if you let me take care of the investigation, since that's what I'm good at. The best thing would be for you to stop asking questions." Zach glared at me.

"I can be helpful."

"If you want my help, you'll stay out of it."

"Lower your voices. People are looking over here," Fab told us.

"What happens if Pavel floats up?" I asked.

"Things get worse for Dickhead," Zach replied. "He could be charged with manslaughter or worse. Who's the boat registered to?"

I lost my appetite. "Me and Brad."

"Brace yourself for a lawsuit from Pavel's family. Do you have insurance?"

"I'm sure we do. I'll have to talk to Brad. I don't know how I can face him."

"I'd talk to him for you," Zach offered, "but that would make it worse."

"When are they releasing the boat?" Fab asked.

"I'm supposed to call," I said.

"Go over to the Coast Guard station and ask to see the boat," Zach said. "Take pictures and inspect for damage. Any chance asshole had an accident out there on the water?"

"It's Dickhead," I reminded him. "When I think back to our conversation, it had been light on details."

"I can get a copy of the accident report faster than you can," Fab said. "I have a friend at the local Coast Guard station. He'll know the latest on the investigation."

Zach put his arm around me. "Don't worry."

My phone rang. "Hi, Mother."

"Honey, we're running behind schedule. I won't be able to make lunch. How about I call you when we dock?"

She sounded as though she was having a good time. "Sure, that'll be fine." I tried not to sound disappointed. "Are you still in Islamorada?"

"We're just getting ready to leave."

"Have a safe trip."

"I'll call as soon as I get back." She hung up.

I put my hands over my face and banged my head on the table. "She's lost her mind."

Zach rubbed the back of my neck. "Is your mother okay?"

"What's going on?" Fab asked.

"I've got a question for the two of you. Would either of you want your mother to date Spoon?"

Fab threw back her head and laughed.

Zach blew his coffee back in his cup. "She's with Spoon?"

"Worse than that. They sailed to Islamorada yesterday, and they're just heading back now."

"She's sleeping with him!" Zach announced.

"Do you have to say it like that? If you don't stop laughing, Fab, I'm going to kick you out of your chair."

"Sorry," Fab muttered.

"The whole prison thing bothers me. Is he or isn't he legitimate now? More importantly, is he totally legitimate? People whisper about his auto body place, not to mention him in general, of course, when he's nowhere around because people are afraid of him."

"Very few people in this town are one hundred percent legit," Zach pointed out.

"It's hard enough thinking about her having sex with Spoon, but I don't want her to end up in jail or worse."

"Sex with Spoon," Fab said. "I bet that's all hot and messy."

"That's not helpful," I said.

"Have a talk with her," Zach suggested. "I can talk to Spoon and tell him under no circumstances does he involve her in anything illegal."

"You leave Spoon to me," I told him. "You know how Brad hated you when he met you and now you're in the tolerable category?"

"Yes." Zach's eyes narrowed.

"When he hears this, I bet he actually starts to like you."

Zach shook his head and laughed. He didn't care what anyone thought of him. "Thanks, I think. I have a meeting back at the office," Zach stood up. "Keep me up to speed." He pulled me out of my chair. "She'll be back in a minute," he told Fab.

We walked to his Escalade. He pushed me up against the driver's side door and kissed me until my mind went blank. "How about a real date this weekend?"

"Dinner, then sex?"

"Or sex, dinner, and more sex."

"I'd love that." I kissed his lips.

"Call you later."

I turned around, and Fab handed me my purse. "It looked like you two were finished. Let's go to the Coast Guard office and see what we can find out."

"How was bodyguarding Israel?" I asked. "He's got that Latin sizzle thing going for him."

"I haven't noticed."

I laughed. "Sure."

"The whole gig was uneventful, which is the way I like it. What's up with you and Zach?"

"I'm trying to be grownup, but I'd like more time for fun. That means I limit the urge to whine."

"I know what you mean. A weekend in Key West would be fun...or anywhere, for that matter."

"Did you woman up and tell Marco what you want?"

She shook her head. "Nope."

"Me neither. We should do that before we get bored with being neglected and move on."

"I'm pretty much there."

I sighed. "What if they turn out to be the loves of our lives and we never said anything?"

Chapter Twelve

Fab jerked the wheel of her Thunderbird hard, skidded sideways into the driveway of the Coast Guard building, and screeched to a halt. She hated the brake pedal and never used it until the last second.

We walked into the office, and Fab went to the counter. "Is Lieutenant Patrick in? Tell him Fab Merceau is here to see him."

We didn't have to wait long before he appeared in his white Coast Guard shorts and shirt. He towered over the two of us. Why wouldn't Fab go for him? Probably too normal.

He looked her up and down, a boyish grin on his face. "Hey, trouble." He swung Fab into a hug.

"This is my friend Madison Westin," Fab introduced.

I wanted a hug like hers, but wasn't going to ask. "Nice to meet you." I nodded at him, unsure of what else to say.

"I need some information," Fab told him.

"Come back to my office." He motioned for us to follow him down the hall. "What's up? Please tell me you're not in some kind of trouble with the Coast Guard."

I chuckled. He obviously knew her well. He had a nice office, no pictures of a woman or children, just one of him and his Akita. His nameplate read Dan Patrick.

"There was a guy overboard the other night, a Pavel Klaus, and I wondered if you knew anything about the case," Fab said. "Madison and her brother are the owners of the boat, although she wasn't on it that night."

"I know we stopped looking for him. We have two reports on file regarding incidents of him jumping overboard and swimming back to shore. The latest was two months ago over on Decker Island. Klaus went with a group of people. They were all drunk, got into a fight, so he snuck off and swam back to the mainland. The friends called and reported him missing. We searched, and the whole time, he was sitting at the Croc, laughing it up."

"You think he's alive?" Fab asked.

"You'd think he would've shown up by now," Dan said. "No one's seen him, as far I know."

"Can we get a copy of the report? And is it possible for us to look at the boat?" Fab asked.

Dan stood up. "I'll be right back. I know the report is done; I'll get you a copy. One question: did Devereaux have your permission to take the boat out that night?"

"No, he didn't," I said.

"We'll note that in the report, and it will help you in dealing with the insurance company." Dan left the office, shutting the door behind him.

"He's very nice," I said.

"And funny and smart."

"Have you…?"

"No. What am I going to do with a nice guy?"

"How do you know him?"

"Friend of a friend. Dan and I have swapped favors a few times. He's one of those people you can ask for help who always says yes."

Dan opened the door. "Here you go." He handed some papers to Fab.

"We appreciate this," Fab said.

"Thank you." I smiled.

"Come on, ladies. I'll take you down to the boat. We have it parked in a holding area down in storage. The captain says you can pick it up tomorrow."

It took several minutes to maneuver the maze of the docks to where the boat sat in the water by itself.

"Is there any damage?" I asked.

"There's minimal damage to the starboard side. We ran a couple of tests and took some wood scrapings. We cleaned out the contents of the boat and bagged it for evidence in case this goes to court."

"Do you mind if I take a couple of pictures?" I asked.

"Go ahead."

I took out my phone, walked around the boat, and took several pictures. I had to look hard to see the damage and there was no evidence of a crash.

Fab and Dan stood on the main dock, laughing and talking.

"What's a good time to send someone to pick up the boat?" I asked. "I'm having it towed back to The Cove."

"I'll have the guys pull it out of the water today, so it will be ready to go anytime tomorrow. I was going to tell you if you were going to drive it back, the waterways can be tricky if you're not familiar with the area. Come back to the office and sign the release form and you won't have to come back tomorrow."

"My aunt used to love to collect favors from people. Her theory was you just never knew. I owe you one," I told Dan.

"That's how Fab and I became such good friends, swapping favors." He smiled at Fab. There was no doubt he liked her.

"Thank you for your help, Dan," Fab said.

We waved to him and walked back to the car.

"What's in the report?" I asked.

"The five of them were drinking, and a couple of them were smoking pot."

I shook my head. "That's a shock."

"When the Coast Guard showed up, they were all drunk off their asses. So far, they only have theories and no real evidence. Pavel sat on the port side, and their theory is that, based on the damage, Jax hit something, possibly a mile marker, and it threw Pavel from the boat. Of course, the other theory is that Pavel decided to jump overboard and swim back to shore. Not a good idea, since he was drunk. However, the shore wasn't far. The fact that he hasn't shown up yet isn't good for Jax."

"If he's alive, now would be a good time for Pavel to walk into a bar and order a beer. If he's dead, the nightmare begins."

"This next part is interesting," Fab said.

"What now?"

"It says here that Jax told the Coast Guard and the sheriff he borrowed your boat, thinking you wouldn't mind."

I shook my head. "In Jax land, he probably thought that was the truth."

"At least you can tell Brad the boat looks okay."

"Did you see the inside? The entire interior and new white upholstery was covered in black marks, and one of the cushions has a large cut. There was actual garbage in it."

"The inside was pretty filthy," Fab conceded.

"Jax likes nice things, but he never seems to know how to take care of them. I'm going to do what I can to get it cleaned and repaired before Brad comes back from fishing. Thank goodness I know everyone who worked on the boat. I can have it looking like new."

"Brad won't blame you."

"He'll blame me and Jax. What if I have to tell him that in addition to his boat being trashed, it gets worse? Pavel could be dead. I'd like to shuffle it off on my mother and bury my head in the sand."

"What's your mother going to say?" Fab asked.

"About the boat, Jax, or Spoon?"

"You probably won't have to call Spoon *Daddy*."

"What?"

"You know…the stepfather thing."

"Eww. Do me a favor and don't ever say that again."

"You can't shoot your way out of this, so you need to find the humor, or you'll go crazy."

"That's my second smile today. The first, I was ogling your friend Dan."

"He thought you were cute, too. I told him I'd let him know when you kick Zach to the curb."

"You're so funny."

Chapter Thirteen

"You're back." I was happy to see that Jax hadn't done anything stupid, like disappear.

"I've been all over this town, in every dumpy bar, and no sign of Pavel," Jax said. "His girlfriend is a drunk, babbling mess. All she could do was shake her head when I asked if she'd seen him. I scoured the docks and talked to his co-workers. He hasn't shown up anywhere."

I had obsessed every moment of the day that Pavel was going to show up any minute. I wanted to be supportive, but I was worn out. "I don't want you here."

"You know I don't have anywhere else to go. After posting bail, I'm a little short on funds." He pulled his pockets out of his shorts to stress his point.

I took a deep breath. "I saw the boat today. You failed to mention the damage. And what the hell did you do to the interior, walk on the white seats with muddy shoes? You're lucky I don't file grand theft charges against you."

"I hope you don't do that, but I can't blame you if you did. 'Sorry' sounds lame, but I am sorry."

I believed he was sorry, but somehow I knew he'd probably make the same choice again. "I need two aspirin, a margarita, or both."

"You need a little loving from Mr. Sir." He smiled.

"Thanks, but I have a boyfriend."

Jax threw back his head and laughed. "Sure you do."

I was surprised when the doorbell rang. My friends all walked in through the back French doors like cat burglars. I walked over to answer the door.

"Hi, Mother." I briefly thought about falling on the floor in a pretend faint, but she would know I was faking and wouldn't see the humor.

I hesitated, then stepped back so she could enter. I wanted the right setting to unload all of the dirty details, preferably public. Her first target would be Dickhead.

"Spoon and I got back about an hour ago. I thought I'd stop by on my way home." She hugged me.

I knew the second she saw Jax.

"What are you doing here?" Mother demanded.

"Hi, Mother Madeline. Happy to see you, too." He stood and hugged her.

"Why don't you sit down, and Jax can tell you why he's here," I told her.

"This ought to be good." Mother sat in a chair opposite Jax and stared at him.

"I'm here because of Madison, to show her how much I've changed and talk about the future."

"I liked you as a son-in-law until your life went off the rails and you seemed incapable of helping yourself," Mother said.

"I remember you telling me you wished me well as someone else's husband."

"Still doing drugs?" Mother asked.

"I've been clean for a year now. No drugs or cigarettes. I still drink, but only beer."

"This is where you might want to get to the good part," I said.

"Look, I hate these family things." Jax stood up. "I'll see you later."

"Sit. Down." He'd never admit it, but part of him was afraid of his ex-mother-in-law. "Madison, why don't you tell me?"

I looked at Jax, and he turned away, but not quick enough. I saw the smirk on his face. He hated confrontation of any kind. The fact that I had to do all the talking was fine with him.

I started from when I found him sitting on my couch. I didn't give her glossed-over highlights; I told her in tabloid headline detail. I stopped the tale just before the phone call from the Coast Guard.

Mother was red-faced with anger. Jax refused to make eye contact. I wanted to puke.

"What in the hell were you thinking?" She wagged her finger in Jax's face. "How could you put Madison at risk?"

To his credit, Jax stayed quiet. He gave me a look that said, "What about the rest of the story?"

"Your lawyer will never get one of his grimy fingers on the deed to this property," Mother said. "Here's a better idea. Use a public defender to get yourself out of trouble."

I jumped up. "I'll get you a shot of Jack. Would you like some ice on the side?"

Mother had suspicion written all over her face. "Do I need a cigar, too?"

"That would be a good idea." I was such a coward, trying to liquor her up before spilling the rest of the story.

Mother whirled and grabbed Jax's arms, forcing him to look at her. "What else have you done?"

Jax stared at her.

"Mother, I…" I fumbled for the right words.

"If there's more to the story, then spit it out," Mother said.

I told her about the call from the Coast Guard, the missing Pavel, and that I'd been to see the boat and it was set for release in the morning.

"How did he get access to the boat?" Mother demanded.

"That's a good question. I'll let him tell you." I pointed at Jax.

"I knew Madison wouldn't care if I took it for the day," Jax said.

"Did you ask? Did she give you the keys? Tell

you where it was docked?" Mother fired her questions without waiting for answers.

"Madison," Jax whined.

"Even if you were still part of the family, this would not be okay," Mother said.

"You're right. I shouldn't have done any of this." Jax hung his head. "I would fix all of this if I could. I still love Madison."

"Love her?" Mother snorted. "Tell me this; would you want your sister married to you?"

"I don't have a sister." He paused. "No, I wouldn't."

"Do you think you're smart enough to scam a lawyer all by yourself? Did you ever ask yourself why the lawyer is doing this? Is there anyone else involved that you've failed to mention?"

"I'm sorry," he said, putting his hands over his face.

She turned to me. "Did you give permission for Dickhead to take the boat out?"

"Of course I didn't."

"Have you filed a police report?"

"It's in the Coast Guard report that he didn't have my permission. I'm going to talk it over with Brad to see what steps we need to take to protect ourselves. I'll take responsibility for fixing the boat, and I'll be the one to tell Brad."

Mother glared at Jax. "You need to leave."

"We were just talking about that. He needs to stick around and help clean up this mess," I said. "Would you mind if I called Spoon and had him pick up the boat in the morning?"

"Why Spoon?" she asked.

"He has the best towing equipment in town, and the boat needs to be moved to Moron's for repairs." With my mother doing whatever with Spoon, he'd be one less contact for me in The Cove. Putting him in middle would be out of the question.

"Don't you think you should wait for Brad and see what he wants?" Mother asked. She was still angry with Jax, but had gone into cleanup mode.

"If Brad was in town right now, then I could do that, but the boat can't sit at the Coast Guard indefinitely. I'm capable of making decisions."

"Well, you have a lot of them to make. How long has he been here?" Her eyes cut to Jax.

"Long enough. I got a lawyer referral from Whit, and my new attorney should be back in town in a few days. I'm going to get all my questions answered and then make a plan. Do you want that drink now?"

"No, thanks. I have a long drive home. I'll talk to you in the morning." She hugged me and whispered, "We'll figure this out."

"I prefer Jax," he said.

"What are you talking about?" Mother asked.

"Do you think you could drop the Dickhead?" he asked.

Mother laughed. "I'll think about it. Don't get too comfortable." She walked out the door. To her credit, she didn't slam it.

I knew she'd been deprived of screaming her frustration, but she was good at not saying things she'd have to take back later. Tears welled up in my eyes, but I refused to let myself cry in front of Jax.

"Please don't cry," Jax said. "If you do, I'll start crying, too."

"The smartest thing you did was make her laugh."

"I thought about telling her one of my stupid knock-knock jokes." He smiled. "I don't remember her being this scary."

"That's because when times got rough, you were scarce, avoiding my family completely."

"What now?"

"You know she's relentless. She'll be back." I started up the stairs.

He turned up the sound on the television.

Chapter Fourteen

My phone rang just as I took a sip of my coffee. Getting a bad feeling, I hesitated before answering.

"Madison, sorry if you're asleep, but I have news I know you'd want to hear."

I was happy to hear Zach's voice. "Good news, I hope."

"I got a call from my friend at the Coast Guard. They pulled Pavel out of the water down by 21st Street."

"So much for the theory he swam to shore. Why did it take so long for the body to show up?"

"There's a lot of reasons. The biggest one being the currents. A man was out on his balcony, drinking his morning coffee, spotted him floating, and called the police."

"That's a terrible way to start the day."

"There's more. He didn't drown. He died of a gunshot wound."

"You mean murdered?" I screeched. The whole situation just went from bad to worse.

"Looks that way."

"Jax would never shoot anyone. He hates guns. He doesn't even own one." Thank heaven I'd locked mine in the safe when he first showed up at my house.

"Did you know any of the people on the boat that night?" Zach questioned.

"No. New friends of Jax. I'm going to sit Jax down and wring specific details out of him about his night of joyriding."

"Why don't you let me do the investigating?"

"I've asked you a couple of times for information and haven't gotten any," I reminded him. "If stonewalling me is your way of telling me to mind my own business, you can forget it. I'm going to be involved. I can ask around, and then we can share information."

"Do you want my help? Stay out of it. I don't want you getting hurt. Someone murdered Pavel, and we've no idea who or why."

"Will you at least keep me in the loop?"

"When are you getting rid of Dickhead?"

"Don't you have an ex-wife? Is that what you would do?" I decided to take a page from his playbook and answer a question with a question.

"When you make up your mind what you're doing, let me know," he grumbled.

"What's going to happen with Pavel now?"

"They're in the process of sending his body to the morgue," Zach said. "They'll notify his family. A detective has been assigned to the case, though my friend didn't know who. You can expect a visit from the police with all kinds of questions."

"I'll call Cruz and have him advise me on how to deal with that visit."

"I don't know what you're going to tell Jax. His problems just got a whole lot worse," Zach said.

"I should tell him they found Pavel. After that, I don't know."

"Did you get together with your mother?"

I didn't want to relive that conversation. "She's good in a crisis."

"What did she have to say to Jax?"

"We both told him not to get comfortable."

"Happy to hear that," Zach said.

"Thanks for being the one to tell me about Pavel." Zach didn't know me very well if he thought I'd sit around and be scared, waiting for the next shoe to drop. "I'll talk to you later." I hung up the phone.

I wanted to pull the covers over my head and stay in bed all day. Pavel murdered! Was there a chance Jax was somehow involved? Zero chance, I answered myself.

I went upstairs and quietly opened the door to the guest bedroom. Jax was nowhere in sight, and the bed hadn't been slept in. I didn't want to deal with him anyway. I wanted more coffee.

Jazz lay on the couch, fast asleep. I noticed his food bowl was full and he had fresh water. No wonder he wasn't weaving between my legs, howling. Jax loved Jazz, and the feeling was mutual. He had a way with animals and small children. I'd wanted a child with him, but it never happened. Later, I realized that was for the better.

I took my phone out and called Spoon.

"Madison Westin, what can I do for you?"

"Would you pick up my boat at the Coast Guard and tow it to Moron's? I've already signed the release."

"I'll give the Coast Guard a call and take care of it," Spoon said. "Anything else?"

"I really appreciate this. Send the bill to my house." There was no need to give Spoon details. He knew the second anything happened in The Cove.

"You remember when I told you I could fix anything? Well, I can," Spoon reminded me. "Keep that in mind." When I first met him, he called himself "The Fixer." That, coupled with the look on his face, had made my hair stand on end.

I called Moron and left a message to expect the boat. No explanation was necessary with him, either. He knew when a tourist stubbed their toe, which always surprised me since he was so unsociable.

Jax walked in the through the French doors.

"You look like crap. Did you sleep on the beach?" I asked.

"I couldn't sleep. The damn sand gets

everywhere." He brushed some off on my floor. His eyes were bloodshot, and he reeked of liquor.

"You need to pull yourself together."

"I want to go pick up the boat and drive it back. I'll work on cleaning it up," Jax said.

"I've already had it towed, and hopefully the repairs will be complete before Brad's boat gets in." It wasn't true, but I didn't want to fight with Jax. He'd never again get near the boat, no matter what I had to do.

"Have you heard anything?" Jax asked.

"I got a call this morning. Pavel's body was fished out of the water."

"What the fuck?" He covered his face with his hands. "I knew the guy for one hour, and he's dead." He looked up at me. "What? What else?"

"The police will be here today or tomorrow with more questions."

"You and I could make all of this go away," Jax said.

This ought to be good. "How's that?"

"You tell the cops you were driving. Everyone knows you don't drink and drive. By eliminating the alcohol factor, they'll write it off as an accident."

"The gaping hole in your fat idea is that I wasn't on the boat that night," I pointed out. "The four other people on the boat know that, and let's not forget the Coast Guard knows it, too."

"Oh, calm down. I'll talk to all of them and tell

them what to say," Jax said with confidence.

"So everyone's going to lie for you and face criminal charges and jail time? And what about me? I can think of several felonies I might be charged with."

"You're exaggerating. A slap on the wrist," he said.

"You're awfully cavalier with my life."

"Just think about it."

"I have thought about it, and the answer is no," I shot back. "In fact, a big no. Do you remember the last time I tried to take the blame for something you did?"

"What are talking about?"

"The drag racing incident? You spinning out of control and smashing into the living room of some old man's house. Ring any bells?"

He shrugged. "All you had to do was say you were driving."

"I did, you bastard. You failed to tell me there were seventeen eyewitnesses, and the police interviewed every one of them. Everyone in the neighborhood had been sitting out on their porch that day. Funny thing, I couldn't pass for a six-foot, blond-haired man. I could've gone to jail."

"You weren't arrested."

"I was handcuffed and forced to sit in the back of a police car for over an hour. They let me think I was on my way to be booked into county jail. In case you care, I decided then it was the last time I would lie for anyone."

"Do this one damn thing. You do this, and the whole situation goes away, and I'll leave town tomorrow."

"I'm not doing it."

"I'm going to go shower. In case the cops show up, I'm sliding out the back. I'll lay low for a few days, and they'll either go away, or they can deal with my lawyer," Jax said.

I decided it wasn't a good time to tell him Pavel died from a gunshot wound. He'd trip over himself getting out the door, leave town, and leave me to answer questions that I didn't have the answers to. He wasn't one to confront his problems head on if there was an easier way, one that didn't include confrontation. He liked being Goodtime Jax. I'd told him one time that a person was judged by their word, and his was crap. He'd smiled and walked away.

He stared at me, trying to decide what his next bad decision would be. He started to speak, changed his mind, and got up and went upstairs.

"Clean up the sand on the floor," I yelled after him. Maybe it would be better if he left town. I didn't know what to think. Eventually, he'd be caught because he wasn't smart enough to stay out of trouble. Before he went anywhere, I needed to get my house issue settled. Ever since the first day I'd found him sitting on my couch, I'd been sucking down yogurt for my chronic stomachache.

I had to get out of the house, away from Jax

and images of a murder I had nothing to do with. I grabbed a couple of plastic sand pails, went out the door, and headed for the beach.

Chapter Fifteen

I stood at the kitchen sink washing my seashells, having collected four buckets full. The long walk in the warm sand with the breeze blowing through my hair had felt good as I bent over every other step, picking up shells. I looked out the window. The gate stood open in the front, and a sheriff's car sat on the other side of the street. A dark sedan pulled up behind it. I shut off the water and ran for my cell phone. I hurriedly called Cruz Campion.

"This is Madison Westin. Is Mr. Campion in?"

"Hi, Madison. It's Susie." Cruz's assistant was always friendly, but I had to go through her to speak to him.

"He said to call when the sheriff showed up, and they're banging on my door as we speak."

"Go open the door and find out who's the investigator in charge. Mr. Campion's out of the office; I'll text him the info."

I went to the door and looked out the peephole. Kevin and Detective Harder stood there. Thank goodness for Kevin. Harder and I had history, and it wasn't pleasant. Harder hated Zach and so, by extension, he hated me.

"Susie, it's Kevin Cory, and Detective Harder."

"Don't say anything, and Cruz will get back to you."

I pasted a smile on my face and opened the door. "Hi, guys."

"We'd like to talk to you. Can we come in?" Kevin asked.

"No." I should've taken Jax's idea and snuck out the back door.

"What does that mean?" Kevin asked, looking uncomfortable.

"Do you have a search warrant?"

Neither of them said a word.

"It means you can't come in," I said. "What do you want?" I looked at Detective Harder.

"Where's the boat?" Harder demanded. "I have questions about the accident."

"My lawyer is Cruz Campion, and he said not to answer any questions until he got here." It wasn't exactly the truth, but Harder didn't know that.

"You got yourself a good lawyer this time. I heard the last one wouldn't rep you for littering." Harder laughed. "Where were you the night of the murder?"

"Like I said, contact Cruz." Harder was talking about Tucker Davis. He'd been my lawyer very briefly, and things didn't end to his satisfaction. Tucker was probably sorry he didn't think about framing me.

"I figured your alibi would be your criminal girlfriend. How is Fabiana Merceau?"

My phone rang, and I jumped for it, the interruption timely.

"This is Cruz. Let me speak to Harder."

"Here you go." I handed Harder the phone. Harder scared me. I was sure he tormented insects for his own amusement.

"Figures she had you on speed dial," Harder said with a half-smile. Cruz must have said something funny because Harder laughed. "You graduated at the top of your class. You know I can take her in and hold her until you show up."

I held my breath. I could hear Cruz's voice, but couldn't make out the words.

"When you show up tomorrow, have the boat with you." Harder paused. "Cruz wants to coach you." He handed me my phone.

"Answer only yes or no," Cruz said. "Is the boat there?"

"No."

"Okay, I'll make him get a subpoena, and you should prepare yourself for the fact he'll get a search warrant for your house. I told him we'd meet with him tomorrow afternoon. Is that convenient?"

"Yes."

"See you tomorrow. You can shut the door in his face." Cruz hung up, laughing.

I looked at Harder. "I'll see you tomorrow." I stepped back to shut the door.

"One more thing." He put his hand on the door. "Where's Jackson Devereaux?"

"I don't know. He wasn't here when I woke up this morning." Technically, I was telling the truth.

"Have him call me." He handed me his business card. "If he doesn't, I'll have him tracked down."

"Okay." I shut the door and breathed a sigh of relief.

I walked into the living room and picked up Jazz. He looked at me like, "What?" I hugged him until he meowed, then I laid him back down so he could go back to sleep. I wanted to lie down with him, but I was in total pace mode.

"Now what?" I said when the doorbell rang. It rang three more times before I could get to the door. "Whoever it is, you're really annoying me."

I opened the door, and my brother was standing there. "Hi, Brad. I didn't know you were back. How was the fishing?" I moved to hug him, but he stepped back.

My brother had sun-bleached hair and a dark tan from the long hours he spent on his commercial fishing boat. He liked to say, "From my boat to your dinner plate."

He glared at me, his face full of anger. "Where the hell is he? Why would you let fucking Dickhead use my boat?"

I had seen my brother mad before, but never at me. "I didn't."

125

"You think I'm stupid? The keys, where it was stored, all takes knowledge. If not you, then who?" He walked inside, slamming the door.

"He figured it out by himself."

"That dumb bastard is not that smart."

"Would you stop yelling? I'm not deaf."

"The boat was not yours to loan."

"Let me say this slowly. I did *not* loan him the boat."

"I got a call that Dickhead was racing around at night, no running lights on, and hit a mile marker. The best part involves a dead fisherman."

"I don't know what happened out there that night. The dead guy's name is Pavel Klaus, and I didn't know him either."

"What in the hell is the matter with you? You're awfully calm."

"I've been living this for a couple of days. Lower your voice or get out. I'm tired of being interrogated. I don't have any answers for you."

A loud thud against the front door brought our yelling to a halt.

"What was that?" Brad opened the door, and Jax fell in the entryway.

Jax lay there battered, bruised, his nose bleeding, clearly on the losing end of a nasty fight.

"What the hell happened?" I asked.

"Help me get him over to the couch," Brad said.

Jax groaned when we laid him on the couch.

"Should I call 911?" I asked Brad.

"What the hell happened to you, you jerk-off? Do you need to go to the hospital?" Brad asked.

"I hate doctors," Jax moaned. "Man, I'm sorry about the boat. I'll work on it until it's one hundred percent."

The man could fix anything. If he didn't know how something worked, it didn't take long until he had it figured out.

"You bet your ass you will," Brad growled. "What does the other guy look like?"

"They look fine." Jax was having a hard time catching his breath. "I was jumped from behind by a couple of fishermen thugs, friends of Pavel who think I murdered him. They told me they were going to beat me to death."

"How did you get away?" Brad asked.

"A guy bigger than both of those two assholes put together showed up. They took one look at the barrel of his gun and took off. He told them there wouldn't be any second warning. He tossed me into the back of his truck bed and dropped me off here. Told me to clean up my mess and get out of town. He said Madison was off limits."

"What's he talking about?" Brad asked me.

"I wasn't there." My money was on Slice, Zach's investigator, but it wasn't the time to ask questions. There was nothing to be gained in aggravating Brad any further. "I'll get something to stop the bleeding." I ran into the kitchen.

"You need to be careful. There are more than a few guys down at the docks that would kill for twenty-five bucks and a twelve-pack," Brad told Jax. "Where's the boat?" he asked me.

"The boat's been trailered to Moron's. He's going to get started right away. I'll pay for the repairs," I said.

"It's not about who pays. I put hours of sweat into that boat. I'll never understand why you let Dickhead joyride around with his lowlife friends."

"She didn't," Jax wheezed.

"Shut up," Brad replied. "Why are you here anyway?"

"Stop it," I said. "His breathing is getting worse. He needs to go to the doctor, whether he likes it or not."

The doorbell sounded. I opened the door, and our mother stood there.

"Oh, isn't this nice?" I said. "You show up after unleashing Brad on me with no warning, when you knew I wanted to be the one to tell him what happened."

"What are you talking about?" Mother pushed past me. "Brad." She hugged him. "What the hell happened to him?" she asked, pointing at Jax.

"A couple of Pavel supporters decided to beat him to death," I explained.

"Can't you stay out of trouble?" Mother took the towel from Jax and gently cleaned the blood from his nose and mouth. "How was your trip?" she asked Brad.

"Trip was good, filled the tanks in record time and came back early."

"It's late for you to be here in The Cove. Another date with Spoon?" I asked Mother.

"Madison, please." And then to Brad. "Is Madison in any danger?"

Brad glared at me. "What the hell are you talking about now?"

"Didn't mother tell you she's dating Spoon?"

"That criminal with the tattoos?"

"Same one." I felt a little bad, rolling mother under the bus.

"There must be something in the water down here. You two have lost your minds." Brad turned to Mother. "You're not going to date Spoon if I have to take him fishing, tie weights to his ankles, and push him overboard."

"I'll help you get Jax to your truck," I told Brad. "I'll come with you."

"You stay here. I'll deal with this."

"You can bring Jax back here if they don't keep him overnight," I said.

"He's coming home with me. I'm going to spell out just how helpful he's going to be in getting the boat back in the water." Brad glared at Jax.

"I'll get it running better than before," Jax said.

"Hardly, since I did the original work."

I remembered when the two of them had restored a turquoise 1964 F-100 short bed truck; it was a work of art when they finished. I never understood why Brad had sold it.

I pointed at Mother. "Take her with you."

"Madison, what has gotten into you?" Mother asked.

"You knew I wanted to be the one to tell Brad and then you did it. No heads-up? Nothing?"

"She didn't tell me anything," Brad said. "I heard about it the second I docked the boat. You, your ex here, and the dead guy were all anyone wanted to talk about."

"Slow down," Jax mumbled as Brad pulled him to his feet. I shut the door behind them.

"I want an apology," Mother demanded.

"For what?"

"It was my right to tell Brad about Spoon, not yours. I'm your mother, in case you forgot."

"I'm sorry. I took all my frustration out on you. It wasn't very satisfying, if that matters."

"What's wrong with Spoon?" Mother asked.

"Would you want *me* dating Spoon?"

"He's a better man than Jackson Devereaux," she defended.

"At least Jax hasn't been to prison," I shot back. I was on shaky ground; Jax had been to jail.

"I didn't come here to talk about Spoon. I'm a grown woman and can decide who I want to date."

"You remember those words. You'll be

hearing them again when I'm telling you the same thing."

I could tell she wanted to send me to my room. I almost wished she would, so I could sit up there with the door locked. I took a deep breath to step back from the drama.

"Don't worry. Brad will calm down," Mother reassured me.

"Jax being dumped on the doorstep cooled down the conversation. I didn't get a chance to ask Brad how long he'll be in port."

"I'll call him tomorrow," Mother said.

"Do you want to spend the night?"

"Stay in the same room Dickhead was in? No thanks."

"It's Jax now, remember?"

Mother laughed. "Did I promise?"

"You can have my room."

"I need to go home. I have an early morning appointment. I'll call you after I talk to Brad. When you get an update on Jax, call me."

Chapter Sixteen

Mother called to tell me that Jax had spent the night at the hospital. He'd been beaten worse than originally thought, sustaining a couple of cracked ribs.

"I've done something you need to know about."

I closed my eyes. "What?"

"Brad's leaving in the morning. He's getting the boat restocked this afternoon. Jax can't stay out in the Everglades by himself. He's not coming back to your house, either."

Brad lived in the Glades in a house that he'd remodeled himself. I almost fainted when I first saw it. I'd thought it was a dump that should've been bulldozed. The transformation was shocking. It had taken him over a year, and he paid attention to every detail. I hated going there, especially in the dark, the bugs chirping and buzzing in your hair was unnerving. One always had to be on the lookout for what might crawl up your leg out of the tall grasses.

I exhaled. "What does that mean? What have you done?"

"I relocated him to The Cottages."

"I'm surprised he went."

"I didn't give him a choice. He tried not to show it, but he liked the idea. I picked him up and drove him over there, and Mac put him in cottage ten."

I resisted the urge to jump in the air. "I'll pack the rest of his stuff and take it over to him." Peace at last.

Mother sniffed. "A thank you would be nice."

"Thank you."

* * *

My SUV was filled with storage boxes. I retrieved four plastic containers from the garage and filled them with Jax's clothes and shoes. He packed light; no other personal items. I guess people on the run didn't have stuff.

I realized I didn't know anything about his life since the day I'd gotten in my car and driven away, pre-divorce. I thought back to our conversations. He hadn't offered up the slightest tidbit. I worried every waking moment about my house and Pavel. I loved life in The Cove, and I wanted Jax out of town. I'd still have The Cottages, but it would drive me crazy to live amongst my tenants. Every one of them was high maintenance.

I noticed everything was quiet when I drove into the driveway of The Cottages. I took the plastic containers and stacked them in the office.

I wasn't in the mood for a face-to-face with Jax. I walked over to Joseph's, and his door stood wide open. He lay stretched out on the couch, watching television.

"Come on in," he called.

"You feeling okay?" His face had a dull, yellowish tint.

"Not really. Doesn't mean I can't talk. Besides, I've been wondering where you've been."

"What have you heard?" I bounced into a chair opposite him, careful not to choose the other chair. The last time I sat on it, a spring shot up my butt.

"Since they drug the foreign dude with the hole in his head out of the water, rumors started flying."

"What's the latest?"

"Pavel came here with his father fifteen years ago from the Czech Republic. His mother still lives there. The father died a few years ago. The Coast Guard was able to track the mother down to tell her about her son, and they're coordinating funeral arrangements with Dickie-Ass."

"You might want to be nicer to the only funeral director in town. When's the funeral?"

"Tomorrow. Are you going?" Joseph asked.

"I don't go to funerals of people I don't know."

"Promises to be a big shindig. Sid Byce, Pavel's boss, is throwing a party afterward, outside in the patio area. If the food comes from The Wharf, it should be good. Sid's paying for the whole thing."

Free food was not incentive enough for me, but party-funeral combos could be a new advertising concept for Dickie. "Any ideas on how Pavel ended up dead?"

"Your husband is the chief suspect."

"Ex-husband. Why would Jax shoot someone he met for the first time when Pavel stepped on the boat that night?"

"Sid's made it clear he wants someone to pay, and he doesn't care who it is."

"He sounds like an ass."

"Where have you been, girl?" Joseph laughed. "Most of the people in this town are assholes."

"You're a cynic." I smiled.

"What's up with you moving your husband in here?"

"Ex. It seemed like a good arrangement."

"Mark my words, girlie; he's going to be trouble. You need to pack his ass up and send him back to wherever he came from. Express!"

"He's been here one night."

"Who kicked his ass?" Joseph asked.

"Why don't you find out and tell me?"

"Grow a pair and kick his ass to the state line. If you can't do it yourself, ask one of your ass-kicker friends. They'll be happy to do it."

"Do you want a beer?" I asked.

"Are you pulling it out of your pocket?"

"No, I'm offering you one of yours, so I can get a bottle of water." I perused the refrigerator, not surprised that it held only beverages.

"I want one from the back because they're the coldest."

I popped the top and handed him his beer. "If Jax leaves now, the police will think he killed Pavel for sure."

"Do you think he had anything to do with Pavel's death?"

I sat down and downed half the bottle of water. "No, I don't. He doesn't even own a gun, and even if he did, he's not a killer."

"What about one of his friends that was on the boat?" he asked.

"He just met them."

Joseph raised his eyebrows. "You sure about that?"

"I'm not sure about anything. What are you trying to tell me? Stop with the questions and tell me what's going on."

"Not long after your mother dropped his butt here, a guy and a girl showed up. I have a nose for trouble, and they're it. Mark my words, you're going to be looking for ways to be rid of the three of them and soon."

"Where are they now?"

"Some skinny, grimy looking, tattooed guy in a van came by, and your husband's two friends piled in and left. A little while later, another car pulled up, and your husband got in that one. I couldn't see who was driving."

"Everything else around here going okay?"

Joseph threw his beer can in the direction of the trashcan, missing by a foot. "It's quiet right now."

"One more thing; do you know a Luc Baptiste?"

"Never heard of him. Why?"

"Elizabeth left him something, and I've been trying to find a guy no one knows. How odd is that?"

"If it's something good, keep it for yourself. Problem solved."

A middle-aged woman poked her head in the door. "Are you ready, Joseph?"

"Hey, Ellie, come on in. I'll get my jacket. I have a doctor's appointment," he told me.

I stood up. "Thanks, Joseph. Call me if you hear anything."

I walked to my SUV, refusing to let everything going on overwhelm me. I pulled my ringing cell phone out of my pocket. I debated not answering, but I knew she'd call again. "Hi, Mother."

"Good news. Brad's calmed down. He and Jax are at Moron's assessing the damage."

"I thought Brad went out fishing this morning."

"A couple of his guys didn't show up, so he had to delay it a day."

"I forgot to tell Brad, the detective on the case

is issuing a subpoena for the boat, so he won't have it very long."

"We're under no obligation to wait for law enforcement to get their act together."

"Mother, if we repair it now, it'll look like we're covering up evidence."

"Madison, did you shoot the guy?"

"You know I didn't."

"Our family isn't involved in this case."

"It could be used against Jax and would look like I'm covering up evidence."

"Stop overreacting. Do you want to get back with Jax?"

"That's over. Don't ask me why I didn't just tell him to go away. I'm giving him credit for warning me. Who knew it would get worse after that?"

"Brad says he's not doing drugs anymore. I was happy to hear Brad believed him. I'm not sure I did when he told me. Now he needs to get sober, and not think he can just be an occasional drinker."

"Alcohol has ruined his life, and he needs to admit it and move on," I said. "I'm happy he's helping with the boat. Brad's a stable influence on him. I think Jax will get along great with Moron."

"I called Jax's mother. She was grateful that we didn't leave her son to twist, even though he's a pain in the butt."

"Every time I thought about calling, things

went from bad to worse. I just assumed he was keeping her up to date because I knew he was calling her every other day."

"She also verified that Jax has been completely off drugs for a year now. Basically, it was a mother chat, worrying about our children."

"Jax and I both got lucky in the mother department. That was nice of you to call."

Jax seemed to be on the right track. I wondered if his mother knew he'd also given up cigarettes.

"Do you want him to stay in The Cove?"

"My guess is he'll go back to South Carolina to be with his family."

"Listen to me. You need to let Jax figure out his own problems. It's character building for us all."

"Who's going to stick up for Pavel? He deserves to have this case solved and the real shooter going to jail," I said.

"Please, just let the police do their job. Stay out of it. Do you hear me?"

"You make it sound so easy. How can I stand by and let Jax go to jail for something he didn't do?"

"I don't want you getting hurt," Mother said. "Brad and Jax are going to work on the boat. You need to concentrate on your own life. You have The Cottages to manage. Stay out of the rest. You better be listening."

"I hear you."

"When Brad leaves Moron's, he's going back to the Glades. His boat's ready to take off in the morning."

"How long will he be gone?"

"You know how it works. It's grouper season, so probably a week or two or until the freezers are full. He's been having good runs lately," Mother said.

"What did he say about Spoon?"

"I told him you exaggerated the situation."

"So you told him I lied." I laughed. "That was probably a good idea."

"Don't be so dramatic." Mother hung up.

Chapter Seventeen

My crappy day turned around when I spotted Zach's Escalade parked in front of my house. I forced myself to walk in a dignified manner, not bolt through the door and jump in his lap.

"Honey, I'm home," I called.

"I'm in the kitchen."

He had on his bathing suit, my two-piece hanging on his finger. He kissed me. "Here, put this on."

"Are you cooking too?"

"I'm prepping a few things for later." He turned to stir a marinade mixture. "I'll have this finished by the time you come back downstairs."

I went upstairs and changed into my black tankini, pulling my hair up into a ponytail. I decided nothing was going to spoil our evening. Before putting my phone on the charger, I turned it off. Any more crises would have to wait.

At the bottom of the stairs, Zach took my hand and led me outside. By the side of the pool sat two glasses of red wine.

"I'm loving this." I kissed his cheek, and we grabbed our wine and sat on the steps in the shallow end of the pool.

"How was your day, dear?" Zach asked.

"All I think about is Pavel. One minute, he's on the boat, and then days later, he's found murdered. I want to go back in time and change that night."

"Go easy on yourself. You had no idea what Dickhead was up to, sneaking around."

"I feel guilty. How am I supposed to feel about this dead guy, a stranger? I'm so fixated on Pavel; he's real to me now. If I had my way, this whole situation would just go away."

"It'll help when they arrest someone, and hopefully, it won't be someone you know."

"Jax didn't shoot Pavel." I shook my head.

"Unfortunately, Harder is lead on this case, and right now, Jax is their only suspect. Considering mine and Harder's past, he's going to play hard-ass with you and Jax. It doesn't help we're still together. We could break up."

I laughed. "Break up what?"

"We'll tell people we're no longer together, and then we'll sneak around."

"I like the sneaking around part. But Harder has several reasons to dislike me that have nothing to do with you, the biggest one being my lawyer, who's always on the winning side."

"Slice is looking into this case, and we should know something in a few days," Zach said. "Slice has contacts on the docks from here to Key West. His brother works for the Miami police department. They get something solid, we'll know. And Kevin will look out for you; he'll keep Harder from going too far over the line."

I was tired of being afraid and jittery, waiting for the bang of the next falling shoe. "What's for dinner?"

"Hungry?" He smiled.

"Yes, and I want you to feed me first."

Zach put his arms around me. "We're having salmon, pasta, and vegetables." He took my hands and pulled me up the steps and out of the pool. "You can sit on a barstool and tell me what to do." He picked up a beach towel and wrapped it around me.

"That should be fun." I laughed.

We sat at the counter and focused on small talk. I started nibbling on the food before it hit the plate. Zach had signed another client. He loved his job; the excitement in his voice matched the expression on his face.

On our way upstairs, he let me know that he wouldn't be there when I woke up in the morning. He had an early morning meeting in Palm Beach. He'd stopped leaving notes when I'd told him if he did it again, I'd have to hurt him.

* * *

I fished out my black lacy bra. I hated wearing bras. I'd never managed to find a comfortable one, but I couldn't attend a business meeting with my nipples on display. I pulled on a black sleeveless dress and a belt, finishing the look with a silver necklace and earrings. I carried my shoes downstairs to put on as I went out the door.

I dreaded the meeting with Cruz and Detective Harder. Harder wouldn't be able to resist scaring me with threats of jail. I couldn't imagine the interrogation being any worse if I were guilty. The difference would be that if I were guilty, I'd end up in handcuffs, but with Harder, that could happen anyway. He'd done it to me once before, and I hadn't been guilty then, either.

I braved the traffic to Harder's office in Miami. Only one person gave me the finger. Cruz had promised to be on time and meet me in the lobby. We'd have to sign in and go through the metal detector. I was already on edge when I lucked out and found parking in the front of the building.

I sat in my SUV and dialed Fab. "Where've you been?"

"Israel flew back in to put the finishing touches on his new album. I just dropped him at Miami International. He exhausts me; I can barely keep up. He burns twenty hours a day."

"Are you up for a girlfriend lunch and some shopping therapy?"

"Always. Anyone in custody for the murder?"

"I wish. I'm here at police headquarters for a meeting with Harder and Cruz."

"Don't mention my name," Fab reminded me. "Harder thinks I'm a criminal. Frustrates him, he lacks proof."

"Imagine that. Someone thinking that about you."

"I'm ignoring you. Call me when you're done and we'll meet." Fab hung up.

* * *

I sat at the conference table, a pained smile pasted on my face. Cruz told me to pause before answering Harder's questions, giving him time to object. He wanted only yes or no answers, and if that wasn't possible, then use as few words as possible.

Harder was of average height, tightwad haircut, and carried himself with a rigidity that suggested a military background. He slid into the chair opposite me, with a well-used legal pad containing notes scribbled erratically. "So, sweetie." Harder's dark eyes bore into mine. "We're here to discuss the murder of Pavel Klaus and what you know about the events of that night."

"Really, Harder," Cruz reprimanded. "*Sweetie* is unprofessional."

The look in Harder's eyes told me that it was game on. To my credit, I managed to stay calm, phony smile in place.

Harder ignored Cruz. "Were you on the boat the night of the twenty-fifth?"

"Stupid questions are beneath you," Cruz said.

Harder looked at me. "Answer my question."

"No."

"Can anyone corroborate that?"

"You have verification in all of the various reports from that night, and if you need more, then contact the Coast Guard or any of the agencies that responded," Cruz said.

"You gave your boat to Jackson Devereaux to joyride in, and you want me to believe you were nowhere around?"

"I wasn't there," I said.

"How did he get the keys?"

If only I could throw up on him. I looked at Cruz and he nodded his head to answer. "He took them off the key rack in my kitchen."

"So he stole the boat?"

"He didn't have my permission to take the boat," I said.

"Have you filed theft charges?"

Cruz interrupted, "Check the report; it was noted that Devereaux didn't have permission to take the boat. I spoke with Mr. Westin, and he's declined to pursue theft charges."

I didn't remember anyone ever calling Brad "mister" before; he's such a laid-back guy.

"Why would you let someone who doesn't

have a driver's license drive your boat?" Harder's voice rose.

Cruz cut in, "Driving a boat doesn't require a license."

"Still, your husband isn't fit to drive a car, but it's okay for him to kill someone with a boat?" Harder asked.

"He has a license. I have a copy here." Cruz took the paper from a file and handed it to Harder.

"The Florida license was revoked when they ran a check and discovered the DUI conviction in South Carolina and that his license had been revoked there. He currently has an ID card. How did that escape your notice? Let me guess, if I ask you if you knew he was wanted in South Carolina, you'd tell me you didn't know that either."

"That's not a question," Cruz pointed out.

"Did you know he was on the run?" Harder asked.

Cruz had known that question would be coming, and he had warned me to be vague. "I didn't know." I was nauseous, my stomach kicking nonstop.

"Did you know your husband is a drunk? That he liked to drink and drive? Amazing he hasn't killed anyone yet, or maybe he has." Harder smirked.

"For the record, Harder, Jackson Devereaux is her ex-husband," Cruz stated. "Madison hasn't had contact with him from the time of their divorce until he arrived in town."

"Duly noted. Did you know Pavel Klaus?"

"No," I said.

"Did you know any of the other people on the boat?" Harder questioned.

"Only Jax."

"Do you have anything to add about the night of the accident?"

"No."

"Okay, Harder, we knew this would be a waste of time, but you insisted," Cruz said. "Miss Westin wasn't there; she doesn't know anything. Is there anything else?"

"Where's the boat?" Harder asked.

"Why?" Cruz countered.

Harder pulled a folder from under his legal pad. "I have a subpoena to pick it up and impound it as evidence." Harder handed Cruz the paperwork. "If Miss Westin doesn't have anything to hide, she'll cooperate."

"Of course she'll cooperate," Cruz assured him. "Where's the boat, Madison?"

"It's at Marone's boatyard in The Cove," I informed them.

"Has he started work on the boat?"

"I don't know."

"I'll call Marone and tell him to stop any work. The boat will be picked up within the hour." Harder picked up his phone and called to give the order to execute two warrants.

"It'll be towed to the police storage yard today," Harder told us.

"When do I get it back?" I asked. What did he mean by two?

"When the case is over. It could be a year or more; your lawyer knows how cases can linger on the court docket."

I wanted to slap the smile off his face. How would I explain that to Brad?

"And here's a copy of the search warrant for Ms. Westin's house." He handed another piece of paper to Cruz. "They're being executed as we speak. The searches should be over by the time she gets home." He looked at me. "Sorry for any mess."

"So that's why you had us come to your office. You're a real bastard. But then, you know that," Cruz said.

"You're having my house ransacked?" I screeched. "What about my cat? He's old." I picked up my phone and called Fab.

"You can't use your phone in here." Harder motioned for me to put it away.

"Where are you?" I asked Fab.

"On my way back to The Cove."

"I said put it away," Harder yelled.

"Harder is having my house searched, and I'm worried about Jazz."

"I'll take care of it."

I pressed *End*. "Look." I held up my phone. "I'm putting it away."

"You hang out with the cream of the crap, and you want people to believe you're Snow White. It doesn't work that way. In my experience, you're no better than the people you associate with."

"Do you have any more relevant questions?" Cruz asked. "If that's all, I have another meeting." Cruz slammed the lid of his briefcase, snapping the locks.

"Sweetie, you'll be hearing from me again. You can count on that," Harder told me.

"You know Ms. Westin has counsel. Contact my office, and I'll make her available."

"You and I both know I don't have to go through you. I can do what I want and inform you afterward."

"I'm playing golf with the chief tomorrow. I'll inform him of your unprofessional behavior," Cruz said.

"Go ahead. He already knows I'm an unrelenting bastard. What's he going to do about it? I'm good at my job, and I put killers behind bars. I don't have a single unsolved case in my file." He stood up. "Sweetie." He nodded at me and walked out of the conference room.

"Where's Devereaux?" Cruz whispered. "At your house?"

"He might still be at Marone's, helping with the boat. My mother relocated him to The Cottages."

"I'm surprised Harder didn't ask about his whereabouts." He pulled on my arm. "Listen to me. Stay away from your ex, and then you won't be put in any awkward situations."

"Don't worry."

"Another thing, don't go playing Nancy Drew with Fab. Don't get me wrong. I like Fab, but she's crazy all day long."

I nodded. I couldn't promise that with a straight face.

"Don't give Harder any reason to harass you. Look, I know Harder, and you're not a serious suspect. This was a jerk-around session so he could execute the warrants without any interference."

"I'm hoping once this is all over, Jax packs up and leaves town." I told him.

"These kinds of meetings are a waste of my time and your money." Cruz snapped his briefcase shut.

Chapter Eighteen

"What are you doing?" I asked Fab. She was sitting on the floor with Jazz, rolling a ball at him. He looked bored.

"I thought it would be fun to play catch."

I laughed so hard I thought I'd fall off the stool. "That's the best laugh I've had all week."

"It has catnip," she said. "The guy at the pet store picked it out."

"If you get Jazz to play catch, fetch, or whatever, I'll buy dinner for a week."

She glared at me. "I ate your salmon, enjoyed every bite."

"Zach cooked dinner for me."

"Ah, lovebirds!"

"I know you're making fun of me." I made a face at her. "But it was nice to spend a quiet evening together. I did suffer momentary guilt over turning off my phone, but who can relax and have spontaneous sex if she's thinking the phone might ring?"

"Eww. I arrived as Kevin and his posse were leaving. Kev said Jazz didn't get off the chair."

"Probably resting up for his play date with you."

She glared at me and fed Jazz one of her leftover peas. He spit it back at her.

"How bad does the upstairs look? Down here, it doesn't look like they were even here."

"Kev was the lead. He wouldn't tell me what they were looking for. He did ask where Boner was."

"You're not funny," I said. "I'm just going to ignore you. Did the police take anything with them?"

"No, and I was surprised. They did ask where Mr. Sir slept."

"Thank heaven for Kevin. That's why my house wasn't tumbled. Nothing in this house belongs to Jax. I got rid of all his stuff the other day."

"Where is he?"

"My mother relocated him to The Cottages."

"I love your mother."

"Wait until she decides to manage your life and you'll rethink that thought."

When the doorbell rang, Fab asked, "Who's that?"

I looked out the window. "Dickie."

"The creepy funeral guy?"

"Yes." I started for the door. "You stay right there and don't even think about sneaking out the back. Sit back down." I pointed to the stool.

Fab made a face. "Why didn't you give me a heads-up?"

"Didn't you have a big funeral today?" I asked Dickie as he walked in.

Dickie saw Fab sitting in the kitchen. "She scares me," he whined.

"You're not wanted, are you?"

Fear crossed his face. "No."

"Then you don't have anything to worry about."

"Pavel's memorial service was earlier," Dickie said. "Afterward, Mr. Byce catered lunch. Turned out larger than your Aunt Elizabeth's funeral, but everyone there knew her. Most of the people who came today didn't have a clue."

"Word flew around town that Sid Byce was catering from The Wharf," I said. "No one around here passes up good food that's free. Funeral or no."

"A reporter from the local paper was there, and she told me I gave her good quotes," he said with excitement. "I'll be at the newsstand first thing in the morning to get all the copies."

Fab snorted and shook her head.

"The girlfriend blew up two pictures of Pavel to poster size. She had them framed and sitting on easels up on the podium in place of where the coffin would've been. I had the urn displayed on a smaller table with the flowers."

"Her name is Kym," I said.

"Crazy girl all strung out, hanging onto another girl. She told me she was poly something, and I think she meant lesbian."

I shrugged. "I haven't met her."

"I felt sorry for the dogs," Dickie said.

"What dogs?"

"Kym brought Pavel's dogs, and they sat in front of the pictures of him and howled, very sad. The noise they made was pitiful. Raul and I wanted to take them outside and play with them, but we had to wait until after the service was over."

"What kind of dogs?"

"Two Golden Retrievers."

Nothing good ever came of drunks having pets. At some point, the pets always ended up neglected.

"You shipping Pavel's ashes to his mother?" I asked.

"His mother gave permission to split the ashes. Kym took her half; she originally wanted to sprinkle them where they pulled him from the water, but instead headed to the Gulf. I told them they needed to go out past the mouth of the inlet and one of her friends, rail thin, jittery guy, told me I was stupid. The other half I'm shipping to the Czech Republic. Mr. Byce picked out a beautiful urn."

"That was generous of Pavel's mother." It saddened me to think about a mother mourning the loss of a son or daughter.

Dickie nodded. "Cremation was a good choice; he was in bad shape with half his head missing, and a few places on his body were pretty well gnawed, where some kind of fish had chewed on him."

"Dickie, we don't need the details."

"I understand cremations, but I prefer a traditional burial. I'm the artist, and Raul is the businessman. That's one of the reasons why we're so good together. My favorite part is the dressing, the hair, and makeup. I do my best to make everyone look natural. This one would've been difficult."

"Any talk about who might've killed Pavel?" Fab asked.

"No one even whispered the word murder. They all acted like they do when an old person dies of natural causes."

"Where was he shot?" Fab asked.

"In the back of the head."

"Someone shot him from behind?" Fab murmured. "That's cowardly."

"Mr. Byce is convinced that your ex-husband is the guilty party. I saw Byce yelling at Kym and her girlfriend, and Kym started crying. Right after that, the two girls stuffed sandwiches and cookies in their purses and snuck out the side door. I watched from the window. They went the wrong way and had to cut through the tattoo parlor parking lot."

"Did Jax show up?" I asked.

"Because I didn't know who he was, I asked around and was told he wasn't there. A good thing, in my opinion. It would've been ugly between him and Mr. Byce. Mr. Westin needs to watch his back."

"Brad?" I asked.

"Jax," Fab said.

"Oh!" I almost laughed. Jax hated it when people called him by my last name. "Did you just come by to tell me about the funeral?" I asked Dickie.

"I came to say thank you for all your help." He fiddled with the button on his shirt. It popped off and rolled across the floor, landing at Fab's feet. "Mr. Campion got my charges reduced. I had to pay a fine and do community service, but in one year, it's erased from my record."

Fab handed him his button. "What about thanking me?"

He looked totally confused.

"For what?" I asked.

"I got Brick to agree to let him turn himself in." Fab smiled. She loved that she made Dickie uncomfortable. I rolled my eyes and shook my head.

"Thank you," Dickie said, unable to make eye contact with Fab.

"How are you and Raul doing?" I asked.

"We're doing good. I took your advice and came clean about everything. Raul agreed to give me another chance if I agreed to couples counseling. He won't be sorry."

"I'm happy for the two of you," I said with sincerity. I found Dickie to be unpretentious and genuinely nice, and I'd never heard him say a bad word about anyone. In spite of that, most people joked about him behind his back, and he had to know.

"Anything I can ever do for you, I will," he told me.

"And me, too," Fab added.

"I have to go. Raul and I are going to dinner." He ran for the door.

I whirled around. "You should be ashamed of yourself, Fabiana Merceau, for intimidating that poor man. I heard his car squeal out of the driveway."

"Why do you get all the credit? I was nice to him, too."

"You sound as whiny as Dickie."

"That's uncalled for," she said huffily.

"Did you forget you beat him up? Which I had to hear from him."

"He exaggerates, slapping him is not the same as beating him up."

Chapter Nineteen

I came back from a walk on the beach, my buckets filled to the brim with seashells. Leaning against my front door was a large manila envelope. Anoui had finally sent over the reports. Her business card stapled to the front said she was an Information Specialist.

I started with the report on Pavel. It didn't contain anything I didn't already know, never in trouble with the law, no known enemies, a regular guy who went to work every day on the docks, never without a girlfriend. In his off time, he stayed drunk and hung out at the beach. Nothing in the report answered the question of why he had ended up with a bullet in his head. She included the photo from his driver's license, which was dark and could be half a dozen other people.

The report on Jackson Devereaux, aka Jax, aka Dickhead, started with his previous DUI conviction, relating how he had jumped South Carolina jurisdiction and had a warrant out for his arrest. All old news. There was no mention of what he'd been doing from the time of the divorce until his arrest. Anoui did note that once he'd left South Carolina, he'd gone off the grid and managed to lie low until the night of the boat accident. That surprised me. An anonymous lifestyle required cash, and he didn't have any.

Anoui also included a copy of the sheriff's initial accident report, which showed me what a lying bastard my ex still was. He knew two of the people on the boat that night. Hell, I knew them, too. His cousin Robert Devereaux had been there, along with Apple Manning, the same girl I'd caught him rolling around on the floor with in a drunken romp at the end of our marriage. That scene was forever burned in my mind.

If those two were in town, and I'd bet Jax's right nut they were, the three of them had moved into The Cottages. That was why I hadn't heard from Jax. I was always the boring one; I never wanted to party with him and his friends. He was always the leader of his band of lowlifes, and somehow that fulfilled him.

My favorite part of the report was when Apple told the Coast Guard she'd been at the Jumpin' Croc all afternoon with Pavel and Kym. The three of them chased their beers with rum shooters, and Pavel and Kym had fought all day. Apple called Jax and told him that her friends needed a break from fighting and to pick them up at the restaurant dock. There was no Mary on the boat. The whole time it had been train-wreck Apple. His evasiveness made sense. The report said she and Kym had sat on the bench at the back of the boat, facing one another and talking. Kym turned to tell Pavel a joke, noticed he was gone, and screamed. No mention of any makeout session between the women. Jax turned the boat around, and the four of them searched the water. There was nothing about them hitting a buoy or anything else. Kym's version was basically the same. Robert and Jax had nothing to contribute as they had been in the front of the boat with their backs turned.

I was underwhelmed by the content of the reports put together by Anoui and happy the package hadn't included an invoice. With the exception of the accident report, the other reports said nothing. Anoui had been overhyped. I flung the reports across the room, mad at Jax for not being truthful about all the details. I picked up my keys, deciding to take a trip to The Cottages and find out what was going on for myself.

* * *

I saw Mac sitting in the office. "What's going on?" I asked, opening the door.

"I picked up the phone to call you several times today and set it back down every time."

She looked nervous, which put me on alert. "Sounds like great news. What didn't you want to tell me?"

"Two sheriff's cars pulled in a little while ago. The cops walked up front and came back with

Jax in handcuffs."

"At least I know where to find him. Wait. Up front? Was he out on the beach?"

Mac looked down at her paperwork. "When your mother brought him here, I put him in unit ten. By the next morning, he'd moved his things into a waterfront unit."

I tried not to yell. "You should've called me right away."

"My daughter Candy filled in for me and she didn't know there was a possible problem. She gave him the key after he told her he lost his. I'm really sorry about this."

Mac had once told me she and her husband gave their kids names with special meanings. They had joked about Coors, and a coin toss later, they named her Candy. I was happy for her daughter. Candy Lane was a stripper name, but not as bad as Coors Lane, which sounded like a street name.

"It's not your fault or your daughter's." I knew if Jax hadn't been able to get a key, he would've broken in, and then changed the locks. "Who else is staying there with him?"

"Two people, Robert and Apple." Mac sighed.

"Where are they now?"

"Apple's still in the cottage. She sleeps all day and comes out late in the afternoon. I saw Robert walking down the street when the cops pulled in. He stopped at the yellow house across the street and sat on the patio, feet up like he lived there, until after they left. Then he walked up the drive just before you got here."

"I'd like to kick those two over the state line while Jax is in jail." I simmered with pent-up anger.

"They know a free ride when they see one," Mac said. "Asking won't get rid of them. Death threats would work with Apple. I'm not sure about Robert."

"This is ridiculous." I stood up. "This is not a redo of the past."

"Sit down." Mac motioned to my chair. "There's more. The sheriff was summoned for noise complaints and a fight. They threw a huge party; add liquor and drugs and you get irate neighbors blowing up the phones to the sheriff."

"I'm going to go have a talk with them." I held out my hand. "Give me a key in case they don't open the door."

I walked outside and called Fab. I got her answering machine, so I left a message. "Can you find out why Jax was arrested and how long he'll be in jail and get back to me?"

I turned the doorknob of the cottage, and to my surprise, it opened. Robert and Apple sat on the couch, watching television.

"Hello, you two," I said. "Just like old times."

"Hello, cuz. You're looking good." Robert winked. His mama would describe him as a good-sized boy, tipping the scales at close to three hundred pounds. His passion was clothes, and he'd adapted to Florida beach style in his shorts and T-shirt.

"Why was Jax arrested?"

"Don't know. I wasn't here," Robert said.

"You were here." I pointed at Apple. "What did they say?"

Apple slumped back against the cushions, a deer in the headlights look on her face, bloodshot eyes, and long dirty hair hanging in her face. "I don't know," she mumbled. She got up and ran into the bathroom in her stained T-shirt worn over a g-string.

"She's weirder than ever," I said. "Did she tell you why Jax got arrested?"

"I don't talk to her."

"Here's the deal. Apple leaves today, and if she doesn't, then all three of you are out. I'm going to wait to find out what's happening with Jax before kicking your ass out of here. In the meantime, don't withhold information, or I'll have you tossed into the street by someone bigger than your ass."

He looked at me and laughed. "You're looking good, Red." He acted like a man without a care. He expected life to take care of him without any effort on his part. For the most part, he had a knack for finding people to sponge off of.

"As of now, the parties and the loud noise stop. If the sheriff comes to this unit again for any reason, your free ride gets terminated on the spot. Understand me?"

"I hear you." He looked me over in a way that made me want to slap him.

"What are you doing here in Florida?"

"You know Jax and I are inseparable. He asked me, I'm here, simple as that."

Jax and Robert were like conjoined twins. They had grown up together and formed a bond. They were known to sleep with each other's women, beat each other up, and do other things sane people would have turned their backs on. They would go their separate ways only to find they couldn't live without each other.

"Don't get used to this." I closed the door behind me. He had a way about him that some women found charming, but it only irritated me.

I walked by Joseph's, and his door was closed. I had almost made a clean getaway when I saw Miss January sitting half-in and half-out of the hedge across the street.

"Ignore this," a little voice told me.

"Go away, I'd never do that," I responded mentally. "Hi, Miss January, do you need some help?"

She poked her head out the hedge. "I need help getting Kitty out of here."

Of course, it would be about her dead cat. "Let me help you up, and I'll see what I can do."

I hooked my arms around her chest and pulled gently. She was bony and frail, and I didn't want to hurt her. It took a few minutes, but I was finally successful. "Are you okay?"

"Kitty," she cried, pointing at the bushes.

"Don't get upset." I looked in the hedge, and sure enough, there it lay, still as dead as the last time I had seen it. "How did it get in here?"

"I was out pushing her in the doll carriage Angie gave me. Kitty loves to ride. I saw that dreadful Kyle boy coming down the block. He tried to take Kitty once before, but I started screaming and he ran off. I knew I couldn't get away, so I hid her in the bushes."

"Why did Kyle want Kitty?"

"He said for target practice. He told me I was crazy. I'm not!" Her eyes filled with tears.

"I promise you Kyle won't ever bother you or Kitty again. You stay here, and I'll go get something to wrap Kitty in to get her out of the bushes."

"Oh, honey, you don't have to worry about that. Kitty likes to be held."

There was no way I was picking up that animal with my bare hands. "I really need to get something. I don't want to hurt Kitty pulling her out."

"Here, use my sweater," she said, pulling it off and handing it to me.

I crawled part of the way through the same hole Miss January had used. I tossed the sweater over Kitty and was able to drag her out. I wrapped her in the sweater and handed her to Miss January.

"You don't mind carrying her back for me do

you?" She handed Kitty back to me. "I don't want to put her in the carriage. You're nice, just like your Aunt Elizabeth."

I didn't think about what I was doing; I just did it. I carried Kitty under one arm and guided Miss January and the carriage with the other. I wanted to run back to her cottage, but I was afraid she'd fall.

I breathed a sigh of relief when we made it to her porch. "Here we are." Miss January settled into her chair, and I handed Kitty to her. She pulled a cigarette from behind her ear and lit up, taking a long drag.

"If you need anything, you call me. Don't worry about Kyle." I practically ran to my SUV. I needed to get home and shower.

For a woman who might die any day, according to the doctors, she appeared to be doing better. I wasn't sure what kept her alive. I thought it would be funny if it turned out to be the vodka.

Chapter Twenty

Fab squealed around the corner and screeched to a stop in front of me. "Get in. I need backup." She had turned in her months-old Thunderbird for a black Corvette.

"For what?" I jumped in, pulling my seatbelt tight.

"This is a quick job for Brick."

"That explains the new car." The black leather seats were comfortable, and the dashboard had every gadget new to the market.

"I'm going to plant a tracking device on a woman's car before she leaves work. A friend of Brick's wants a clean and easy divorce," Fab said. "The soon to be ex-husband wants his wife to agree that they each take their own toys and go their separate ways. He says it's been the worst two years of his life. Nice guy marries high maintenance."

"Are we following her?" I asked.

"Brick is handling this one."

"He doesn't strike me as a hands-on guy."

"This is a favor for a friend," Fab said. "Besides, he got his PI license when he opened the bail bonds business. He used to track his own skips back in the beginning."

"What will I be doing?"

"Run interference. It doesn't take that long to attach it to the underside of the car, and I don't want to attract any attention."

"Do I get paid?"

"You haven't worked off your current IOUs," Fab reminded me.

"Will I ever?"

"You have to ask for them back."

"There's nothing written down."

"Hard to keep track of then, huh?" Fab smiled.

I shook my head and made a mental note get my own IOUs. "What have you heard about Jax?"

"I called Kevin. Jax was picked up because he's on Harder's 'person of interest' list. Originally, they were going to hold him on the probation violation. But guess what? South Carolina said the case was closed. Harder's plans to hold him in jail indefinitely fell through."

"So sometime tonight, he'll be back at The Cottages," I said.

"How do you feel about that?"

I sighed. "I'll be glad when this case gets solved."

"Kevin said Harder was going to jerk Jax around, and it would be an all-night interview. I asked him to let me know when they let him loose." Fab paused. "Do you mind if I spend the night?"

"The guest bedroom and bathroom is free of Jax cooties. You can stay tonight and any other night. It's not as if you need a key. Is everything okay with Marco?"

"He's never home. Besides, I like your couch, and I don't feel like driving."

I sat there running through my options of what to do about Jax.

"What are you thinking about?" Fab asked.

"You'll think I'm crazy."

"Seriously? Crazy? Tell me already," Fab said.

"Life gets back on track when we figure out who killed Pavel. Harder chasing Jax is a waste of time."

"We? Do you have a plan?"

"Not entirely. That's where you come in."

"So you need me, do you?" Fab swung into the parking lot and jerked a ticket out the machine.

"What do you want me to do?"

"The car's right over there, one row over and three cars down." Fab pointed in that direction. "Stand guard in the aisle and let me know if anyone comes this way."

I pulled my keys from my purse.

"What are you doing?" Fab asked.

"If I see anyone coming, I'll act like I'm looking for my car. Then, I'll alert you and walk this way."

"It's a bad sign when you start coming up with your own ideas."

Fab planted her tracker in less than five minutes, and we left the garage and were back on the street.

"Since this is Brick's case, why didn't he plant his own tracker?"

Fab laughed. "Brick doesn't crawl under cars."

"You're the one experienced at this investigation thing," I said. "I need your help."

"You need to leave this to Zach."

"Why? It's the same old song. Protect Madison from herself. Guess what? I've proven I can take care of myself. Keep your damn eyes on the road." I pointed through the windshield. "So I'm not you. I could be a Fab-in-training."

She laughed, but her expression told me she was thinking about the idea. "Who would want Pavel dead?" She slammed on the brakes at a red light. "I think we can cross off the four who were on the boat. They didn't know him, the exception being the girlfriend, and I can't see that pale, boozy girl killing someone without maiming herself."

"There's no evidence Pavel was killed on the boat. It didn't look like a bloody crime scene to me."

Fab pulled up to my house and parked, blocking the driveway. "I called Dan today at the Coast Guard, and he told me no blood was found on the boat, inside or out. You don't blow off a guy's head without blood and tissue ending up everywhere."

"What if Pavel jumped overboard? Only this time, the joke doesn't have a happy ending. He swims to shore and someone shoots him." We got out of the car and walked into the house.

"That makes more sense than him being murdered by Jax."

Tossing my purse on the kitchen counter, I looked at Fab. "I say we conduct our own investigation. I want the truth so it doesn't haunt me forever."

"Zach and your mother will hate this when they find out."

"We don't tell anyone."

"It'll work for a while." Fab shook her head. "Then it will explode on you."

I ignored her words of advice. "We need to talk to Pavel's friends to see if they can give us more information than the reports Anoui sent over. What kind of reports were those anyway? Three reports, one on Pavel and what a regular guy he was, the one on Jax said nothing, and a copy of the initial accident report. They're sitting on my desk. Help yourself."

"That surprises me. I know Anoui, and she's good."

"I better not get a bill."

"What did Pavel do for Byce?" Fab asked. "All kinds of illegal activity goes on up and down the docks in the Keys."

"He was a full-time employee. When the fishing boats docked, he unloaded them into the warehouse. The fish was then sent to Byce's seafood stores and restaurant."

"I say we start there. We need to be careful Byce doesn't find out," Fab said.

"What do you know about Sid Byce? I'd never heard of him before the accident and hadn't eaten at his restaurant, though I've heard good things about the food."

"His family ran this town back in the day. When his father died, his mother took control of the family holdings. The Byce family is all about power, and they get what they want. Mrs. Byce controls the family with an iron fist. I met his mother once, a tall, big-boned woman with beady eyes, and a lot tougher than her son."

"Dickie told us Byce blames Jax and wants him to pay," I reminded Fab. "Why wouldn't Byce want the real killer behind bars and not the first guy he can pin it on?"

"When the cops arrest someone and it makes headlines, then 'Oops, sorry, wrong guy,' no one believes it. The mentality is if he was arrested, then he's guilty. First one accused is the culprit, and lots of people never change their minds."

"It's all fun with the finger-pointing until it happens to someone you know," I said.

"Where did Pavel live?" Fab asked.

"He lived in an apartment behind the Pass boardwalk; the only access is from the alley. We also need to ask around about Kym. I think it's a long shot, but maybe there's a link to her."

"We don't have much to go on here," Fab said.

"We know he wasn't killed on the boat."

"Look, Fabulous-wannabe, we have to be careful who we ask questions. There's a killer out there, and a real possibility of kicking the proverbial hornet's nest."

"I'm not going to be a 'Wannabe' because we both know that's what you'll shorten it to."

"Fabulous Two. Is that better?"

"Madison's good."

"You're no fun," Fab said. "We need to find someone else to get the information. We ask one question ourselves, and it'll be all over town in an hour."

"We need our own Information Specialist. I want information on Kym and Byce without Zach finding out and putting a stop to it."

"It has to be someone connected to the local area and who won't attract attention. We need a dock connection, and that will probably cost. I'll check around," Fab said.

"I just realized I have my own Anoui, and he always has way better information than what I read in her reports."

"I'm afraid to ask."

"Joseph can get us the info we need," I said.

Fab sniffed. "He's unreliable and always has his own agenda."

"If you'd have sex with Joseph, we wouldn't have any problems with him," I managed to say with a straight face.

She glared at me. "You're lucky we're friends, or I'd shoot you."

"I am lucky."

"Have you skipped down the road in that thought process of yours, 007?" Fab continued. "What happens when we find the murderer? You do remember that we're chasing someone who has killed at least one person, right?"

"At that point, we give the information to Kevin or Zach."

"And that's where Zach kills us both," Fab said.

"Zach can just get over himself."

"And the rest of your family?"

"We agreed we tell no one. Especially my mother and brother. There's always going to be the issue of me not doing what I'm told."

"You're walking a thin line. They're all going to find out, and being the good friend that I am, I'll be the first to say I told you so."

Fab was right. My family cared about the outcome, but not at the expense of my getting hurt. The others had agendas having nothing to do with truth. "Once we find the killer, then I'll blame it all on you," I told her.

"I'm glad you think that's funny because I don't."

"If we're going to be partners, you need to know I'm a regular comedian."

Chapter Twenty-One

Fab's phone rang. "Hi, Kevin. Any news?" The call lasted under a minute.

"Jax was released," Fab told me. "He was questioned by Harder for a couple of hours, along with his attorney, Tucker."

"Tucker Davis? How in the hell did those two hook up?"

"I imagine Tucker salivated over the thought of representing your ex-husband."

"Tucker would love to serve up a huge payback to me, ever since the shopping mall project got scrapped. And his fixation on owning this house goes back to when Elizabeth died."

"You shouldn't have gone against him at the city council meeting." Fab shook her head. "Your impassioned speech on his mall project being not only a blight in The Cove but the entire Keys had people listening. Plus, you organized all the store owners to show up en masse. You were so good even I paid attention."

"I wish I could take credit for the project being dumped. I heard from Zach that Tucker lost a lot of his influence when his seedy reputation turned into headlines. His backers pulled out. They were scared their names would get muddied in all the negative publicity Tucker was generating."

"I wonder if Tucker found Jax, or the other way around," Fab said. "I'm putting my money on Tucker doing the finding."

"Insert Tucker into the Jax fiasco and everything makes sense. How some unknown lawyer found out where I moved to, about the house, and my life in general. Jax is a smart man, but he's not a scammer. He wouldn't do this on his own. Enter Tucker using Jax against me."

Fab grabbed a waffle from the freezer and popped it in the toaster. "The upside for Jax is that none of the plan so far has been illegal, just a nuisance."

"My aunt lived in The Cove her entire life. It astounds me that she used Tucker to draw up her will. She had to know his reputation."

"Elizabeth probably didn't know how obsessed Tucker was with her, or how he'd insinuate himself into your life after her death," Fab said.

"I'm confident Tucker will get Jax off if there's something in it for him. You and I both know that 'something' is my house."

I left Fab feeding Jazz waffle pieces that he chewed on and spit back at her. He knew the difference between waffles and turkey.

* * *

I pounded on Jax's door like an impatient cop with a warrant in my hand. I knew the blood drained from his face when he heard the knock. The thought put a smile on my face.

The blinds moved. "Why in the hell do you knock like that?" Jax said, opening the door.

"Like what?" I asked.

"It's early."

"We have a lot to talk about. Give me a good reason why I shouldn't kick your butt to the curb right now." I looked around; the place was a wreck. The ashtrays overflowed; empty beer cans and wet beach towels were everywhere.

"I'm not hard of hearing," he said, sitting on the couch. "Give me a break. My head hurts. Why are you yelling?"

"You're so loud," Apple whined from the chair next to the couch. Her face was chalky, and her long hair hung in a ponytail. She pulled a blanket over her head.

"Get her out of here today. If you don't, you're out tomorrow."

Jax covered his ears. "You don't understand."

"Oh shut up with the 'I don't understand.' Get dressed and come outside so we can talk."

He looked at the clock. "We'll have to do this later. I'm meeting with my lawyer."

"Tucker? Tucker Davis? Tell me, is he your lawyer on the lawsuit?"

He stared at me, obviously trying to decide how to answer. "He is now."

"Our agreement was that I would be the first to know if anything happened. Who made the first contact, you or him?"

"He did, referred by Lloyd Samuels," he said, looking away. "I don't like him, but his fee is right: free."

"Jax, you've jumped in bed with a snake. He's going to screw you good."

"Why? And tell me, what's the deal with your house? It's nice, but why doesn't he just buy one that's available?"

"It's a long story that goes back to my aunt. Please don't do anything that will jeopardize my property."

He tipped my face to his. "I won't. I have to go. I have an appointment with the snake, and then I'm going to Moron's." He walked into the bathroom. "Have you talked with your lawyer yet?" He didn't wait for an answer before slamming the door.

"Call me when you get back!" I yelled. I left knowing he wouldn't call. He hated confrontation. Fab and I would have to track him down and tie him to a chair.

I walked across the yard to Joseph's unit and knocked on the door.

He answered with a beer in his hand. "Want one?"

"I can't chase waffles with a beer and not throw up."

Joseph shook his head. "I'd still be asleep if you weren't out there yelling at your husband."

"Ex-husband, and I wasn't yelling."

"My ass. You woke half the neighborhood."

"I need a favor," I said.

"What else is new?"

"You owe me, and you need to start returning favors, or the next time you need a ride home from jail, you can use your thumb."

"Let me guess. Spy on the trio over there." He pointed to Jax's cottage. "And report back."

"I can do that legwork myself." Jax had never been able to hide anything from me indefinitely. When we were married, I turned out to be a quick learner.

Joseph sighed. "So what now?"

"I need to find out everything I can about Pavel and his girlfriend Kym. And I need this information yesterday without anyone knowing I'm the one doing the asking."

"You're freakin' crazy. You're going to get my ass kicked."

"If you do it right, no one will suspect. You're not dealing with rocket scientists."

"What about me?" he asked. "I'm a sneaky, cagey bastard, but I'm not a rocket person, either."

"Who were Pavel's friends? Was he doing anything illegal? Did he owe anyone money?

This is what we know. He was a nice guy, squeaky clean. How does that translate to a bullet in his head?"

"As soon as I ask the first question, Sid Byce will hear, and he'll flip out all over me. Everyone knows I live here, and you own the place. Plus, people think…" He paused. "You and I…um…"

"You and I what?"

"I tell people we're close."

"When that gets back to Zach, he won't be happy." I was pretty sure all Zach would do was laugh, and no one would believe Joseph anyway.

"Anything else you want?" Joseph asked.

"I want to talk to someone who worked with Pavel. A friend or a co-worker would be great, or someone that knows everything that goes on down at those docks. I don't care about anything illegal except how it would relate to Pavel."

"This is a piss poor idea," Joseph declared. "You need to rethink this plan of yours. You'll end up dead like Pavel, but only half of you will float up in the Gulf and the other half who knows where."

I leaned forward. "Too damn bad! Pavel deserves to have the real killer in jail, and Jax isn't going to be railroaded because it's convenient. You know who to ask without Byce finding out."

"Jax is a big boy. You need to stay out of it. You're not involved."

"The hell I'm not. Your buddy Harder is lead

on this case. He's had my boat impounded, searched my house, and questioned me until I thought I'd scream."

"News flash, Harder and Byce are good friends," Joseph said. "Byce wants a quick resolution to the case, and your husband is in his crosshairs. Byce's hopping mad that no further charges have already been filed."

"Come on. I know you can do this for me without anyone becoming suspicious."

"You'll owe me big."

I opened his door. "Thanks, Joseph. You wouldn't want someone to railroad you into jail for something you didn't do."

I saw Mac down the drive and waved to her. I walked by Miss January's porch, where she was sitting in her chair sound asleep.

"Miss January isn't usually up this early," I said to Mac. "She usually sleeps until noon." I looked over at her.

"She slept there all night," Mac said.

"That's horrible. She doesn't even have a blanket. The nights are cooler now. Do you think she's dead?" I asked.

"I checked her pulse; she's still breathing. I think she's a tough old bird, but she belongs in a home." Mac shook her head.

"Good luck to that. I heard some friend of hers suggest that once, and she cussed her like a hardened truck driver."

"You could make it happen. She does need

someone to look after her."

"That's Miss January's choice." I narrowed my eyes. "She has a home here as long as she wants one. Everyone here looks out for her, and I can be called anytime night or day."

"The regulars all like you. How did you get them to trust you?" Mac asked. "They treat me like I have a contagious rash."

"I had the advantage of knowing Joseph and Miss January from when my aunt was alive."

"There's more good news," Mac said.

"Seriously?"

"I had to tell Julie Cory that she and her boyfriend had to take their fights inside."

"More details." I had worried about the boyfriend since my last talk with Liam.

"Nothing else to tell. They were screaming at each other over where she parks her car. When he grabbed her arm, I interrupted the lovebirds and told them I was calling the sheriff. The boyfriend yelled at me to mind my own business."

"What did you do?"

"I told him it was in his best interest to talk to me, and then I pulled open my jacket to show him my 9mm Ruger."

"Have you seen her since?"

"The next morning, she looked fine and thanked me for not calling anyone. She didn't want her brother to find out; he's overprotective and hates her boyfriend."

"That sounds familiar." The big difference was Zach didn't hurt women.

"I told Julie I wouldn't stand by and let Dirt Face hurt her. I'd either shoot him, call the sheriff, or both," Mac said.

"How does a nice girl like her pick a boyfriend from the bottom of a hole?"

"If you can figure out the answer to that question, you need to manufacture a pill. I predict stardom and riches in your future."

We both laughed.

"Back in the day, I used to date my fair share of felon bad boys," Mac said. "My goal was to reform them."

"How did that work out?"

"I got arrested in a drug sting. The charges were eventually dropped. Some weren't so lucky. I went running back to my high school boyfriend, who was a very nice guy. We married and lived happily ever after."

"What's your number one suggestion for a happy marriage?"

She laughed. "Lots of sex."

"When do I get to meet Mr. Mac?"

"When you get married. How are things with you and your PI boyfriend?"

"Married? Why do I have to wait that long?"

"I don't trot my husband around single women. He's mine."

I smiled and shook my head.

"Liam asked when you were coming around

again," Mac said.

"He okay?"

"Looked fine, just unhappy."

"He has my phone number," I said.

"Told me someone stole his phone. His mother was super mad at him because she thinks he lost it."

"Who does he think stole it?" I asked.

"I asked him the same question. He thinks it was Dirt Face, but he hasn't told his mother because he doesn't have any proof."

"Five bucks says he has his phone back by tomorrow. You on?"

"This time tomorrow?" Mac asked.

"Yeppers."

"You're on."

We sealed the deal with a handshake.

Hearing my name called, I turned to see Gardener Girl walking up the drive. "Hi, Jami. I'm happy with what you're doing around here. The plants are looking good."

"There's a problem, Miss M," she started. "I went to the shed a minute ago, and the lock was missing and all of the gardening equipment was gone."

I followed her back, opening the door of the shed. "Gone where?" It had been stripped bare, only a few chemicals left behind. "When did you last see everything?"

"Last week on my regular day. I swear I don't know what happened. I know I locked up; I wouldn't forget. I always double check."

Mac walked up behind me. "I'll call the police."

"I'll take care of this." I headed to Jax's cottage. I pounded on the door, but no one answered. I had the key Mac had given me on my ring. I tried it, and it only took me a few seconds to realize the lock had been changed. I hadn't seen Jax leave, but he could've gone down the beach and walked out onto Gulf Boulevard.

I walked back to where Jami and Mac stood staring into the empty shed.

"I'm sorry," Jami said.

"I know you had nothing to do with any of this. Do what you can today, and next week you'll have all the equipment you need." I turned to Mac. "No police, I'll handle this. In fact, don't tell anyone we know. Both of you promise me."

They both nodded. Jami waved goodbye and rode off on her bicycle.

"I'm so sorry. I don't know how this happened," Mac said. "I never thought to check the lock. I will from now on."

"It wouldn't have mattered how often you checked. This happened when no one was around, or I'd have known before today."

"Anything I can do to help?" Mac offered.

I pointed at Jax's cottage. "Have you noticed when the three of them leave at the same time?"

"Afternoons, they sit on the beach and drink beer."

"Do any of them have a job?" I knew that was a long shot, but I asked anyway.

"Jax leaves every morning early and gets back mid-afternoon from working with Moron. The other two are free-loading slugs."

"Call me the next time you see the three of them hit the beach."

Chapter Twenty-Two

"Oh, good. You're back." Fab was sitting on my couch, pounding away on her laptop. "I need your help."

"I'm not agreeing until I hear what you need *help* with." I threw my purse on the floor and kicked off my tennis shoes.

"That's not the attitude of a Wannabe."

"I knew you'd shorten it."

"How long have you been waiting to say that?" Fab asked a slight curve to the corner of her mouth.

"I was lying in wait, looking for my first opportunity."

"Ride with me down to Key West and drive my car back." Fab snapped the lid shut on her laptop.

I turned to look at her. "You're letting me drive your car?"

"You're the only one I'd let drive my car. I wouldn't ever ride with you as a passenger. Your driving makes me crazy."

"Love you, too."

"Don't smile at me. I'm letting you drive

because you're the kind of driver other drivers give the finger to."

"There's nothing wrong with following the speed limit. How are you getting back?"

"I'm picking up a Ferrari for Brick."

"Nothing with Brick is that simple. What's the Cliff Notes version?"

"He rented a Ferrari to some spoiled rich-kid brat, and it's a week overdue," Fab said. "The guy's not picking up his phone or returning calls. Brick's sending me down to find the car and bring it back."

"We're jacking a car? That sounds like fun."

"Calm down. I have a key." She picked up a key ring from the table and put it in the pocket of her jeans.

"Why are you limping and have Band Aids on four of your fingers?" I asked.

"I jumped from a second-story bathroom window this morning into a dumpster. There wasn't as much trash in it as I hoped. I ripped my fingernails off, and there was no soft landing. Not to mention the smell."

"Why not use the door?" I admired the fact that she thought fast on her feet. I couldn't see myself taking a dive out a window.

"I got trapped in the bathroom, and speed was of the essence."

"Did you get what you went for?" I asked.

"Hell, yes."

"It's clear you're going to make me ask."

"I went to retrieve a sex DVD. A friend of a friend of a...you get the picture. Trust fund baby of a billionaire thought she had herself the catch of the year, a spoiled less-rich brat from Palm Beach. Turns out, he only likes to screw and record it. When she realized she'd been taped and couldn't retrieve it on her own, she paid me huge to get it back. Seems as though Daddy thinks she's a virgin."

"What is she, twelve?"

"How old were you your first time?" Fab asked.

"Thirty."

Fab looked at me and laughed. "So you lost your virginity last week?"

"Did you get combat pay?"

"I billed her triple and told her I'd give her a discount if she'd pass along my name to her other friends with money to burn."

"Next time, take me," I said. "Perp comes home early, and I'll create a diversion. I could've created a scene before he got to the door."

"Perp? You need to cut back on the television. I predict one of these days you'll have your own trashcan to jump in."

"I want all the cases that don't fall into the felony category."

"Yes, there was a legal issue," Fab said. "But this narcissistic piece of crap had about fifty DVDs, all marked with different girls' names. To not fall into one of the categories you mentioned, you'd have to call in the police. The guy goes down, maybe, and all those women get their names smeared in the newspaper."

"What about the other DVDs?" I asked.

"I filled a pillowcase, threw them into the trash before I jumped, and now they're in my trunk."

"Good thinking. Another happy ending," I said.

"Not so happy. When your family finds out that you're running around like PI Jane, they'll send you to a convent."

I knew she was right. They'd feel compelled to save me from myself. That could get ugly. "Promise me you won't give up until you get me out of the convent."

"Pinky swear." We linked fingers.

Fab rocketed down the Overseas Highway, a two-lane road running north and south over the water that ran through the Keys. I gripped the hand rest, my knuckles turning white, and looked out the passenger window because looking out the windshield made me nauseous. We made the two-hour trip in a little over an hour.

Driving into Key West, Fab was forced to use the brakes. It turned out to be a beautiful, sunny day. The sidewalks and streets were crowded with people, bikes, scooters, and skaters. Fab squealed into the driveway of a hotel and handed the keys to the valet, along with a big tip not to park it, but leave it up front. We walked the two blocks to the Pier House on famous Duval Street.

"Can we stop for something cold to drink?" I asked. "Something with a cherry."

"We're here on business. You can get your children's drink later." We took the elevator to the third floor. "Wait here for me."

I stood by the elevator and watched as Fab spoke briefly with the maid. They disappeared inside a room. Minutes later, Fab was on her way back down the hall. "Well, that was fast," I told her.

"He'd already checked out. The housekeeper called a friend at the front desk and found out that he moved across the street. He's trying to hide a car and leaves a forwarding. Not very bright."

It was a short walk to the Ocean Resort. "It's parked second one in, third row." Fab pointed. "Wait until I get to the valet desk, drive out in your pokey fashion, and no one will notice." She tossed me the keys.

The car was absolutely gorgeous, cherry-red exterior, black leather interior. "If you ask me, a Ferrari's a man's car," I mumbled, sliding behind the wheel. I pushed the seat forward as far as it would go, and it was still a stretch to reach the pedals. I exited the hotel parking lot, and no one even looked in my direction; the nerdy-looking valet guy was busy flirting with Fab. I parked at the end of the block in front of Fab's car and waited.

A short time later, the passenger door opened, and Fab jumped in.

"That was easy," I said.

"I had a message to deliver from Brick," Fab said. "But when William Clayton didn't answer the door, I picked the lock. Clothes, tighty-whiteys strewn all over the floor, and he was nowhere in sight. I found the rental contract and keys inside his briefcase. I grabbed them and left."

"This was fun. I'm loving this new secret life of mine."

"I'm wearing off on you." Fab looked at me. "That's not necessarily a good thing. Your family expects you to behave the way they tell you." She smiled. "How has that worked for them in the past? Girlfriend, you're a 'crazy' junkie."

I started to say she was wrong, but she cut me off. "I see the rush you get. And your excitement builds with each new job. I know we were going to meet at your house, but I need a ride back from Brick's."

"I won't be arriving right behind you, so don't call me every five minutes," I told her.

Fab sighed. "I'll try to be patient."

I got in her car and adjusted the seat forward. I looked in the rearview mirror. A hollow-eyed thug who looked like a drug dealer who snorted his profits, approached the window of the Ferrari and shoved a gun in Fab's face. My eyes were glued to the unfolding scene as I reached across to the passenger seat and slid my Glock out of my purse. I was too shocked to panic. Fab and I opened our car doors at the same moment. The guy took a step back, and I took aim and blew a hole in his left hand.

He screamed, the gun fell to the ground, his hand covered in blood.

"Take one step," I yelled, "and I'll shoot you dead! Fab, are you okay?"

The guy grabbed Fab, who had one leg out of the car, twisted her around, and shoved her in my direction, and then he took off running.

"Where the hell did you get a gun?" Fab demanded.

"You're welcome." I reached down, giving her a hand up off the ground. "Are you okay?"

"Dumbass was going to jack Brick's car. Once the GPS was activated, I would've went after him for free."

"I need to get my phone to call and report this to the police."

Fab grabbed my arm. "No, you will not." She walked to the trunk of her car and retrieved a plastic Ziploc bag. With the bag over her hand, she picked up the carjacker's gun and put it in the Ferrari. "How are you going to explain having a gun? Trust me. That dirt bag isn't going to be showing up at any hospital."

"I have a concealed permit. Everything I did

was legal."

"I don't want to be the last to know anything, I'm not your boyfriend," Fab said. "You're one accurate shot."

"Leave the gun. I'm calling the cops. If jacker dude's bullet wound gets infected, his arm falls off, and then he dies, I'm not getting arrested for murder. You can leave. I'll take care of this."

"Hold off making that call until I call Brick." She phoned Brick, explained what had happened, answered a few yes-or-no questions, and hung up. "Brick said to wait here. The cops are on their way. I'll be parked across the street at the corner."

A few minutes later, a black Jeep Wrangler pulled up and two men dressed in shorts and tropical shirts jumped out. They looked as though they'd spent a few nights sleeping on the beach.

"Madison Westin?" the scruffier of two asked.

I stepped back. "Who wants to know?"

"I'm Paulo, and this is my partner Grove." He lifted his shirt, showing a police badge and a police-issue Glock 45. "We got a call about a shooting."

I related all the details. I lifted my shirt, showing him my gun, and handed him my concealed carry permit.

"Hurts my feelings; Fab's sitting in a car all by herself." Paulo laughed and waved in her direction. "Where's the other gun?"

I opened the trunk of the Corvette and pointed to the plastic bag.

Grove walked over and took it out. "Did you touch it?"

"No," I assured him.

"We'll take it from here," Paulo said. "If we need any more information, we'll contact you through Brick Famosa."

"That's fine," I said getting into the Corvette. I made a U-turn, pulled up behind Fab, and got out of the car. I put my arms around Fab and hugged her. "Just so you know, if he'd shot you, I'd have emptied my magazine into his skinny frame, blowing pieces of him all over the street."

"You're going to make me cry," Fab said. "Drive carefully. Brick has a couple of cousins who are detectives in the Miami police department. They'll work with Heckle and Jeckle back there to trace the gun so Brick knows where to send the thank you."

"Did you and Paulo ever…?"

She grimaced. "It was one weekend, and I was drunk. I never think about it."

"Your indiscriminate sex is safe with me." I laughed.

* * *

Turning onto the Overseas Highway, Fab blew by me, top down, her long hair blowing in the wind. She looked as though the Ferrari was made for her. I hoped I looked as good behind the wheel of her Corvette.

On the drive back to The Cove, my phone rang.

"Jax and his mangy friends just left in a truck with two other guys," Mac said.

"Did you know the guys in the truck?"

"No, but they've been here before. The last time, Jax didn't come back until the next morning."

"When does Liam get home?"

"He's here now, moping around."

"Tell him not to go anywhere. I'm sending a surprise."

I knew Spoon would help me, but I'd made him off-limits since he started sharing cigars with my mother. Asking for favors and keeping secrets was beyond my comfort zone. Instead, I called Slice, Zach's chief enforcer. I'd seen him in full intimidation mode, and he scared me, even though I'd never been the object of his fury.

"I must have dialed wrong," I told Zach when he answered the phone.

"You didn't. Slice handed it to me when your name came up on his screen. You scare him."

"No one scares him." I laughed. "I need a favor."

"What are you up to now?" Zach asked.

I wasn't in the mood to share. "Put him on the phone." I sighed. "He can say yes or no for himself, or I can call someone else."

Silence followed. "Where are you?" Slice asked. "I'm on my way."

"Calm down. I'm not in trouble."

"You never call me," he said.

"I need some Slice expertise."

"I'm afraid to ask what that means."

"One of my tenants, Liam, is twelve and very special to me. Had his cell phone stolen. I think it can be recovered if acted upon quickly, and it has to be found in twenty-four hours for me to win my five-dollar bet." I filled him in on all of the details. "Liam is there now."

"How far do you want me to go?" Slice asked.

"Don't kill anyone."

"I'm doing this because I want an IOU."

"Done. If you need to get permission from the boss, I can hang on."

"Very funny. You can start your own fights with him." Slice disconnected.

My next call was to Fab. "Change of plans. On the way home, we need to swing by The Cottages."

"What's going on?"

"Jax and his friends just left the property, and now is a good time to search their cottage for what belongs to me."

"My lock pick case is in the glove box."

"I have mine in my purse. I'm prepared like a Girl Scout. You're my lookout for a change."

Fab hesitated. "Are you sure?"

"Yes, I am."

Chapter Twenty-Three

"Brick told me to tell you he owes you one for your discretion," Fab told me. "He laughed when he said it. He couldn't believe he was indebted to the 'crazy redhead,' as he likes to call you."

"I'm not squandering his IOU on something inconsequential. It'll be big." I laughed. "I hope today's drama doesn't come back to bite me."

"When I left, he was on the phone calling his brother Casio, a hard-ass detective. Carjacker dude picked the wrong car to steal."

"He needs to be in jail before he shoots someone," I said.

"You didn't think about sharing when you got your concealed permit? What's up with that?" Fab demanded.

"It just came in the mail. Billy at the gun range has been after me to get one. I'm glad I stopped resisting. Today could've turned out differently."

"Seriously, thank you. He looked like he was jonesin' for a fix, and that makes an addict dangerous."

"Careful of the dip," I told Fab. "Drive in like a normal person, so we don't attract attention." I opened the door. "Call me if…"

"I know the drill. Mac and I will gossip while you're busy."

I snuck around the corner of the building and slid the pick into the lock. It took longer than I expected, but the door finally opened. It was a two-bedroom unit, and I knew in a second which bedroom Apple had slept in, as a g-string hung on the doorknob. I wrinkled my nose. I didn't care to have the added benefit of butt floss in my underwear. I went straight to Robert's room.

Robert had always been neat, everything put away, even the bed made. I opened every drawer until I found what I was looking for in the last one. The pink and yellow receipts were clipped together. He'd used three different stores to pawn the lawnmowers, blowers, and yard tools. Everything else he'd sold to a secondhand store for less than he'd get at a yard sale. He had a big ring of keys, but I had no clue as to what they might open. The Iowa driver's license issued to him under another name surprised me. I found it interesting that he'd made a stopover in Iowa. I held the license up to the light to see if it was real, and it had the state seal. I spotted a wooden box on the dresser. I opened the lid and, to my shock, there was a credit card with my name imprinted on it. I only had two activated cards in my wallet, and that wasn't one of them.

I quickly went into Jax's room, carefully avoiding the g-string hanging on the doorknob. Stepping over the dirty clothes, I walked to the dresser and rifled through the drawers. I found more pawn receipts. From the descriptions on them, he'd hocked his father's watch and ring, but then had redeemed them.

The rest of the cottage was clean, which I knew was courtesy of Robert. The smell of stale cigarettes and alcohol lingered in the air. I looked around to make sure I'd left the place as I found it, pocketed the receipts and the credit card, and then slipped out the door.

Fab and Mac were seated on the wrought-iron bench outside the office. I held up the pawn receipts. "At least I know where all the garden equipment is. You need to keep a close eye on things around here," I told Mac.

"I'm going to be right up their asses," Mac said.

Fab and I turned to leave. "What about Liam?" I asked.

"A big, burly guy named Slice showed up. Scared me. I had 911 on my phone ready to push the button. Next thing I knew, he and Liam started laughing and walked to the pool area," Mac related.

"How long did he stay?"

"Half hour. He stopped by on his way out, gave me his card, and told me to call if I had any problems. I loved his big blues and sexy lips; he was yummy. I put him on my do list."

After you get past scary, I could see sexy. "Do list?"

"You know, just in case the husband decides he wants a tramp wife," Mac said.

"Does he have a list?" Fab asked.

"Mostly movie stars. Mine's more realistic," Mac said.

"Anything else I need to know about?" I asked.

"I forgot to tell you, Jax fixed Liam's bicycle. I see the two of them together on occasion, and he has the kid laughing."

"Kids like him." I smiled.

"I like Jax minus the other two," Mac said.

"The only reminder of Apple was a pair of her underwear." I told Mac.

"Do you have time to take me to Star Pawn?" I asked Fab when we got in the car. "If not, take me home, and I'll get my car."

"There's no way I'd miss this."

I thought about all the pawn receipts, realizing Robert had screwed me again. Fab cut through the side streets, screeching into a parking place.

I rang the bell. We stood outside the door of the pawnshop, waiting to be buzzed in. A man turned to stare before releasing the lock.

We walked inside, and I produced the ticket for the riding lawn mower. "What's the amount to get this back?"

The burly man wore a wife-beater shirt and had tattoos up both arms. "You don't look like a Robert. Do you have identification?"

"I'm not Robert Devereaux, but this is my

lawn mower, and I'm here to get it back."

"I can only release the item to the person named on the receipt."

"He stole this from me." My voice was on the loud side. "I want it back."

The doorbell buzzed again, sounding like a swarm of bees. A young girl stumbled through the door. She wore dirty pajama bottoms, four-inch high heels, and a tank top that accentuated her flat chest. She sported a black eye and her stringy hair hung in pigtails with skull clips. "I have some jewelry to sell," she mumbled, standing too close to me.

"Hold on a minute," the man said.

He looked at the newest customer. "Over here," he motioned. He walked into the backroom and came out with a miniature female version of himself.

"How much are you looking for?" the woman asked her.

The guy came back and stood in front of me. "Now about your supposed ownership of the lawn mower." He leaned across the counter, getting right in my face. "If it's stolen as you say, call the sheriff and file a report. Then you still won't get it back."

I forced myself not to step back. "Why's that?"

"When Robert tells the cops this is a scam and says you're lying, you'll both be arrested. The cops will pick up the mower, and it'll stay in impound until the court case is settled, and then it'll be sold as unclaimed property because both of you will be in jail." He smiled, displaying gold front teeth.

"How'd Robert get it in here?" Fab asked.

He eyed Fab, his gaze lingering at chest-level. "He rode up on it, in the middle of the day. Pretty ballsy for something you say he stole." He stared at me.

"Do I have any other options?" I asked.

"Yeah, go get your buddy Robert. The two of you come back with c-a-s-h. He pays, signs off, and we'll release it. We don't give a shit who takes possession."

"What's the amount?"

He looked at the paper and used a calculator. "Twelve hundred sixty dollars."

"You gave him nine hundred. Less than two weeks later, you want twelve sixty back?" I asked.

"Does the sign out front say charity? I'm a businessman with expenses. Cha-ching, cha-ching, the amount goes up by the day. That's how it works when you borrow money."

"Thanks for your help."

Fab started laughing when we walked out the door.

"Stop laughing. Thanks for warning me how awful that would be. Now what?"

"I looked at the receipts; they're all legitimate shops. You'll need Robert to get everything back," Fab said.

"You knew all of this and didn't say a word. Why?"

"For my own amusement. I wanted to see how you'd hold up against the owner, and you did good, girl."

"You need to work on the whole friend thing," I told her.

"You knew I was a beginner when we met," Fab reminded me.

I sat in the car in a sulk, running through my options to come up with something other than bringing Robert back to the shop. If I called the police, then I might as well go buy new yard equipment.

"What are you going to do?" Fab asked.

"Get the c-a-s-h. Do you suppose that spells cash? Take Robert back, and get my stuff."

"How are you going to get him to do that?"

"He'll do it. He has no shame. He won't be one bit sorry or even embarrassed."

"Why aren't you surprised by all of this?" Fab asked. "Is this a familiar road?"

"Stuff used to disappear all the time. The first time, it was my diamond tennis bracelet, a gift from Jax. Thankfully, I noticed it right away. Then, it suddenly reappeared. Another family member told me Jax found it in Robert's backpack. It didn't surprise me because I suspected Robert from the beginning."

"What did Dickhead have to say?"

"Jax never held his friends responsible for

their actions. I confronted him a couple of times about Robert, and the response was always the same. 'You don't understand about family.' You don't know how much that bugged me."

"I don't understand Jax," Fab said.

"It's simple, really. He doesn't believe in himself."

"What are you going to do about Jax? I hear Moron likes him, and you know he doesn't like anyone. Says he knows his way around a wrench. You need to lose the cousin and the girlfriend," Fab told me.

"Amen, sister."

Chapter Twenty-Four

Whit, my CPA, called with the information I needed. "Do you have good news for me?"

"The law is on your side, but…" Whit hesitated.

"I don't want to hear a 'but.'"

"I played golf with my friend Chet, the real estate lawyer I told you about, and we had a long talk about your situation. This is mainly a nuisance lawsuit. You being on the title before your divorce doesn't make it community property in this state. In addition, you inherited it as your sole and separate property."

"That's good news."

"Jackson can't claim it as his homestead, which would've given him certain rights because neither of you claimed it as your primary residence and you didn't contribute financially. Thankfully, both of you claimed another residence as your primary. In a nutshell, he has zero claim on the Cove Road house."

"And the 'but'?" I asked.

"Even a lawsuit going nowhere can be expensive to defend."

"What do you suggest?"

"Since Jackson is cooperative, get him to sign a dismissal dropping the lawsuit."

"He told me one hasn't been filed," I related.

"If anything does get filed, get him to sign off while he's in a cooperative mood."

"The lawyer behind all of this was Tucker; the one in South Carolina was a shield."

"Both lawyers are bastards." Whit snorted. "Tucker doesn't have a down and dirty reputation for nothing."

"Even if I could get Jax to agree to drop the lawsuit, Tucker would never let him back out."

"What's on Tucker's agenda this time?"

"Same old, he wants my house. Why? I don't know. Let's face it; there are properties with better locations, better lots of things. Seems to me he just wants something of Elizabeth's for some reason."

"Maybe he thinks if he has her house, it will transfer the respect people around here had for her to him," Whit said.

"Or I'll have to spend so much on lawyer fees I might have to sell The Cottages. If I can get Jax to drop his lawsuit, can it be done without Tucker finding out?"

"Normally, Jackson's lawyer would be doing the filing," Whit advised. "In this case, since he is willing to burn Tucker, Chet can draw up a dismissal, and you file it with the court. The clerk will mail Tucker a copy, making her the bearer of the good news. My money's on you, girl. One more thing."

I groaned. "There's more?"

"Chet won't be your attorney of record in this dismissal. He's not interested in a fight with Tucker. That's why you'll have to take care of the filing."

"I really appreciate this, and I can get it filed," I assured him.

"Keep me informed. Now that I've lifted the ban on gossip, I've become a junkie. When there's nothing good going on in The Cove, I have Hollywood websites bookmarked."

I laughed. "I really like you. I can see why my aunt loved and respected you."

"I know everyone in town. You need help, call," Whit offered.

"I do have a question. What do you know about Sid Byce?"

"Aren't you full of surprises?" Whit laughed. "He's the big league in this town."

"Byce is demanding Jax be arrested," I said. "Jax didn't kill anyone. I want to find out who did."

"Byce is power in South Florida. Nothing happens he doesn't know about. It frustrates him that he can't run it as his own little country. He has powerful friends around town: police chief, mayor, all the members on the city council."

"What do you know about him personally?" I asked.

"He's known to be a straight shooter," Whit continued. "Hardnosed businessman, no personal scandals."

"Is there a Mrs. Byce?"

"She died; they had one son, Alexander. He was arrested for drunk driving a couple of years ago; crashed into a couple of parked cars, and spent over a month in the hospital. The kid garnered sympathy because he spent some time in the hospital and then hobbled around on crutches and then a cane."

"Anyone hurt?"

"No one else was injured, late at night, streets deserted. After he got out of the hospital, he posed for every photo he could for the local paper. Looking remorseful, promising to change." Whit snorted. "Blah-blah nonsense, no doubt written for him."

"Any problems at his restaurant or with his employees?"

"The food's great. I never pass on the dessert tray. His restaurants get featured in travel books with five-star ratings. The young ones line up to work there. I hear it's a fun place, and the money's good."

"This murder makes no sense," I said.

"In what way?"

"Pavel was a straight-up guy, no criminal record, friends speak well of him, a harmless weekend drunk, and we both know a lot of those in this town."

"So, why kill him?" Whit asked.

"Exactly! He worked for Byce. The girlfriend had a couple of arrests for drunk in public, open container. How does any of that answer your question?"

"Maybe it's as simple as random," Whit suggested.

"In this town? I checked out the crime stats: an occasional break-in or stolen car, mostly drunk in public and DUI arrests. The last murder was two years ago. Eighty-year-old Betsy Winters shot her husband when she walked in and caught him in bed with a younger woman."

"I remember that." Whit laughed. "The other woman was twenty years younger and survived."

"What happened to her?"

"People turned on her. Everywhere she went, people called her a home wrecker and blamed her for that horny old bastard Winters' death. After she recuperated, she moved to West Palm."

"And Betsy?" I laughed at the idea of shooting Jax; not killing him, but making sure Mr. Sir was rendered ineffective.

"Aah, Betsy. I have it on good information that she faked out the District Attorney with a dementia defense. She never went to trial and was instead sent to a senior home where she died a year later."

"I hope you're wrong about the random thing because then we may never find out what really happened." I shook my head. "In the meantime, Byce has decided he wants Jax to pay for the crime, and Detective Harder seems willing to go along."

"Harder? I forgot about him. They've been friends for years. Harder's one of the people in the power circle."

"What's up with that? Harder's the only detective to investigate murders in Dade County?"

"Good friend of Byce's. Byce probably called in the favor, and the police chief would've assigned Harder to the case."

"You know what this town needs? A girls' network that rivals the boys'."

"I like that idea."

"Please keep this conversation between us. No one can find out I'm asking questions."

"No one will hear anything from me," Whit said. "I'll keep your secrets, like I did for Elizabeth, and take them to my grave."

"Secrets? I'm going to take you to dinner, get you drunk, and pry those secrets out of you."

"I'd like that." Whit laughed. "I'll get a dismissal drawn up by Chet and send it over, and you get Jax to sign. Chet's name won't be on the document. He wouldn't screw Tucker openly because he doesn't want a war, but it'll hold up in court, if challenged."

"I appreciate the info. Jax promised I would be the first to know about anything regarding the case, and that would include the filing of a lawsuit. He'll sign the paperwork, and I'll get it filed immediately."

"Jackson's a lucky man to have you watching his back. I hope he appreciates it."

"I think he does. For the record, I'm doing it for my own self-serving interests."

"Keep me updated," Whit said.

Chapter Twenty-Five

"Get up, you fat prick!" I kicked Robert in the leg as hard as I could.

"Huh? What?" Robert poked his head out from under the blanket. He blinked slowly as he focused on me. "How did you get in here?"

"Walked. Now, get up. You and I are going to the pawn shops to get my garden equipment back."

"I don't know what you're talking about." He rolled over to go back to sleep.

I leaned down and cocked my gun in his ear. "Yes, you do. I have the pawn receipts right here, signed by you."

"Get away from me, you crazy bitch." He eyed my gun pointed at him. "You broke in and are threatening me. I should call the cops."

"Would you like to use my phone? I'd like to hear you explain how you stole my stuff and pawned everything."

"What's going on in here?" Jax asked, standing in the doorway, clad in a pair of boxer shorts. He always looked much better than I did in the mornings, and I still found it irritating.

I pointed at Jax. "Get out."

"I told you she was crazier than when we were married," Jax said to Robert, eyeing my gun. "Think about my mother before shooting him. She doesn't like him either, but she wouldn't want you to kill him."

"I wouldn't kill him, but I can blow his foot to bits all over this room." I hit Robert's foot with the gun.

"Oww. Get her out of here, Jax!" Robert yelled.

"You're on your own." Jax closed the door behind him.

I turned back to Robert. "You've got ten minutes. I'll be waiting outside. You'll do this, or I'll shoot you and then call the cops."

"Jax knew all about this," Robert said.

I walked out of the bedroom to where Jax stood, slamming the door as hard as I could.

"Look, honey." He pointed at his crotch. "Morning dick, like the good old days."

"You stooped so low as to steal from me!"

He looked me in the eye. "I know you won't believe this, but I didn't know until after the fact."

"Why didn't you tell me?"

"After everything that's happened? I didn't have the money to buy the stuff back. Honestly, I was hoping you wouldn't find out."

I shook my head. "I'll deal with you later."

"Thanks for not shooting him," Jax said.

I slammed the front door in his face. It was

childish, but felt good. Mac was standing under an open window next to the building. "What are you doing?" I asked.

She jumped back, hitting her head. "Ohhh! The window was open, and once I heard 'fat prick,' I stopped to listen. I know I shouldn't have, but who can pass up a good ass chewin?"

"What's happening I don't know about?"

"When does that happen?" Mac pointed to the cottage I had just left. "If we got rid of Robert, there'd be no complaints."

"Ms. Madison, Mac." I turned, and saw Creole walking in from the beach. Tall, lean, and muscled, he made my heart race. Water drops clung to his chest, making me think indecent thoughts.

"Creole." I stared at his mouth, recovered my manners, and smiled.

He barely broke stride and continued down the drive, disappearing inside his cottage.

"He winked at you." Mac nudged my arm. "Half-naked like that, he gives me a hot flash."

"Makes you want to see the rest," I said. My cheeks burned.

"Listen to you. I wonder if his you-know is…"

"Stop. We've already agreed he's hot."

I needed to focus, not fantasize about Creole all day. Besides, Zach wasn't exactly chopped liver. A night of hot, sweaty sex with Zach, and it would be Creole who?

Robert came outside. "Someone broke into our

cottage," he told Mac, staring at her boobs, which were stuffed into a child-sized shirt.

"You should call the police," Mac said. "Be sure you get rid of the pot first." She smiled and walked away.

"Did I tell you you're looking really good these days?" Robert asked.

"Get in." I pointed to my SUV.

"No, really. I've seen you skinny, fat, and skinny again. This in-between look is much better on you. Nice ass, sticks out in the back."

"Thanks." Had he just told me I had a fat ass?

"I wouldn't kick you out of bed."

"Look, we're going to three pawn shops. I pay to get my stuff out of hock, you sign, and you load it in the back. I haven't figured out how I'm going to get the riding mower back."

"Fill it up with gas, and I'll ride it back," Robert offered.

"I don't trust you not to stop at another pawn shop and hock the thing again."

"Give me twenty for my trouble, and I'll give you my word."

"Your word!" I snorted. "You're hilarious."

He looked at me suspiciously. "This isn't an ambush is it, where I end up in jail?"

"No, Einstein. Then how would I get my stuff back?"

"I'd have to tell the cops about Jax's part in this; he's a co-conspirator." Robert had that sneaky smile on his face that made me want to beat him senseless.

"You're dumber than a bag of barber hair. And here's one of the many differences between you and Jax; he doesn't steal. Your signature is the only one on the receipts, so it looks like your co-conspirator left you hanging."

"Jax knew if you found out, you wouldn't call the cops," Robert said.

"You lucked out because I want everything back, and I don't want to wait until you're in jail."

He looked over at me. "I like fat fuck."

"What?"

"You used to call me fat fuck. I like that better than fat prick."

I laughed. "I've cleaned up my language post-divorce."

"I remember when I first met you and what a prissy chick you were. After a year with Jax, you were using 'fuck' three or four times in a sentence. It used to impress me how you could load a sentence with four-letter words and have it make sense."

"Those were the good old days."

Pawnshops all looked alike and operated the same. The first two were uneventful, no drama. All they wanted was the money. I paid cash, Robert showed his identification, and signed the paperwork. I got back my garden tools, blowers, and a push mower. They'd paid him next to nothing. The interest was loan shark rates that I didn't know were legal.

Our last stop was Star Pawn. "I'm back," I said in a loud voice when Robert and I were buzzed in the front door.

"Hi," I said to the woman as I walked past to her husband.

She glared at me and started in my direction. Her husband walked in front of her, grabbing her arm. "I'll take care of those two."

"I was in the other day…" I started.

"I remember you. I didn't figure I'd be seeing you again."

"This is the thief who stole my lawnmower, and I'm here to pick it up," I said.

He eyed Robert. "I want to see the cash first, then the paperwork. I planned on keeping that mower for myself."

Teflon Robert smiled. He couldn't have cared less about anything going on. He didn't concern himself with legal or otherwise.

I opened my purse, pulled out my reading glasses, the cash, and handed it to the pawnbroker. "I bought it at Home Depot. They still have them in stock."

The owner turned away and went in his office. I was ready to start screaming, 'Where the hell are you?' when he reappeared.

"Robert, sign here," the man said.

"I didn't know you wore glasses," Robert said to me.

"I need them for the fine print."

"I love the librarian look you have going. Sexy." Robert winked.

"I knew this was some kind of scam," the pawnbroker hissed. "You two figured you'd walk in and say the mower was stolen, and you'd get it back. Doesn't work that way, girlie."

"What are you talking about?" I asked.

"You two are banging each other. Robert here looking at you, licking his lips. You thought you'd concoct this story, thinking you were going to screw me."

"I need the key," I told the guy.

He slammed the key on the counter. I picked it up and handed it to Robert. "I'll meet you at the gas station on the corner."

"You say he stole the damn thing, and then you give him the key to ride away on it. Get out of here, and don't either one of you come back in my store again."

"Thanks for all your help." I pushed open the door and left quickly.

I waited for Robert to come riding around from the back. "Madison!" Robert yelled. "Not that I don't trust you, but I need the twenty up front!"

"You're a piece of work."

"My mother taught me to get paid before doing work."

"Your mother?" I was surprised because he never mentioned his family.

"I know what you're going to say, you can

save it," Robert said. "If she was here and I told her I had nothing to do with this and you were a liar, she'd kick the crap out of you."

"I didn't know you had a mother. For some reason, I thought you were found under a bush."

"As much as my mother would like to downplay it, she's completely at fault for making me the pretentious son of a bitch that I am today," Robert said.

That bit of honesty left me speechless. "Here's your twenty." I ripped it in half and handed it to him. "You'll get the other half when you deliver. I'm going to follow you back, so take Gulf Boulevard. The nearest gas station is two blocks down."

He waved his half of the twenty, smiled, and put the mower in gear.

The drive back to The Cottages was slow, going down side streets at one mile an hour. I backed into the driveway and stopped in front of the garage.

"Drive it in here!" I yelled to Robert. "Then help me unload this stuff."

"Is there extra pay for this?" He held out his hand.

"No, there isn't." I pulled the other half of the twenty out of my pocket and gave it to him. "Consider yourself lucky I don't throw your clothes in the road."

Between the two of us, the work took less than five minutes.

"Thanks for helping." I'd forgotten how easy going he could be. Nothing bothered him. In the past, many times his charm had worn me down, and we would sit and laugh it up. "Let me make this clear. You steal from me again, and I'll have you arrested *after* I have both your arms broken."

"I enjoyed our little outing." He winked. "We should do it again." He turned and went out to the beach.

"Robert!" I called. "See this?" I held up a large lock. I'd already given Mac a key. He laughed and kept moving.

I hadn't cleared the driveway when Joseph walked out, waving his arms. I pulled back in and got out of my truck.

"I've got an update. I'll meet you out on the beach. I don't want anyone to see or hear us."

I took off my shoes, threw them in the back of my car, and pulled out a bucket. I couldn't wait to get out to the beach.

"We're talking, not picking up seashells," Joseph said.

"We could go down by the water and do both." It felt good to sit on the white sand, digging in with my toes and fingers and letting it sift through. "Are you okay?" I asked.

Joseph's breathing was labored, his face pale. "I'm feeling better now that I sat down. You know it's day by day with me."

"How about more sun and less beer and cigarettes?" I suggested.

"You're not my doctor."

"No, I'm not, but I'm your friend."

He gave me a strained smile. He looked as though he needed a pain pill. "Byce told his employees if they want to stay employed, not one word about Pavel. He's got your husband in his sights and doesn't want to hear about anyone else. Doesn't look good. You're smoking the Kool-Aid if you think you can go up against Byce and win."

"Why wouldn't he want the real person to be charged?"

"He thinks Jax's the shooter. I don't know why." He shook his head. "Everything I've heard, doesn't add up to me."

I sighed. "Any good news?"

"Nope. Pavel's girlfriend left town, and in a hurry. Kym was seen yesterday morning picking up her paycheck, and then she packed her shit and left no forwarding."

"Why would she do that?"

"I heard she was walking home with Apple the night after the accident, both of them sloppy drunk, needing the other to stay upright. They were overheard saying that Pavel's murder was planned. That went down the docks like wildfire."

"Do you believe that?" I needed to keep antacid in my purse.

"Just sayin'. Word has it, Kym trashed the place where she was living, taking only what she wanted. A couple of Pavel's friends went over to check on her and found her gone. The dumb bitch left the two dogs locked in the apartment."

"Are they okay?"

"Good thing Pavel's buddies went when they did," Joseph said. "The dogs were out of food and water."

"What happens to them now?"

"Lilly the rescue chick has them, and she's frantic to find them a home. They're high maintenance. Do you know anybody?"

"I'll call everyone I know." The dogs didn't know it, but they were better off without Kym.

After seeing how she left them to fend for themselves, I hated to think where they might've ended up if she'd taken them with her.

"Cathy down at the Back Room Bar told me that when Kym came in for her last check, she was acting weirder than usual."

"Any luck with finding someone to talk who worked with Pavel?"

"There's a guy who worked on the docks with Pavel. He says he'll talk to you, but wants money for a trip out of town. Wants to go back home."

"Does he have anything worth paying for?"

"Don't know that. He'll probably give you an earful on both Sid and Alexander Byce. Hates them and hates working for them."

"Give him my number. Tell him to call me and we'll work out an agreement. I want to hear a sample before I pay."

"Good idea. You stay here and vandalize the beach." Joseph sucked in his breath when he stood up. "Keep me out of all this."

"Thanks, Joseph. Go home and take a nap."

"Yeah, yeah. You owe me."

I watched him hobble up the beach. I continued to sit there and sift through the seashells. I thought about everything Joseph had said. Byce had a hatred for Jax, nothing new there. Kym splitting town makes her what? Scared or guilty. And last but not least, a disgruntled employee. One-step forward was one-step back to where I had started.

Chapter Twenty-Six

"Anybody home?" I called out. A small meow greeted me. I couldn't believe there wasn't anyone sitting in my living room or kitchen. "Just you and me," I said to Jazz, picking him up and scratching his neck. "This has been a long day, black cat. I didn't find out one thing that would help Jax."

Fab walked through the French doors. "You went to the pawnshops without me, didn't you?"

"I handled the whole thing really well. Everything is back at The Cottages and locked up with a more intimidating lock."

"How did you get the riding lawn mower back?"

"I had to pay Robert twenty dollars to drive it, and then I followed him, just in case."

Fab pouted. "I wanted to drive the damn thing."

"I thought you were working. You can go over anytime, pick the lock, and drive it around the neighborhood."

"You paid him?"

"Yes, and he wanted the money up front."

"Now that I like." Fab shook her head. "If

something goes south, what do you care? You have your money."

"Those two owners are scary. The man told me not to ever to come back. He thought Robert and I were a couple and we were trying to scam him."

"I'm tired of missing the good stuff."

"Please, I'm always one step behind. I need your help on Jax's case."

"Almost forgot. Jax's in jail."

"Aah!" I pulled the ends of my hair. "Now what?"

"Kev says they picked him up this afternoon. He's now the number one person of interest. Harder's offering a deal to reduce murder one charges to manslaughter in exchange for a full confession."

"And if he doesn't confess?"

Fab shrugged. "He goes to trial, a good lawyer will get him off, case closed. Shuts up the folks demanding an arrest."

"What happens now? He sits in jail until the trial? How long will that take?"

"You know Tucker as well as anyone. He's a good criminal lawyer. My guess is he represents him pro bono."

"Tucker and free aren't synonymous. I say we rip a page from Tucker's playbook, the one that says, 'Use him and screw him.'"

"I want in on this," Fab said.

I told her everything Joseph had told me.

She shook her head. "That's a bunch of useless nothing, except the dock connection."

"With Kym gone, there's one less person to testify who could corroborate Jax's story."

"Pavel was very drunk that night," Fab said. "He had a .28 blood alcohol. Jax didn't blow, but the other two did, and their blood alcohol levels were in the low twos. They proved to be too drunk and too stupid to keep their mouths shut. The statements they gave the police were rambling and disjointed, rendering them useless. A good DA will use that to their advantage."

"Five people on board, and no one sees or hears a drunk go overboard? Explain that. It's amazing someone that drunk managed to get to shore and not drown."

"Pavel didn't have his pants on."

"He was naked?"

"His belt was unbuckled, and his pants were down around his ankles when they fished him out. This is a small town," Fab pointed out. "Everyone knows everyone else's business even if you've only lived here five minutes. Someone gets murdered, and no one knows anything. Big red flag!"

"No one's talking openly about Pavel or the murder. That's why we need to talk to an insider, friend or co-worker. The girlfriend would've been nice. Her skipping town caught me by surprise."

"Normally, murder would be the talk in every

bar in town," Fab said. "A local bar is a great clearinghouse for information."

"Unless they're afraid they'll end up the same way. More likely afraid it'll get back to Byce." My phone rang. "It's Joseph," I said.

"The guy I told you about doesn't want to talk anymore. He's leaving town." Joseph sounded agitated. "Something spooked him, and he's hanging for his paycheck on Friday and going back home."

I covered my phone with my hand. "Joseph's friend from the docks doesn't want to talk," I whispered to Fab.

"Tell him I'll meet him out of town so no one will know," I said to Joseph.

Fab shook her head no to me. "I'll find out who he is. Hang up on that ass."

"He was firm," Joseph said.

"Thanks for trying," I told Joseph.

"You remember I told you about Pavel's dogs?" Joseph asked.

"What's going on with that?"

"They need a new home right now. Crystal was taking care of them, and they're too much for her. They're here at my place, and there's not enough room for the three of us. Apple said she would take them, but she can't take care of herself."

"They can't stay at The Cottages," I said. "You know the rule, one dead cat per household."

Fab and I laughed.

"I'm on my way over," I told Joseph and hung up the phone.

I turned to Fab. "Don't roll your eyes at me. You're coming." We took my SUV. There was no room for two big dogs in Fab's sports car. Besides, she wouldn't let a dog in her car, even if it were an ankle biter. "I have a crazy idea."

"That's shocking."

"Sarcasm doesn't become you, and it isn't necessary." I picked up my phone. "Dickie, this is Madison Westin."

"Did someone die? We can send out a car to pick them up, and you can come in tomorrow to make arrangements."

"No, no one died. This isn't a business call."

Fab started laughing.

"Sssh," I told her.

"Do you remember the dogs at Pavel Klaus's funeral?"

"Yes," he said. "They were great dogs."

"Long story short, they need a home. Did anybody show an interest in the dogs at the funeral?" I was hoping he'd offer to take the dogs, since I didn't have the nerve to ask him outright.

"Raul liked those dogs. He's mentioned them a couple of times, wondering how they were doing. We'll take them."

"How soon could you pick them up?"

"I can go now," Dickie said. "I just finished dressing Mrs. Weathersby. I didn't think the dress was the right choice, so I adjusted her makeup so she'd appear more natural and not so pale."

"Dickie, about the dogs. Are you sure? Pavel's girlfriend left town, leaving them behind. They need a stable home, and it'd be nice to keep them together. At some point, I fear they'll end up at the pound."

"Give me the address, and I'll go get them. I'll surprise Raul. Moonshine, our Labrador, died about a month ago, and this will be a great surprise."

"Dickie, I forgot to ask the dog's names."

"Don't worry, I wrote them down. This will work out fine."

I gave him the address of The Cottages and told him I'd call Joseph, so he'd be expecting him.

Joseph answered on the first ring. "I found them a permanent home. Dickie's on his way to pick them up."

"That cretin from the funeral home?"

"Stop it. Those two dogs just hit the jackpot with Dickie and Raul as their new owners."

"I suppose," Joseph said.

I knew Dickie creeped him out, but I also knew the dogs would shortly drive him over the edge. "This is the perfect solution for the dogs. Dickie's on his way now. Promise me you'll be nice." I made a U-turn in the intersection and headed back home.

"You're finding homes for dogs now?" Fab asked.

"Those dogs deserve a good home, and they got one. Every animal should be so lucky."

"Softie."

"You make it sound like a skin condition or something."

Chapter Twenty-Seven

"Hi, honey. I'm home," Zach said as he walked in the same doors Fab had come through earlier. "What are you two up to?"

"Getting drunk in the middle of the day," I said, holding up my iced tea. "Any news for me?"

Fab and Zach did the silent dance. They glared, looked one another over, nodded, and relaxed. I felt guilty that I was the one to put a wedge in their relationship. Zach disapproved that Fab and I had become such good friends; he complained all the time that Fab was a bad influence.

"I took Slice off the case and assigned Winston to investigate. He hasn't come up with anything new," Zach informed me.

"So that's it?"

"In the meeting this afternoon, the consensus was stranger murder," Zach said.

"Stranger murder?" I shook my head. "Are you saying that the murder might never get solved? This isn't the way to get me to stop asking questions."

"What questions?" Zach demanded. "You

promised to stay out of this case."

"I asked Joseph to ask around, and he knows as much as you do. Nothing!" So what if it wasn't the truth? "Who the hell is Winston, anyway?"

"New guy. Good connects," Zach said calmly. "He did a thorough job, looked into Pavel's life and background, and came up with no reason for someone to shoot him. Hence, the stranger angle. And he's not going to make up information just to satisfy you. Your mother was happy that you asked me to investigate."

"What about my mother?" I asked.

"She was worried you'd go snooping around and get in over your head. I reassured her you were letting me do the investigating, and that calmed her down."

"How nice you two could reassure one another. I don't need rescuing, and it's getting old," I told him. "Aren't you supposed to be a top-notch investigator?"

He narrowed his eyes. "What do you mean by that?"

"I mean you have zero information. What do you charge your clients for work like that? Even the reports that Anoui sent over were useless. She couldn't even include a decent photo of Pavel; I had to print it off the internet." I could see he was struggling to stay calm.

"Look, I know you want to help out Jax, but he's only charged with BUI, and he's guilty. It is what it is. My company isn't going to manufacture evidence to get Dick Weasel off. Let him man up and handle his own problems."

"Breaking news: Weasel's in jail on a possible murder one charge," I said.

"There's no other viable suspect. I'm not going to accuse someone else to make you happy." His jaw clenched. "Shouldn't you be at home waiting for Marco?" he asked Fab.

Fab gave him the finger and slid off the stool.

"Sit back down," I told her. I turned back to Zach. "She's spending the night. So you're telling me there's nothing. Case over. Any dock gossip?"

"Like you said, this case is closed," Zach said evenly. "You're pretty involved with someone you divorced."

"It's not that simple." I sighed. "He was a part of our family, and he has a family of his own who are worried. No one wants him going to jail for something he didn't do. In a small town, the story would forever be that my ex-husband murdered someone on the family boat. Do you think Pavel's murderer should walk away? What happens if the person kills again?"

"Do you mind if we have some time alone?" Zach asked Fab.

Fab picked up Jazz. "We'll go out by the pool."

Once she left, I said, "You like Fab. Why are you being so rude to her?"

"I do like her," Zach said. "She's better backup than most men I know. What I don't like is you two running around asking questions. You take crazy chances when you're with her."

"I don't need to be reprimanded like I'm six years old. I don't do anything I don't want to do."

"You woke up one morning, said to yourself, 'I'll go with Fab while she jacks a car from a felon who owes Brick money.'"

"I don't believe he had a record, and there was no jacking involved. Besides, we had a key." I would've lied, but he knew too many details.

"What if rich boy had caught the two of you?" Zach demanded.

"He didn't. Besides, he stopped paying for the rental, which makes it grand theft auto under Florida law. Are you sticking up for that?" Good thing he hadn't heard about the shooting.

"Seriously, you must not be smart enough to know when you're in a bad situation. Or you don't give a damn. Is it all fun and games for you to worry your family constantly?"

I stared at him, shocked. "It must be my stupidity."

"Don't sulk. You know what I meant. Let's table the discussion on Fab. I want to spend what's left of the evening with you. We could go back to my place. I thought you could start spending more time there."

"What are you talking about?" Suddenly, I felt

claustrophobic. He was tightening the reins, and I didn't like it.

"Taking our relationship for a test drive," Zach said. "Spend more time together, as in living together."

"At your place?" I squeaked.

"We would have privacy, and no people walking in and out."

"Hmm. Well, I... uh... hmm." He was definitely off his game if he thought I was going from occasional dating to being guarded.

He glared at me. "That's not quite the response I expected."

"I thought maybe we could go bowling, eat more Mexican food." I hesitated. "You just sprung it on me. I need time to think about the idea."

"How much time?"

"I don't know. That's a big decision to make in five seconds."

He leaned forward. "Come home with me now."

"I can't. I'm not bailing on Fab, and I'm waiting to hear about two dogs I'm trying to find a home for."

His look told me he thought I was lying. "What dogs?"

"Kym, Pavel's girlfriend, abandoned his two dogs. They needed a home, and I think I found them one."

Zach threw his hands in the air. "Why does it

have to be you? If you were living at my place, I could help you with the word 'no,' and you wouldn't be bothered with these kinds of calls."

"It's not a bother. I love animals. Just because my choice is cat over dog doesn't mean I wouldn't help if I could."

"One of Pavel's friends would've stepped forward," Zach said.

"I found the dogs a better home than going home with another drunk."

"You can't meddle in everything in town."

"How does living at your place control who I say yes or no to? Are you going to lock me up and take away my phone?" Zach lived at the top of an old warehouse, modern, slick, and fifty steps straight up to the front door.

"You're deliberately picking a fight."

"Why don't you leave before we both say something we can't take back?"

He stared at me for a long moment, a vein raised on the right side of his head. He turned and stomped out of the front door.

Living together was a bad idea. Not to mention the fact I didn't want to live at his place. "You can come out, Fab. You're lucky he had his back to you, or he'd of seen you eavesdropping."

"I'm not losing my touch. There just wasn't another good place to hide," Fab said.

"I knew you'd never resist listening."

"The conversation went downhill after your lackluster response to moving in."

"There was a moment or two there when I thought I might cry. Seeing you standing there gave me strength not to sink to such a girlie level."

"You're tougher than you give yourself credit for."

"I love my house." I looked around the room and knew I wasn't moving anywhere. "He doesn't have a pool. My house is comfy and has double-dipped chocolate ice cream bars in the freezer. Who would come visit me over there? No one. Everyone's afraid of him."

"Weren't you just telling me you wanted more time with him?"

"Did you hear me say one word about moving in together?" I asked. "Dates, dinners out, shooting pool at the bar, late night swims, and sex. That's what I meant."

"When you said bowling, I almost laughed."

"We can do all that without shacking up," I said.

"I would have said sex first."

"I'm sure you would." I smiled. "I move in with him, and I spend all my time waiting for him to come home from being superspy. And I'm not living somewhere where a guy died."

"That would creep me out, too. What if his ghost is still hanging there?"

"Oh, stop. I'll never want to go there now."

"How are you going to tell him?" Fab asked.

I sighed. "I don't have to think about it tonight."

"Okay, Scarlett, what are you thinking about?"

"What did you think of Zach's report? I think he doesn't give a damn. He acts like he's got competition from Jax, and he doesn't."

"I almost laughed when you nailed him with the zero information," Fab said. "The problem here is that you are loathe to do what you're told." She shook her finger at me.

"Did you believe he wasn't able to dig up anything?"

"I believe he's investigating like he said. My guess is whatever information he's found out, he's keeping to himself. He's trying to keep you from getting hurt."

"He has a few things to learn about women," I said.

"The stranger murder angle has merit. When there's no connection between killer and deceased, it's a hard case to solve. At that point, you need someone to talk, DNA, or a gun with prints on it."

I reached for my ringing phone. "Joseph again," I told Fab.

"Dickie came and got the dogs," Joseph said. "As soon as Dickster walked in, the dogs jumped all over him. He's weird as fuck, but you're right about him and the other guy giving them a good home."

"That would be Raul, and I'm happy that the

dogs have a new home. How are things there?"

"Quiet now that Jax's in jail. Apple's back. Of course, she didn't go far, only across the street to the weed dealer, Chuck. His stuff is cheapass; he sells stems and seeds. She's passed out in a chair by the pool, and Robert left dressed like a pimp."

"She's not close to the pool, is she?"

"No, she's over in the corner. Wouldn't that be something if she drowned?" His laugh was wheezy and brittle.

"That's not very funny."

"You know what they say, don't you? It drizzles, then it pours."

"Good night, Joseph."

"So the little bastard is at home. I'm going for a ride," Fab told me.

"Not by yourself." I grabbed her keys before she got to them. "You drive, and I'll hide in the car. You promise not to hurt him?"

"Why do you have to take the fun out of everything?"

"It wouldn't be a fair fight even if he was in good health, which he's not," I pointed out.

"Don't worry. He's turning out to be useful. He does manage to dig up good info. You have to remember number one is king with him and factor that in."

"After, I want to go on a joyride," I said.

"Where to?"

"I want to do the murder tour, drive down to where the boat accident happened, and then to where they pulled Pavel out of the water. After that, we can go to the docks where he worked and lived. It's a different perspective at night."

"Your promise lasted ten minutes," she sighed. "I know you don't want to accept a possible stranger angle, but you might have to."

"Stranger? That's bull. And besides, did you hear the word promise?"

"I'm going to get the blame for this," Fab warned.

"After you're done terrorizing a sick old man, I'll go to the other places by myself."

"Oh no, you're not."

I turned away and smiled. I knew there was no way she'd be left out.

* * *

"Back into the parking space by the office," I directed. "I can hunch down and see what's going on and no one will see me. Remember, don't hurt him."

Fab jumped out and slammed the door. Everything appeared to be quiet, no one milling around. All the units were booked, but only about half of them had on lights. People either were out or had gone to bed early.

Miss January sat on her porch, Kitty in her lap. She suddenly stood, looked around, then bent over the railing and vomited. Afterward, she wiped her mouth, picked up Kitty, and went into her cottage.

I watched as Creole came out of nowhere and walked to his front door. He stood under the porch light, put his key in the lock, then turned around and waved at me. How had he known I was in the car? I was huddled in the dark and positive no one could see me. He disappeared inside his cottage.

"Good news, bad news," Fab said, getting back into the car. "The guy's name is Tomas. Here's his phone number and address." She handed me a piece of paper.

"Bad news?"

"Right before we got here, a brick went through Joseph's bedroom window. The note tied to it said, 'Shut up, old man.'"

"Is Joseph okay?"

"He's okay. The brick landed on his bed. He told me to tell you to stay away, no more favors. We have a new understanding," Fab said with confidence.

"Does he think there's sex in his future?"

"I'm going to take the high road and ignore you."

"Let's go see Tomas before he leaves town."

"Not we. Me," Fab said. "I'll go first thing in the morning and catch him by surprise before he's woken up. You need to lay low and stop snooping."

"I don't like this."

"Too bad. If someone connects you and Joseph, it won't be good for him or you. He's really afraid right now."

I knew Fab was right, but that didn't mean I was going into time-out without a lot of kicking and screaming.

Chapter Twenty-Eight

"Turn here," I directed Fab. "According to what Jax told me, the last time anyone saw Pavel alive was when they were on the boat headed through this part of the channel."

"There's nothing much to see at night. If he went over here, I can't believe a guy that drunk could swim half a mile and then pull himself out of the water."

"We don't know that he wasn't shot in the water," Fab said. "Although you'd have to be damn lucky to shoot someone in the back of the head in the dark and no lights."

"He floated up about two miles north, where the expensive waterfront condos begin. How far does a body drift before surfacing?"

"It depends on the tides," Fab said. "Logic would say he went over farther down the channel. Let's face it. He could've been killed anywhere and dumped along here."

"I don't know what I thought we'd get out of seeing this in the dark, but I wanted to see it anyway. I knew the nighttime would give us certain anonymity; we could sneak around without anyone seeing us." I pointed across the channel. "Isn't Byce's warehouse down that inlet?"

"It seems close from here, but you have to drive over the bridge and make the U-turn underneath to get there." Fab made a turn in the middle of the street. "Why do you want to see Byce's warehouse?"

"Because Pavel worked there. I went by Pavel's apartment a couple of times and, day or night, the area is quiet, which I found interesting, considering the people who live back there. It's a pay-by-the-week area. There's also a seedy motel that advertises flop for the night if you have cash."

"That's what the sign says?" Fab asked.

"Close."

"I'm acquainted with a couple of low-level dealers who live back there. I talked to them a week ago and got the same story—nice guy, no trouble." Fab turned down a narrow two-lane street, which ended in a dead end. "Pavel smoked pot, but he had his own connection elsewhere. He didn't deal or sell anywhere in the area. He never even asked about their product, and they sell the best weed in the Keys."

Byce's warehouse occupied one side of the lot, and a large boat storage business was on the other side. We parked at the back of the storage yard, got out of the car, and walked down a slim pathway along the docks, giving us a view of Byce's place.

"This was a good idea, no chance of being seen from this side of the property," I said.

"Nothing going on down here, not that I expected anything." Fab turned on her flashlight. "All the businesses here are only open during the daytime."

"Fab, listen. There's a boat approaching. Can you hear the engine in the distance?"

"At this time of night? That's a surprise, unless they took a wrong turn."

"Wow, look at that," I whispered.

"Yeah, and it's heading our way."

A sleek white cigarette boat slid alongside the dock in front of Byce's warehouse. Two men jumped down, grabbed the ropes, and secured the boat to the cleat on the dock. It looked out of place; the boats docked nearby were well-used fishing boats, reeking of fish stench.

"I want to get a closer look at what's going on," Fab whispered.

"I'll follow."

"You stay here and watch what's going on up and down the canal. Stay out of sight. If I'm not back in fifteen minutes, call the cops and tell them you heard gunshots. Then, take the car and get the hell out of here. Pick me up at Roscoe's across the bridge." She tossed me her car keys.

The rolling door in the warehouse squeaked its way open, and the light illuminated two more men. The two men still on the boat stacked small boxes on the back end, then one disembarked, stacked them on the dock, and the two from the warehouse disappeared inside with them.

The second Fab was out of sight, creepiness settled over the area. I wished I hadn't had this idea. What was going on wasn't a good thing. From where I stood, the whole setup reeked of illegal.

Fifteen minutes flew by, and all the boxes disappeared inside the warehouse. Thankfully, I hadn't heard any screams or gunshots. I walked the opposite way from where we had entered, thinking it would be a shortcut around the building and back to the parking lot. Instead it turned into a weedy, overgrown dead end.

I spotted a skinny path down the other side of the building where the weeds were knee-high and old boat parts were scattered around. Another dead end. Trying not to obsess on how scared I was, I turned and walked along the dock where the stored boats were launched into the water.

I jumped at the sound of a scratching noise. Out of the corner of my eye, I caught an outline of a person holding something large. I screamed, and then felt the impact. Pain raced across my back and shoulder blades. My right shoulder took the next blow sending me airborne into the water.

After several seconds of disorientation the lifesaving classes my mother had insisted on kicked in, and I floated on my back. The pain in my arm was excruciating. Three one-armed strokes later, I clung to the dock pilings with my legs wrapped around the pillar. After a brief rest and another few strokes, I grabbed onto the steps that would take me to the dock above. I ignored the pain and pulled myself around, ending up under the stairs, hanging onto the bottom step, waiting and listening for footsteps or voices.

I heard a boat start in the distance. The boat approached slowly; a high-beam light scanned the water. When it was a half-length away, I took a deep breath and went under.

I held my breath as long as I could, then resurfaced quietly. They'd already passed, and I breathed a huge sigh of relief when they didn't double back. I waited for what seemed like an eternity, ignoring that the water smelled gross and felt unbelievably slimy. Picking off whatever had stuck to my skin, without looking at it, I tossed it as far as I could. I stayed quiet and continued to listen for sounds on the docks, trying to gauge when it would be safe to get out.

"Madison? Madison?" Fab called in a loud whisper.

I tried to whisper and ended up yelling, "I'm over here!" After several tries, I pulled myself around to the front side of the steps. Pulling myself up with one arm was harder than I thought it would be; I could only manage the first step. "I need help getting the rest of the way up the stairs."

Fab reached down to help.

"Careful. I think I broke my left arm."

She helped me the rest of the way up the steps. "What the hell were you doing in the water?"

I exhaled loudly when both my feet hit the dock. "I decided to go for a late-night swim in gasoline and feces-infested water."

"I meant, what happened?"

"This burly guy hit me from behind. I caught a brief glimpse of him just before he connected, and I think that's why he missed my head, but he hit me hard enough to knock me into the water."

"It was probably this." Fab picked up an oar from the dock. "Let's get out of here."

"My arm or shoulder is broken. The pain is bad."

"I'm taking you to the hospital."

"No! Everyone will find out, and how do we explain this? I'll call Doc Rivers and see if he can come over." Doc Rivers was retired and made house calls without asking questions.

"He'll tell Zach," Fab said.

"Not if I ask him not to. Besides, we'll come up with another story."

"The boys club is a tight one," Fab reminded me. "If he thinks he's saving you from yourself, he'll tell."

I sucked in my breath. "Then take me to a hospital in Miami."

"Great idea. I know the head of emergency services at Miami General. He works the night shift, and even if he's not there, you can get treated and no one will be the wiser."

"Who's this mystery doctor?"

"Dr. A, or Stan as I call him. We met while he was in medical school. He was my first. Every woman deserves to have her first time be special. He took me from a naïve virgin to a woman. There are so few of those kinds of lovers, you hold them in a special place in your heart."

"My first one was like that. He was older and much more experienced. Every time I think about him, even all these years later, I smile. You're right about there being few special ones."

* * *

Thanks to Fab's friend, we cut to the head of the line and were in and out of the emergency room in two hours. Disheveled and tired-looking, Dr. A had a seductive smile and jet-black hair. He was clearly a lover of women. He smiled at me in a way that made my imperfections seem perfect.

I told him I had fallen into the water after a friend accidently hit me with an oar he'd been unloading from his boat. He X-rayed my shoulder, arm, and back. He came back with the good news that nothing was broken, just severely bruised. He fitted me with a sling, gave me a shot for the pain, and a prescription for pills.

On the way out, Dr. A whispered, "Be more careful in the future. I know Fabiana pretty well, so my guess is that there's more to this story." He winked at me as I left.

Chapter Twenty-Nine

"Where have you been?" I asked Fab when she walked into my kitchen.

"Hey, grumpy. Good morning. Did you make some real coffee?"

"There's a whole potful in the same place it always is." I handed her a mug. "I wanted to go, by the way."

"How's your shoulder?"

"Hurts like the devil. What'd you find out?"

"Tomas didn't respond well to waking up and finding me standing there," Fab said. "Once I assured him I wasn't there to kill him, he got more cooperative."

"Where was your gun?"

"In my hand."

I shook my head. "Fabiana Merceau, you're lucky he didn't have a heart attack."

"Calm down. I left him in one piece, and we worked a deal. He gave me information, and I gave him money. We're lucky I went this morning because his bags were packed and sitting by the door. He planned on leaving once he got his paycheck this afternoon. He didn't want anyone to find out he'd left until Monday, and he'd be back home by then."

I refilled her mug. "So what's he running from?"

"He's running from Byce and his drug friends."

"Why would a successful businessman be involved with trafficking drugs? Which, by the way, carries a life sentence in this state. I read an article the other day about someone who got twenty-five years for far less than what they're doing."

"Byce Jr."

"The son?" I gasped.

Fab nodded. "Alexander Byce III. Only son to the heirship."

"Start at the beginning with Tomas's story and how Byce Jr. fits in."

"Tomas works as an assistant chef at The Wharf. He and Pavel were good friends. One night, they were sitting on the docks, drinking beer and swapping stories, and they watched as a boat came up and unloaded." She poured herself another cup of coffee. "Tomas's story matches what we saw last night, including the description of the boat. The two of them watched the guys unload the boxes and carry them into the warehouse. After the boat took off and everyone left the warehouse, Pavel used his key to go in and look around. They looked in the boxes, and they were all full of white powder.

Pavel helped himself to some of it, figuring no one would notice. They had to leave in a hurry because Byce Jr. showed up with a half-dozen other men."

I shook my head. "Screwing drug dealers was a really bad idea."

"Tomas warned Pavel that, no matter how little he took, they would find out."

"The Byce family has millions. Why would Junior peddle drugs?"

"Greed is the usual motive," Fab said. "When Pavel turned up dead, Tomas decided it was time to go back home to Louisiana and work in the family business."

"I can see where ripping off drug dealers would get you dead. I remember a dealer came by the house once and told me he was going to kill Jax over three hundred dollars. I asked him, 'You're really going to kill someone over three hundred dollars?' He said, 'Pay up or he's dead,' gave me a friendly wave, and left."

"Let me guess, you paid the bill."

"I paid and threatened if I ever saw his face again, I'd call the police and report him as a dealer. In retrospect, the threat was probably a bad idea. That's what happens when you lack drug dealer social skills."

"What'd he say?"

"He laughed and told me I was 'ballsy and stupid,' but I never saw him again."

"Tomas thinks the shooting was related to the

drugs. He doesn't know for sure, but he's not taking any chances that he might be next," Fab said.

"Why didn't he pack up and leave immediately?"

"Pavel talked him into laughing it off. Pavel assured him no one saw them, but then he was murdered. Tomas didn't want to draw any attention to himself. He's afraid if they knew about Pavel, then they know he was with him."

We sat in silence for a moment.

"Tomas wants to become a pastry chef," Fab said. "I told him to go home and make his name in the family business. Blow the doors off one dessert at a time. Make a successful Cuban restaurant even more so."

"Sounds like really good advice," I said.

"I can rise to the occasion. Here's another guy, never been in trouble, now he's in over his head with drugs he didn't even use."

"You really surprise me sometimes, and in a good way."

"So who shot Pavel?" Fab asked.

"Who knows? How long between the time they broke into the warehouse and Pavel turning up dead?"

"Two days."

"What can we prove?" I asked. "All we have is Tomas's theory, which makes more sense than stranger murder. They're running an import-export drug business off those docks, and Zach's man turned up nothing? He should be fired, or Zach's full of it."

"My guess is the latter."

"I wonder what else he didn't bother to tell me. He knew how important this was to me personally, and he lied to my face. That's just great."

"Don't look at me for an answer. Here's a better question. You think Zach's a bastard now, what happens when he finds out about your shoulder? How are you going to lay low long enough for it to heal?"

"I'm not hiding from anyone. Here's our story, and we're both sticking to it."

Fab rolled her eyes. "Oh, brother."

"Look, friend of no faith in my stories, we stay unified and stick to the plan. No one, and I mean no one, is going to find out we were snooping on the docks in the middle of the night."

"Let's hear your story," Fab said.

"You and I went to lunch and shoe shopping at Aventura Mall. I started down the steps, a little kid bumped into me, I lost my balance, fell, and landed on my shoulder."

"You're blaming it on a kid?"

I shook my head. "Oh, don't even try to look shocked. If you knew anything about kids, you'd know it's the perfect story."

"I know about…"

I tried not to laugh. I could see she was trying to figure what she did know about kids. "It's not like I fingered a particular kid, and said, 'Hey, it was that one.' The story works because little kids never watch where they're going. What part of the story isn't believable?"

"Actually, I think it's good," Fab conceded.

"Does Zach know about Dr. A?"

"No, and I don't want him finding out."

"Good, we'll keep him as our own secret. Having a doctor, lawyer, and CPA on speed dial is a good thing."

"I have a surprise for you. I forgot to tell you last night."

"A good one?" I asked.

"I wouldn't put it in the *good* category, but you're going to want to hear it anyway. I got you a visitation appointment for tomorrow with Jax at the jail."

"How'd you do that? I called this morning, and the soonest I could get an appointment was next week."

"Connections, girlfriend. My manicurist's brother works the counter at the visitor center. I gave her a sad story about how you lovebirds were trying to work out your relationship, and you were going crazy not being able to talk to him."

"Once again, I'm impressed." I smiled.

"How's the whole Jax drama going to work out for you?"

I shrugged. "I get what I want, and he gets my help."

"What about his lawyer? You remember Tucker Davis, don't you?"

"I'm going to end run around Tucker and hope he doesn't find out until I want him to," I said with confidence, though the idea filled me with dread.

Chapter Thirty

I threw my arm sling onto the passenger seat of my SUV before walking into the Miami jail visitor center. I produced my identification for the guard at the desk. After checking in, he directed me to one of the cubicles. All of the television screens were turned on, and I could see the inside of Jax's jail pod. A couple of impatient-looking tattooed inmates sat on each side of where Jax would sit. They looked on edge waiting for their visitors to show.

Jax was probably eager for the visit; this place was dreary. Who else would come? Apple couldn't stay sober long enough to make it past the guard desk, and if she made the mistake of showing up drunk, they'd arrest her. Robert had an old outstanding warrant from Virginia; the beauty of a warrant is that it seldom goes away. Besides, he would never put himself out for someone else unless there was something in it for him.

When Jax and I were married, the sheriff had shown up early one morning. Robert was sleeping on the couch in our living room. I got up to answer the door, and Robert had disappeared.

The sheriff was collecting money for a children's charity. I laughed when I found Robert hiding in the pantry closet. He told me about the warrant for unpaid child support for two more children he neglected. He had fathered five children and still hadn't been neutered.

Jax walked into his side of the visitor cubicle, looking as if he hadn't slept since his incarceration. With his pale face and bloodshot eyes, he looked sick. His orange jumpsuit was an unflattering color on him, but commenting on that would start a fight. We both picked up our germ-ridden red phones. The visit was a maximum forty minutes from the time the visitor picked up their phone. The screen would eventually flash the two-minute warning, and once we reached the allotted time, the screen would go black.

"I'm so glad you came to visit," he said, resting his head on his hand. "I hate it here."

"Are you sick?"

His face was damp with beads of sweat. "I've been barfing all night. They gave us hotdogs last night, and half of us started puking. I think mine is combo food poisoning and nerves."

"I stopped by the cashier across the street and put money in your commissary account." Twice a week, inmates could place orders for miscellaneous clothing, toiletries, and junk food.

"I love you," he said.

"A part of me loves you, too, but it's not

enough. Is it?" I felt sad.

"You were the best thing that ever happened to me." His eyes filled with tears. "When I get out of here, think about giving me another chance."

"You get your life together, and then give me a call." I figured that was a safe answer.

"Get me out of here."

His tears made me uncomfortable, but that place would make any person an emotional wreck. "What the heck happened? Why did they hike your bail?"

"They deemed me a flight risk, that fucking violation of probation in South Carolina. Then, when Harder found out the case was settled, he lost his excuse to keep me locked up and boosted the bail. That Harder dick keeps threatening me with more charges. He really dislikes you."

"That's not a newsflash."

"Watch yourself. If he could put you in here with me, that would make his year."

Talk of Harder made me nauseous. "What's Tucker doing about a bail reduction?"

"I'm pretty sure that bastard wants me to stay in here. That way he knows where I am, and I can't skip town."

"If I get you out of here, what assurances do I have that you won't be skipping anywhere?" The word *skip* filled me with anxiety; I'd have a whole new plate of problems.

"If I run now, they'll file murder charges

against me for sure, charges I wouldn't be able to beat. I didn't murder Pavel, and I don't want to spend the rest of my life in prison. Or worse, be introduced to Sparky."

"You could choose lethal injection," I said. "After a few incidents of people's hair catching fire instead of electrocuting them to death Sparky turned into a public relations nightmare for the state."

Jax hit the wall with his fist. "Is that supposed to be reassuring?"

"Calm down, you jerk. All you succeeded in doing with that display was to hurt your hand."

He cupped his hand over the phone. "Get me out of here."

"I'll get you out. But listen up. If you so much as get in spitting distance of the county line, there won't be anywhere you can hide, and you'll go back to jail and rot there for all I care. I've made a few interesting friends since moving here, and I'll sic them on you."

"There's one more thing that you're not going to like."

"What now?" I demanded.

"In exchange for Tucker representing me for free, he demanded that I sign the papers for the lawsuit. He's filing it today."

"I wonder why that took so long. I've had legal advice, so I'm not as worried as before. Whether you like it or not, this will be the one time that you're going to keep your word. You know the old 'wash my hand and I'll wash yours'?"

"You mean 'wash my back.'" He smiled.

"I'm having a dismissal of the lawsuit drawn up by my lawyer for you to sign. Just to be clear, it will include a clause that says there's no chance you can re-file."

"I can't do that," he said.

"Why not?"

"The only reason Tucker is representing me for free is because he wants your house. When he finds out I signed a dismissal, he'll drop me, and I'll be stuck with the public defender. Unless you can get Cruz Campion to represent me. I hear he's better than Tucker."

"Cruz won't represent you for free, and I'm not paying that bill. Here's the deal. You sign the dismissal, and I won't file it until your BUI is resolved in court. That way, you get to keep your free lawyer. He's a sleazy bastard, but a good lawyer."

"Do I get out today?"

"More like tomorrow, if you hold up your end. My lawyer will come over with a notary to get the dismissal signed. And I need to make arrangements to post the bond."

He smiled. "Thank you. I really mean it."

"Why did you join ranks with Tucker to begin with?"

"Samuels was a front man for Tucker. He doesn't want you knowing about this side deal, or all bets are off. If it makes a difference, I was never going to let this case go to court, and I still won't. In the interest of disclosure, Tucker offered me money to make sure I kept quiet. I'm giving you half of it for the pawn fiasco."

I needed to stay calm. Trying to con a couple of unscrupulous lawyers was making me sick. "Well, I should leave."

"Don't leave until the end of the visit." He reached out and touched the screen.

"We know how the food is," I said, hoping to make him smile. "What goes on here?"

"It's noisy. Nobody shuts up all night long. Maybe if I could get some sleep, I'd feel better."

"How'd you hook up with Tucker?" I asked.

"He found me right after the boat accident and offered to make all my problems go away."

That was more honesty than I'd expected from him. "Why does he want my house?"

"He said you stole it from him, that it was all meant to be his. He talked about your Aunt Elizabeth. I think he had it bad for her and she wasn't interested. It all went sour between them over a business deal."

"So Tucker was scorned." He couldn't get back at Elizabeth, death cheated him, so he wanted to get his revenge through me. "Did it bother you at all you were screwing me?"

"I was so desperate to get out of trouble, and I thought I had it handled. I didn't really think it through."

Of course he didn't. I would be happy when all the papers had his signature on them. "What do you do all day?"

"Nothing." He shrugged. "I lay on my bunk. We got television privileges taken away because one of the numbnuts got caught smoking in the bathroom."

"I thought they did away with smoking in jails."

"They did. One of the guys was out on work detail, and a friend of his from the outside smuggled him cigarettes. When you get back to the jail, they make you strip and then give you a clean uniform, so he shoved them up his ass. After he cleared check-in, he and his high-IQ friends went into the bathroom and lit up. The smoke set off the alarm."

"I've got to ask, does the whole pack fit up there?" The image made my butt muscles clench.

He laughed. "You wrap the cigs in a piece of plastic and then insert."

"How desperate do you have to be to do that?"

"That would've cured me of my habit a lot sooner." He shook his head.

"Staring at the ceiling must be a bore."

"They have a book cart, and I found a couple of spy novels to read. Not many of the guys here read."

The screen flashed the two-minute warning. "You hold up your end of the bargain, and I'll get you out of here."

"I'll sign, and I won't leave town." He put his palm on the screen.

"In that case, I'll be here when you're released." I pressed my palm to the glass. "You know our usual spot in the waiting room."

"Somehow, I'll make this up to you," he said, and the screen went black.

I'd already planned my escape. I cut down the side aisle, so I wouldn't get caught in the crush of people racing for the exit. "I made it out," I mumbled as I walked away from the building. I was happy to suck in the fresh air and have the sunshine on my face, not to mention the freedom to go where I wanted.

Chapter Thirty-One

"I'm calling to check in on you," Mother said. "What are you doing?"

"Sitting out by the pool, making out a to-do list." She didn't need to know the list was what Fab and I knew about Pavel, and the questions we still had. My notepad was filling up fast.

"I wanted you to know, Brad called. He came back with a full catch, unloaded, then got the boat cleaned and stocked and went right back out."

"That was fast. I haven't talked to him since he dragged Jax out of my house," I said. "Is he still mad?"

"No, he's not. He made a point of saying so. He's working hard, running back-to-back trips. He plans to take off a couple of months at the end of fishing season."

"I guess he forgot my phone number."

"Don't be like that. He wanted me to tell you that we talked and he said hello."

"What's up with him and Jax? According to Mac, Jax doesn't hang around The Cottages very much."

"Jax has been working with Moron on someone else's boat since ours was towed. I'm wondering if we'll be sued," Mother said.

"For what? I didn't murder Pavel. I want this case solved so our family isn't forever linked with murder."

"I would like it to be over. A little normal would be nice," Mother said. "I asked Jax what his plans were when the court case was over. He told me he's going back to South Carolina."

"When was that conversation?"

"Jax and I talked when I stopped by Moron's to see the progress on the boat for myself. I ran into Zach at the Bakery Café and he thinks you took his advice and stopped snooping around asking questions. I think he has a lot to learn." Mother laughed. "You're in big trouble if you get hurt."

"Don't worry so much." I couldn't think of anything else that wouldn't start a fight.

"Spoon and I have decided that we're better off just being friends. So when my friend Jean asked if I wanted to take a road trip to go gambling in Seminole, I said yes." Jean Stewart was one of her blue-haired friends who lived down the street from her in Coral Gables.

I was so relieved, I struggled to be sensitive. "Are you okay?"

"I need the diversion. It'll be fun. We'll gamble, shop, and overeat."

"Play a twenty for me at the blackjack table. When are you coming back?"

"A few days. I'll have my phone with me. I hope because we don't see eye to eye on this Jax situation, you won't use that as an excuse to hide things from me."

"I'm getting pretty good at keeping you up to date," I said.

"I'll call you when I get back."

I hung up feeling conflicted. I was snooping around even more than Mother would've guessed.

"What the hell happened to your arm?" Zach yelled, stomping into the backyard.

I laid my notepad facedown and covered it slightly with my towel. "I'm guessing you're not here for a swim."

He had on black suit pants, a dress shirt, and a gorgeous pair of black leather loafers. I'd been in his closet, and he was clearly a shoe whore.

"One of my guys saw you get out of your car at the jail with a sling on. Visiting Dickhead? You still have a thing for him?"

"Could you lower your voice?" I wanted to add, 'and mind your own business'. "We had business to discuss."

"And your arm?" he demanded.

"Actually, it's my shoulder. I'm fine, thanks for asking."

"Where did this happen?"

His voice told me he wasn't going to believe

whatever I said. "The way you're firing questions at me, do I need a lawyer?"

"What are you guilty of?"

"Paranoid much?"

"Stop stalling. What the hell happened?"

"I fell at Aventura Mall."

"What's Fab's part in all of this?"

"She didn't push me if that's what you're asking. We were there for lunch and shoe shopping."

He gave me a scrutinizing stare, meant to scare me into confessing. I wanted to laugh and tell him he was wasting his time if he thought I'd spill. "This wouldn't have happened if you were living with me."

"How do you figure that? Is it because you'd lock me in your warehouse and never let me out?"

"Don't be ridiculous. I want to believe you, but I know you two."

His suffocating attempt at control was giving me a headache. I realized if I did live with him, there'd be no spontaneous swims. I'd really miss my early morning laps. "You're making too much out of a simple fall."

"You give any thought to moving in with me?" Zach asked.

"When I said I wanted to spend more time together, I meant dinners out and late-night swims. I'm not ready for playing house. If you were honest, even you know this is too soon.

Your motives are not about love, which, by the way, you've never said, but about protecting me."

"I've got to get back to the office." He leaned down and kissed my cheek.

"You look nice, by the way," I called as he walked away.

His lack of response to the word "love" hadn't gone unnoticed. Was I ready to say those three little words?

His goodbye kisses usually made me hot and tingly. The cheek kiss was disappointing. I knew one thing for sure; I wasn't signing up to be controlled. It would be a constant battle to come and go without endless questions.

Once Zach found out Jax was getting released, one phone call later and he'd know I bailed him out. That would be another fight, or at the very least, snotty comments traded back and forth.

I'd arranged with Brick to post the bail, hoping to keep my identity a secret. He cut his exorbitant fee in exchange for an unspecified favor to be determined at his will. My only ground rule was he wouldn't ask me to do anything illegal.

He had laughed in my face. "You're one ballsy redhead."

In the fine print spelled out by Brick, "If Jax takes off, you find his ass. No one skips on Brick."

My phone rang, and I wanted to throw it in

the pool and sail to the Bahamas, but I answered anyway.

"Jackson signed the dismissal," Whit stated. "I took it over to the jail myself and everything went according to jail protocol. We had a long conversation, and I liked him. I was having trouble with my icemaker on the refrigerator, and he told me how to take it apart and fix it myself. Saved me a service call from the hack I had out the last time."

"Thank you for doing this."

"You're now protected all legal-like. The witnesses were jail guards," Whit said.

I called Brick and gave him the green light to post bail.

Chapter Thirty-Two

My shoulder only hurt with sudden movements. I took two aspirin, got in my SUV, and drove straight to the Bakery Café for a caramel latte, with extra whipped cream, which I hoped would also lessen the pain. I sat at a table on the sidewalk, people-watching, shaking off the effects of a night with little sleep.

Fab screeched up in another new car—a black BMW. She slid into the parking space so fast, I thought she'd jump the sidewalk and end up at the table. "Always easy to find," she said, crossing the sidewalk. She handed me a manila envelope. "Look at these while I get a double espresso."

Before I could open the envelope, Sid Byce walked up to the table. "I know you think that piece of shit you married isn't guilty, but you're wrong." He slammed his fist on the table. "Bad things happen to people who don't mind their own business." His face was red with anger. "Stop asking questions. Your husband's in jail, where he's going to stay."

"Step back from the table," Fab growled from behind Byce. "You want to fight? Pick on someone your own size."

Byce snickered. "That someone would be you?"

"Yes." Fab pulled up her top, showing the gun in her waistband.

"Are you threatening me?" His veins threatened to pop out of the side of his head.

"Madison wouldn't shoot your nuts off, but I would." Fab gave him a creepy, deranged-looking smile. "Don't you ever speak to her again."

"Both of you listen to me," Byce said. "Stay off my property. We shoot trespassers."

"You know what I think?" Fab asked. "I think you shot Pavel."

Byce stared at her with pure hate. "You crazy bitch." He turned and walked away.

"Yes, I am!" she yelled.

"Your part in that drama made my hair stand on end," I said. "That's my way of saying thank you."

"What did he want?"

"Told me to stop asking questions and that Jax's in jail where he belongs. What he doesn't know is that all the arrangements have been made to bail Jax out," I related. "He knew we'd been snooping around his property asking questions."

"If he thought we knew about his drug import business, we wouldn't be sitting here sucking down espresso," Fab said.

"Do you really think Sid Byce is the shooter? What about Byce Junior?"

"My money's on Sid," Fab said. "Alexander does what he's told."

"Byce is a pillar of the community. Murder and running drugs is a stretch, isn't it? If we told anyone what we thought, everyone in this town would laugh in our faces."

"Jax's screwed," Fab stated.

I opened the manila envelope and pulled out photos of the dock area around Byce's warehouse. "When did you shoot these?" Byce was lucky; if Fab had finished her espresso, he might've limped away minus a nut.

"Last night. And before you start whining about not going along, be serious. Your shoulder was almost amputated." Fab smiled.

"Dramatic much?" I shook my head. "It's not hurting now. What else went on down there that I missed?" I ran my finger through the whipped cream on my drink. I used to save it for last, but I didn't like the runny lumps that were usually left.

"Exactly the same as what went down the other night," Fab said. "Amateurs. Doing the same thing over and over is going to get you noticed. The boat even showed up at the same time. I got the bow number. Running drugs in that quantity usually makes the people involved nervous and paranoid. No signs of that with these guys. I put in a call to Patrick at the Coast

Guard to find out who owns the boat."

"These were shot at a different angle. Where were you when you took them?"

"I was across the channel on the north side. Good thing, too. Before the drop, two guys walked the property, including the boat yard."

"Girlfriend, at some point we're going to have to admit we're in over our heads," I said.

"That time would be now. We're in dangerous territory and should step back."

"We just walk away?" I asked. "Pavel's real for me. We haven't found one person who's had a bad thing to say. He's a person who didn't deserve to end up dead. His murderer doesn't get to walk."

"I agree. There are still a couple of missing pieces," Fab said. "They get regular shipments of cocaine, then what happens to it? They're not stupid enough to store it there for very long. Judging by the size of the shipments, they've got a major business going on."

"I want to call in Zach and his guys, but our last encounter didn't go well," I said.

"What happened?"

"I hadn't been wearing my sling and I wore it to the jail. I realized aspirin helped more and took it off, but not before one of Zach's men saw me and reported back to him. He comes over and demands to know what happened. He didn't believe the mall story at first, but I held my ground. Then he brought up living together, and

I told him no thanks."

Fab banged her coffee mug on the table. "Why does the good stuff happen when I'm not there to eavesdrop?"

"Do you have a plan?" I asked. "Zach doesn't know about us snooping around Byce's, or he might've cuffed me and dragged me to a guarded location."

"I'll tell Zach everything I found out last night," Fab offered. "I'll tell him I'm the one who's been checking around."

I raised my eyebrows. "How are you going to sell that I've been sitting back doing nothing?"

"You tell him you asked around, and everyone said the same thing: no one had a reason as to why Pavel would end up dead, blah, blah. You can think on your feet."

"So I'm hanging you out to dry?"

"He expects this kind of behavior from me," Fab said. "He'll be fine if we convince him you're not involved."

"When are we doing this?"

"I have a bodyguard job tonight. I'm one of four who're chaperoning sixteen-year-olds for a birthday party. Daddy's paying for overpriced babysitting to make sure there's no drunkenness or drugs and no one gets arrested. Let's make it tomorrow night. We'll get him to meet us at a restaurant; he'd never create a scene in public."

"I like the way you think."

Chapter Thirty-Three

Since the last time I was at the jail to pick Jax up, they had renamed the main building the Welcome Center. There was nothing welcoming about the cold, sterile room with its gray walls and steel bars. I sat in the same plastic chair I did the last time, close to the exit, and fidgeted to get comfortable. I could look one way and see what was going on at the main desk, and the other way I could see when the inmates came out the door to their freedom. An interesting assortment of people filled half the chairs, I settled in for the wait, which felt like an eternity after the first five minutes.

I had stopped by Whit's office and picked up the agreement. I noticed Whit notarized it himself. He laughed, saying it was his way of getting to meet Jax. I told him about the deal I'd made, and he told me as soon as Jax's case was settled, I should go straight to the court clerk and file my documents.

The jail door opened and closed; chairs emptied and filled again. Finally, Jax walked through the door. He looked like a bone a dog had chewed on, dragged through the yard, and was no longer interested in.

He walked straight over and picked me up in a tight hug, crushing his lips to mine in an intense kiss. I kissed him back, taking me to a time when we had been happy. I had once loved my husband with everything I had to give.

"Thanks for getting me out of here." He kissed me again.

"Were you on the beach when they arrested you?" I asked, noting that he wore bathing suit bottoms and a T-shirt.

"I came back for a beer, and two sheriffs were sitting on the couch, waiting for me. I told them they hadn't been invited in and were breaking the law. They told me to prove it and laughed."

"You're out now." I looked down. "Nice shoes." He still had on his jail-issue slip-on orange tennis shoes.

"When they handcuffed me at the cottage, Robert's flops were sitting by the door. I slid into them quickly after they told me I couldn't get my tennis shoes out of the bedroom. I guess all flops look alike in this hole, even though they were XXXL bitch size. When the property room lost the cheap things, they tried to pass off someone else's flops, but when my heels hung off the back, they had no choice but to let me wear these. They can't discharge anyone barefoot, even if you come in that way. Assholes." He shrugged. "Anyway, what did I do to deserve you?"

"I asked myself the same question in reverse. What did I do to deserve you?"

He pulled me into a hug, and we both laughed and walked to the parking lot. I breathed a sigh of relief when we passed the guard.

"Does Tucker know you're getting out?" I asked.

"Hell no." He opened the driver's side door for me before going around to the other side. "I didn't say a word when he showed up for an early morning visit. I worried every second, until the guard called my name, that somehow Tucker would find out and block my release. I honestly thought one of the guards would tell the bastard."

I sped out of the parking lot. "How do they decide who goes first?"

"They get a list, and it depends on where your name comes up. My luck, mine must've been down at the bottom."

"You need to watch your back with Tucker," I said. "He's a good lawyer, but if he thinks you're standing in the way of him getting what he wants, you're screwed."

"What about the papers I signed?" Jax asked.

"Tucker won't know about those until after your case is settled."

Jax waved his middle finger out the passenger window. "That guy honked at you and flipped you off."

"That happens on occasion." I laughed.

He shook his head. "It's no wonder. You drive like you're ninety-nine. I could give you driving lessons."

"You're not funny. I'll match my driving record to yours any day."

"On second thought, don't listen to me." He laughed and tussled my hair. "Can I stay with you?"

"Stop with the hand gestures before someone shoots at us."

"The next time someone honks at us, I get out at the signal and beat the hell out of them." He flexed his muscle.

"You only act like that when you're trying to make someone think you're a tough guy."

"Yeah, you're right, so I guess I'll calm down."

We laughed and he took my hand holding it tightly. Images of many moments like this crept through my mind as I drove. It made me think about good times.

"I'm taking you to The Cottages, and you need to stay out of trouble. There are a few people who aren't going to like that you're out."

"Tucker told me during the meeting this morning that he's working on a plea where I'd get six months, out in four."

"That's a great deal," I said.

"Would you visit if I agreed to four months?"

"I uh…" That was the last thing I wanted to agree to.

"I'm going to make this up to you. I'm going

to start by paying back both you and Brad."

I stared at him. "Does this mean you're not going to run and leave me on the hook?"

"I don't want to go to jail, but even I know this a good deal that won't be offered again if I run."

"I need something in return."

He frowned. "I don't have anything to give you."

"I want you to get rid of Robert. And make it clear to Apple that she can never set foot on my property. Robert can stay until the day you go to jail, and then I want him out, same day. Agreed?"

"Robert's already made plans to move out. He's sticking around the area, got a job at a stripper bar."

I raised my eyebrows. "Doing what?"

"He'll be working the door."

"Wasn't the first wife, the one he beat the crap out of, a stripper?"

"Only wife, or are you confusing her with the girlfriend who bashed his head in with one of those black frying pans, sending him to the hospital?"

I laughed. "I love these sweet family stories."

"The only reason I helped Apple was because she was homeless. I have no illusions about her. She'll go down to the Croc and hook up with the first guy who buys her a drink."

"When is your next court hearing?" I asked.

"Next week, and if I accept the plea deal,

they'll take me into custody from the courtroom."

"Seriously, watch yourself," I said, pulling into the driveway.

"When I get out of jail, I'm going to put my life back together and show you why we should be together."

"Don't do anything stupid. If you think you're going to, call me."

He leaned over and kissed my cheek. "Harder told me you murdered someone and got off. I didn't believe him, but he seemed sure of himself."

"I killed someone," I sighed. "It was self-defense, not murder. That's an ugly memory I've tried to block out. Thanks for bringing it up again."

"I knew he was full of shit. Did you know Harder and Tucker are friends?"

"Unfortunately. I try to avoid them both, and yet, here we are. I believe you didn't murder anyone, either, Jackson Devereaux."

"Watch your back. Harder wants to keep his distance from Tucker, but they're in bed together on some business deal from what I could piece together." He opened the car door.

"Thanks, Jax." I leaned out the car window and yelled, "I call dibs on the shoes!"

He laughed. "You're crazy." He walked back, took them off, and handed them to me.

"I remember when it was psycho bitch."

"I drove you to it." He winked and walked barefoot down the driveway.

I looked down and smiled. It wasn't every day a girl got her own pair of jail-issued orange shoes.

Chapter Thirty-Four

I loved eating out, especially in new restaurants, but not tonight. Fab had arranged a meeting for us with Zach. The Grotto was the newest seafood restaurant in town and was like walking into a giant aquarium with its floor-to-ceiling views of colorful tropical fish. A sign said there were over one hundred species from the all over the globe. I wondered if the fish knew some of their friends hadn't made it into the giant fish tank, but were dinner instead.

Fab and Zach sat at a table facing the entrance, along with Slice.

"I'll have a margarita, rocks," I told the waiter as I sat down. Fab and Slice looked uncomfortable, and Zach seemed irritated.

"Imagine my surprise when Fab called and asked to meet for dinner," Zach said.

"Hi, Slice. Thanks for your help with Liam." I leaned over and kissed his cheek.

"I'm here for backup." Slice had a completely different personality off the job, easygoing and always in a good mood. There was no mistaking that underneath the charm, he was lethal, much like his partner.

"Me, too," I confided. "Fab, since we didn't flip, you go first." The waiter set my drink in front of me, and I had to stop myself from gulping it down.

"Okay, here's the deal," Fab started. "I've been asking a few discreet questions regarding Pavel and have uncovered some information." Fab had finished her drink and her fingers wrapped tightly around the stem of her glass, a bad sign.

Zach glared at Fab. "Nobody talks to you. It must have been her." He pointed at me.

"You're right, it was me." I narrowed my eyes at Zach. "I asked Joseph to find out what he could about Pavel. Fab and I have information, and it's more than the two of us can handle."

"I knew you wouldn't stay out of it and let me do my job," Zach growled.

"Didn't you tell me case closed? You came up empty-handed. Unless you lied to me."

His dark blue eyes turned to slits. "What did you find out?"

I related everything Joseph had discovered, and that he had put me in touch with one of Pavel's co-workers, who had since left town. I made it sound like Tomas had told me about the things Fab and I had seen on the docks.

"No one in this town is going to make a move against Sid Byce based on the word of a disgruntled co-worker who's left town," Zach said.

"Lower your voices," Slice said. "The whole

restaurant doesn't need to hear you accusing Byce of murder."

Fab patted me on the shoulder.

"When did you get so touchy-feely?" Zach asked Fab.

I interrupted before Fab kicked him out of his chair. "Zach, it's okay with you that drugs come into The Cove via our docks?"

"That's not what I said. I know Sid Byce, and frankly, I don't believe any of this. He would never allow drug trafficking out of his warehouse."

"I'm not a liar. I didn't make this up."

"You may not be a chronic liar, but you only tell the truth when it suits you and only what you think I want to hear, which you've been doing a lot of lately."

"Takes one to know one."

Fab and Slice laughed.

Zach looked at me as if he wanted to strangle me. "That was childish."

"You only tell me what you want me to know, which is nothing," I said. "It's always in my best interest. Didn't you tell me I was stupid? Madison needs a keeper if she leaves the house?"

Zach leaned forward. "That's right."

There was complete silence at the table for a full minute.

"Let's get back on track," Slice suggested.

"For you to believe me, you'd need to catch Byce with a suitcase full of drugs in one hand

and a briefcase full of cash in the other," I said.

"We can get that kind of proof," Fab spoke up.

"You two keep up your snooping, and you'll both end up a missing person's case that never gets solved," Zach hissed.

"Why are you involved in this, anyway?" Slice asked me. "You've no part in any of this case, or am I wrong?"

"Wouldn't you want your murder solved? The real killer on trial?" I asked. "But hey, I guess if Byce murdered someone and deals drugs, it's okay with everyone in this town. Who am I to speak up?"

Zach looked at me with disgust. "Sid Byce didn't kill anyone. You're delusional, and I'd stake my reputation on it. That's how well I know him. And another thing, if Tomas really saw drugs being unloaded, that doesn't equal murder."

"Drug dealers want to move their product in peace," Slice said. "The main goal is to stay under the radar of the cops. What you're suggesting is pretty brazen."

"If this is where I apologize for getting involved, don't hold your breath," I said. "If you're half the investigator you advertise, Zach, even you can see this makes more sense than no-motive Jax killing Pavel."

"It all comes back to the husband." Zach smirked. "Isn't that sweet?"

"Ex," I said loudly. "What's with you? You're

like Byce: blame anyone you want."

"Keep it down, you two. People are staring," Slice reminded.

"If it makes you feel better, I heard the same drug *rumors*. I spoke to Kevin, and detectives were assigned and are conducting an investigation," Zach said.

"Why not just say from the beginning that there's an open investigation?" I asked.

Zach shrugged. "I needed to find out what you knew."

"All I ever asked was for you to be straight with me, keep me in the loop," I said. "You created this situation with your inability to be truthful."

"Yeah, okay, blame me," Zach said. "I was up-front when I told you to stay out of it. This situation is being handled by professionals, which you are not."

"You're a bigger bastard than ever," Fab said.

"When did you speak to Kevin?" I asked. I found it hard to believe that Fab and Zach occasionally worked together on cases in the past.

Zach shot Fab a dirty look. "I forget the exact date."

"Was it before you came to my house, looked me in the face, and said you knew squat?" I asked.

"What matters here," Slice intervened, "is that there's an active investigation going on now. No one else needs to get hurt or worse. Can you two agree to let the police handle this and stay out of their way?"

Frustrated, I counted to five so I wouldn't yell. "With Sid Byce's connections, the drugs and any evidence will be swept right out into the Gulf, and nothing will come of it."

"It's nice that you have Sid tried and convicted," Zach said.

"Just like Byce did Jax," I shot back. "But then, Byce's your friend, and Jax isn't."

Fab cut in, "Slice is right. If the police are involved and there's any connection to Pavel's death, they'll figure it out. Kevin's one hundred percent straight up."

Slice nodded. "Are we ready to order?"

"No, thanks." I stood and walked out of the restaurant. It depressed me to think that there might never be a resolution to the murder case.

Chapter Thirty-Five

I stood at the kitchen sink and watched the postman walk across the courtyard, an oversized envelope in his hand. I opened the front door before he could knock.

"Too big for your box," he said, turning to go back to his truck.

"Thanks, Henry."

After going back in the house, I studied the envelope. There was no return address. I opened it, stripped away the bubble wrap, and pulled out a DVD. A note was taped to the case. 'I knew you would be the right person to send this to. Thanks for your help in getting home.' Signed "Tomas."

I put the disk in the DVD player and hit *Play*. Two men appeared on the screen, sitting in what looked like an office. I recognized the dark-haired one as the one who had sent me airborne into water that night on the dock.

"What in the hell happened last night?" The blond-haired one sitting behind the desk asked. He was clean cut, wearing a polo shirt and expensive Topsiders, which were kicked up on the desk. He had the spoiled, snotty look down to a tee.

"I saw Pavel sneaking around. When I came around the building, he stopped to take a pee in the channel, and I shot him. I shoved him into the water with my foot," the dark-haired one replied. His hair slicked back into a ponytail, and he sported a black beard. He looked ready for a fight with a gun holstered to his left side. "You said to take care of any problems."

"Are you fucking crazy?" Blondie shouted. "I didn't tell you to kill anyone."

"He won't wash up." The dark one sounded confident.

"You're not much of a thinker, are you? Did you weigh him down and take his body out to the middle of the Gulf? No, you didn't."

"He's a nobody. No one's going to care anyway." The dark guy shrugged.

"When the cops find out Pavel worked here, they're going to be all over this place, dimwit."

"What do you want me to do?"

"I want you to stay out of sight and not open your trap to gloat to one single person about what you've done. In short, shut up. Got that? Now get out of here." The blonde guy pointed at the door. "You wait to hear from me."

The dark-haired guy practically ran out of the door.

"And stay out of the bars!" Blondie yelled. He leaned back in his chair and picked up the phone.

"Big problem. I need some help, and Dad can't find out."

Whoever was on the line must have been yelling, because Blondie held the phone away from his ear. After a second, he said, "The guy they pulled from the water worked for us. Keep the cops away from here. In fact, make all of this go away."

After a pause, Blondie said, "I didn't kill him." Another pause. "Thanks, I owe you big for this." He smirked. "Remember, not one word to Dad."

Once he hung up, his phone rang again. He checked the screen and didn't answer. He jumped out of his chair, picked up his jacket, and flew down the stairs.

I hit the rewind button and watched the DVD again. Afterward, I picked up my phone. "Where are you?" I asked when Fab answered.

"I'm on my way home."

"You need to turn around and come to my house. I have something you need to see." I hit the rewind button.

I sat in my overstuffed chair, a favorite of my aunt's. Jazz leaped onto my lap, and we waited for Fab. Twenty minutes later, she walked through the French doors.

I handed her the remote control. "Press *Play*."

She sat in the chair opposite me and watched the tape. "What the hell was that?" Fab asked as she hit rewind. "So trigger-happy didn't even know if Pavel was on to them? This is the smoking gun we needed."

"Do you know the blonde one? The dark-haired guy was the one who hit me on the docks."

"The blond-haired one is Alex Byce, heir apparent. I've never seen the other one before. My guess is if he's smart he's no longer around."

"Who do we give this to?" I asked.

"I think we should hand it over to Kevin. Zach won't like being the last to know, but oh well."

"I thought of Zach as basically a good guy. Now I wonder if he knew about the drugs and looked the other way because Byce is his friend."

"It's more involved than that. When you try to catch a big fish like Byce, you have to cover your bases and check and recheck them. To complicate matters, Sid and Zach are friends."

"As it turns out, it was never Sid Byce, but Alexander," I said.

"Even more complicated, Byce's over-the-top reaction says he either knew about Alexander's involvement or suspected. In the end, will Zach do the right thing?"

"I agree with you. Give it to Kevin," I told Fab.

"What's up with you and Zach anyway?"

"Nothing. Jax kissed me today, and I kissed him back." I sighed.

"Do you want him back?"

"We can't make each other happy. We tried and failed. But I don't want anything bad to happen to him."

"What was today all about?" Fab asked.

"Guilt. I still feel guilty I couldn't fix our marriage."

"Why do we women always blame ourselves?"

"Good question. Jax and I were a lot alike. We had the same interests, the seemingly perfect couple, or so I thought. I loved his family. He introduced me to NASCAR, for which I dumped my old love of football."

"I don't do sports."

I didn't see Fab as a spectator, more like she'd race her own car and crew chief at the same time. "You can stay the night."

"I think I'll drop this DVD off to Kevin. I feel like waking up in my own bed."

"Call me if you hear anything."

Fab stopped and looked at me. "I know that look. What are you up to?"

"I'm going to go ask Joseph tomorrow for the lowdown on Alex."

"You're going to hear he's a big piece of shit," Fab said. "I'll call you tomorrow. I'm serving move-out notices on a flop house building in the morning."

"You're so funny. Be careful."

"The building has a new owner, and his motto is pay or move."

A couple of minutes later, I heard a knock on the door. I wondered what Fab had forgotten, and why she didn't just walk in.

"What did you forget?" I asked to an empty doorstep.

I walked into the courtyard, and chills went up my spine. I turned to hurry back inside and saw a knife stuck in the middle of my door. I looked over my shoulder, then pulled the knife out of the wood, grabbing the note it held before it could fall. Inside the house, I slammed and locked the door.

This is your last warning.

I ran to the kitchen windows and dropped the blinds, and then I moved to the patio doors, closing and locking them. I picked up the side table that hid my floor safe. I opened it and took out a loaded Glock.

I sat at the bottom of my stairs, wondering what to do next. I had no one to call. I knew Fab and I had rattled cages. I'd rushed headlong into danger. So there I sat, gun in my lap.

Chapter Thirty-Six

The next morning, I slid my SUV into a space at the back of the main beach parking lot. I kicked off my shoes and walked the three blocks to The Cottages.

I snuck alongside the garage and cut between two cottages. Turning the corner, I was grabbed from behind, one arm across my chest, another clamped over my mouth. I struggled, and the grip tightened.

"Calm down," a male voice whispered in my ear. "Don't scream." He slowly took his hand away his hand from my mouth. "Why are you sneaking around?"

He loosened his grip and turned me around to face him. Creole smiled down at me. He pushed my back against the side of the cottage, covering my body with his. He wrapped his finger around a strand of my hair. "I like red curls."

My face pressed to his chest, I wanted to run my hands under his shirt and rip it off him. "Let me go." I tried to sound stern. Instead, it came out a throaty whisper, my post-sex, out-of-breath voice.

"You tell me what you're up to, and I'll think about it." He ran a finger across my lips.

"I own this property, and I can come and go as I please."

"I'm disappointed. I thought you'd do better than that."

He reached into my shirt pocket, sending a shock through my breast, and pulled out my cell phone. "In case you ever need my help." He programmed his number and put the phone back in my pocket.

"I always enjoy running into you." He lowered his mouth to mine, and then kissed my cheek and walked away.

I stumbled back against the wall of the cottage, exhaled slowly, and forced myself to breathe. I could still feel the imprints of his hands.

* * *

Joseph's door stood open. "Anyone home?" I called.

Joseph walked out of the bathroom, zipping his shorts. A cigarette was stuck between his lips. "Wanna beer?"

"I want information on Alex Byce." I pushed some newspapers aside and sat down.

"You need to stay away from him. He's an unstable S.O.B." He looked out the door. "Did anyone see you?" He kicked the door shut and threw the bolt.

"Paranoid much?"

Joseph was looking a lot less like death, and his ankles were back to their normal size. He'd gotten sun on his cheeks, giving color to his usual putrid pallor.

"Where's your pimp ride?" he asked, looking out the window.

"It's out there."

"Limo tint, squatty antenna on the back, your ride is as recognizable as your friend's." He stared at me.

"It's over in the main lot."

He looked me over. "From one paranoid to another, you need to do more sneaking around. I like this side of you."

"Can we get back to little Byce?" I asked.

"Your smart mouth needs to stay out of his way."

"I save this mouth for special people."

Joseph rolled his eyes. "He's spoiled. What's his is his, and what's yours is his. He's a poor imitation of the old man; looks are all they have in common. The DNA definitely got watered down in the next generation."

"I need another favor."

"No, no, and no," he yelled. "I'm done. Someone's going to get hurt, and it isn't going to be me."

"Hey, I came through on the dogs, didn't I?"

"Ellie brought me back from a doctor's appointment earlier, and we stopped at Tropical

Slumber. There were no cars in the parking lot, so I went in to see for myself that Astro and Necco were okay."

"And?"

"You did good. Raul was out in the back tossing a Frisbee with them. The dogs were jumping around, having a great time. Dickie seems less weird when he's with Raul, if that makes any sense."

"You're becoming such a softie." I smiled.

"What's the favor?" he grumbled.

"Find out what you can on Alex."

"Hey, I'm not asking one single question to anyone about Alexander Byce. Is that clear enough?"

"Why not?"

"You start with the questions, and you're going to become worm food." He shook his finger at me. "I'll die when I'm good and ready, and it won't be this week."

"I'll think about it."

"Think quick. In the meantime, you'd better learn to walk with one eye looking over your shoulder. Tell me you're going to stop all the questions. Both Byces will find out," he warned. "You're on your own."

"You can't desert me now."

"If you die, I might have to move."

"Don't you want to know what really happened to Pavel?"

"No." He covered his ears with his hands. "La, la, la."

After he stopped chanting, I asked, "Does Alex deal?"

"There's talk, but he doesn't deal at the street level. I'm not saying…" He hesitated. "I've heard when he gets in a shipment, he puts out the call to his distributors, and they show up within the hour. Drugs gone, stacks of cash left behind, business closed."

"That's efficient. If there's talk, why hasn't he been arrested?"

"The family's powerful. The cops will continue to turn a blind eye until they're forced into action by someone at the top of the police food chain."

"Thanks." I stood to leave.

"When are you getting rid of the big butthole next door? After everyone else has moved out?"

"He's gone in two weeks."

"I'm marking my calendar."

Before leaving, I peeked out the window. Seeing no one, I waved at Joseph and slipped outside. I cut around the backside of his cottage, down a small path, and out to the beach.

Chapter Thirty-Seven

"Zach is having me followed," I told Fab. I sat at my kitchen counter with a bowl of caramel ice cream, made healthy by adding fresh raspberries and a touch of whipped cream. The can said only fifteen calories.

"Then this is a bad idea." She picked out one of the raspberries, ran it through the whipped cream, and devoured it.

"It's your job to make it a good one." I had to eat my raspberries fast, or they'd be gone.

"You owe me again."

"Stop with that. Friends don't owe friends."

"I knew this friend thing would come back to bite me."

"Leave, and I'll turn off the lights. Pick me up down by the hourly motel. Make sure you're not followed." I went out the French doors and cut through my neighbor's yard to a narrow pathway that only residents knew about. I kicked off my shoes and ran down the beach.

"News from Kevin," Fab said, as I slid into the passenger seat. "The DVD had an abnormality in it and has been discredited."

"Now what?"

"There's more. Kevin said he was ordered by his superior to stay out of it. Kevin knows we're telling the truth, but he doesn't want to get involved. He lives in this town. In a couple of hours, we'll have all the evidence we need to prove what we're saying. What about your promise to stay out of it?"

"After tonight, I won't drive by these docks every day."

Fab looked at me as if I'd lost my mind. "You come down here every day? Someone had to see you."

"I didn't turn down the one-way road. I parked across the channel and used binoculars."

"What'd you find out, Sherlock?" Fab asked.

"Sarcasm is unnecessary." I paused. "Nothing, but it made me feel like I was doing something. I hate waiting."

"I bet you opened your Christmas presents early."

"You bet I did. I was in college before I dropped that bad habit. What about you?"

Fab looked a little sad. "I didn't bother. I never got what I wanted, anyway. I got what my parents wanted me to want."

"I've had a few of those gifts, and they blow."

"We're parking here and walking back." Fab pointed at a small parking lot in front of a deserted section of the docks. "I'm planting a bug in the phone, and one under his desk." She held up a boat figurine. "This is a camera, so we can listen and watch from my laptop."

"How long will it take?"

"A few minutes. If we get separated, we'll meet back here."

"Let's hope that doesn't happen."

We cut across someone's backyard. Music blared from the opposite corner of the house next to an overgrown vacant lot. I was happy I had changed into sweatpants. They kept the skin on my legs from being ripped off by the waist-high weeds and concealed the Glock holstered at the small of my back. We'd figured out the delivery schedule, and the path where we stood ended at the back corner of the warehouse.

Fab turned the knob on the steel door. I was surprised when the door opened. Fear shot through every muscle as I followed her inside.

The only light in the warehouse came from an office at the back. The door stood open, male voices coming from inside.

"What do we do now?" I whispered.

"I say we get out of here," Fab said.

"Get out of my office," a male voice shouted. "And close the door."

Fab pushed me behind some wooden crates. I stepped into the small space and Fab squeezed in beside me.

Three men armed with automatic weapons walked down the stairs into the main warehouse. "He's an asshole," one of them said. They looked like triplets, dark hair, olive skin, and tattooed. What was it with the wife-beater shirts?

"I'd love to kick his ass, but that'll have to wait for another time." All of them laughed.

One of them hit a switch on the wall. The warehouse roll door started to go up, and all the lights came on. Alex Byce walked out of the office, a watered-down version of his father. Dressed in expensive shorts and a short-sleeved shirt, he looked like someone you'd see on the tennis courts of a country club, not a drug dealer.

A speedboat approached the dock, but it was different from the white one we had seen. It was cranberry-colored and twice the size as the previous one.

"That's not the regular boat," one of the men said.

"Don't worry. I've got this under control." Alex walked out to the dock.

Fab clicked off a couple of pictures with her cell phone.

"Who's that woman over there?" One of them pointed at Fab. They all turned to look. One of them pulled his gun and shot at Fab.

I drew my Glock and shot back, intentionally missing. I only wanted to give us time to get away.

"Run." Fab shoved me.

"Why's Alex getting on the boat?" Another one of them yelled.

"I smell a setup. Let's get the hell out of here." The three men split up and took off in different directions.

Fab disappeared, and I headed straight for an illuminated exit sign down a long corridor. Someone pushed me from behind. "Keep moving. We need to get out of here." Creole grabbed my hand, and we ran to the door. He hit the long silver bar, shoving open the door. The building exploded. Creole and I went flying across the parking lot. I landed face down in the dirt with Creole next to me.

"Are you okay?" Creole asked. He stood up, then picked me up, and set me on my feet. He kissed me gently on the lips, holding my face in his hands. "I've wanted to kiss you for a long time, minus the explosion. Can you walk?"

I demonstrated I could move my arms and legs. Where in the hell had he come from? "I broke all my bones."

He brushed the dirt off my clothes, spit on his fingers, and applied pressure to my cheek. "You're bleeding; expect to feel sore for a few days. You took a hard hit." He tipped my face to his. "Listen to me. Get out of here now, and don't look back."

Tears filled my eyes. "I don't know how."

He gave me a shake. "You can do this. Follow the chain-link fence over there." He pointed to the left. "When you get to the end, you'll see the opening. Squeeze through, and you'll be in a

307

junkyard. There's never anyone around there. Cut straight across and go over the fence; boxes are stacked for you to climb. Once you get to the top, it's a short jump. Go home and mind your own business."

"My Glock is missing," I said. "I don't know what happened."

"You brought a gun to a gunfight?" He smiled. "That's such a turn-on. Don't worry. If it didn't blow up, I'll find it."

"Thank you." I hugged him. "I want to come with you."

"You don't want to be involved. I'm going to collect for this." He gave me a long kiss. "I'll be mad if you hurt yourself. Now go."

Adrenaline propelled me to the fence. Squeezing through wasn't easy; ten pounds more, and I'd have been screwed. Another explosion rocked the ground, followed by a smaller one. Flames ripped through the roof of the warehouse, and sirens blared in the distance. I knew Fab would've gotten out, but she also needed to be one-step ahead of the police. If either of us were caught, what would we say? I didn't know what Creole was doing there, and I didn't care. I was beyond grateful, and I'd keep his secret.

Surrounded by wrought-iron furniture pieces and sky-high piles of old metal cans, I had landed in junk heaven. I spotted an old wrought iron table with chipped white paint, circa 1940. I had to have the table and two of the pink rocking chairs.

A dog barking brought my salivating over the finds to a halt. Or was it more than one? The teeth of the Doberman were the first thing I saw when it rounded an old pile of bicycles. Another one was right behind. Their heads were the size of melons. In front of me, sat an old pontoon boat, surrounded by wooden chicken feeders and mesh fishing traps. I jumped to the top of the pile, hurling myself into the back of the boat. I felt a sharp tug on the back of my tennis shoe, but managed to pull it away. My attacker stood, barking and growling, showing me all of his teeth. The other stood quieter, only letting out the occasional bark. The first dog jumped on the wire cage I had used to get inside the boat. The cage wobbled back and forth. I grabbed one of the old oars piled inside the boat and swung it in the air over his head. He backed up, fell off his perch, and continued to bark.

I reached in my pocket for my phone, but it wasn't there. Attack dog went around to the other side of the boat and jumped on a wooden box in another attempt to gain access. I picked up the oar again and hit the side of the boat to scare the dog. The oar splintered, the pieces landing at the dog's feet. The dog jumped down, sniffed the wood, and sat down. His stare unnerved me, and I was the first to look away.

Darkness wasn't far off. I could see the other

fence from where I stood, but I couldn't possibly outrun the dogs. Screaming seemed futile. My body ached, and the aspirin I had taken earlier had worn off. Frustration overwhelmed me, and I started to cry. I said a short prayer that morning would come quick. I was certain Fab would come looking for me, but how would she know to look in an old junkyard?

My hope was that the dogs would get bored and go back to where they came from, leaving me time to clear the fence. Instead, they settled on the ground, staring up at the boat. I had a bad feeling they were in for the long haul. I sat in the rotted captain's chair. With several oars by my side and the help of the full moon overhead, I could keep an eye on the dogs until they went to sleep. I didn't think it was possible to hurt as much as I did. It hurt to move, to sit still, and to think. My head banged with pain. I didn't want to make a sound for fear of waking the dogs. I wouldn't be able to fight off an attack, if one of them managed to get on board. I fell asleep despite myself, slipped out of the chair and slammed into the deck. Both dogs barked a few times, then lay back down. I gripped a rotted oar just in case.

I sat on the floor in the corner of the boat and watched the beginning stages of daylight appear in the sky. The dogs looked fed and cared for despite their lack of hospitality, so I figured their owner would appear at some point. But how would I explain sleeping in the boat?

"Princess! Duke! Time for breakfast!" a man called.

The dogs jumped up, never looking my way, and ran around a corner and out of sight. I didn't waste time. I grabbed an oar, sucked in my breath, and jumped to the footboard. My left foot missed and sent pain shooting through my body. I grabbed hold of the side bar to keep from falling on my face and slid to the ground.

I paused to listen. Hearing nothing, I ran along the back fence. The crates were exactly where Creole had said they'd be. I stepped on the first one, testing it with my weight. When it appeared to hold, I scurried to the top and climbed down the other side of the fence.

Running across an empty field, I headed for the street. Less than a block away was a convenience store, and I hoped I could get help there. Ignoring my pain, I snuck down the side street that paralleled the main highway, fearful of attracting attention.

A walk that would've normally taken five minutes seemed to take forever as the adrenaline wore off, and I limped along. At least Princess or Duke hadn't been able to take my shoe. The gas station sign was a welcome sight. Finally, I'd get help.

"Gas only. Store's closed," a pimply-faced kid said over the intercom.

"Would you make a local call for me so I can

get a ride home?" I asked.

"There's a pay phone down the street."

"I buy my gas here all the time."

"Are you buying gas now?" He looked at the empty pumps.

"I don't have any money. My purse got stolen. If you could call for me, I'll pay you when my ride gets here." I hoped the stolen purse story would get me some sympathy.

"You need to leave, or I'll call the police." His look told me he thought I was full of it.

"I'll pay you for the call."

"I'm calling the cops." He held up a phone.

The last thing I wanted was to explain to the cops why I was covered in dirt, with cuts, bruises, and dried blood on my arms and legs. I ran across the street, turned down a side street, and doubled back to sit on the porch of an empty house. I watched as a sheriff's car pulled into the parking lot of the convenience store.

"Little prick," I mumbled.

The sheriff parked and got out of his car. The clerk let him inside the store.

I decided to split while the cop was inside the store. I refused to focus on the pain, and instead put my energy into not getting caught. I ran far enough down the street so they couldn't see me crossing the road from inside the store. I ignored the *No Trespassing* sign in the parking lot of a seedy motel, cut across, and walked out onto to the beach. I sat behind a trashcan to catch my breath. No one walking by would see me unless they came very close. I would never make it the mile or so home on the soft sand; I'd need to walk down by the water.

It had been a bad idea to sit down, as getting up was a painful ordeal. My muscles were screaming loudly in protest, and it was hard to ignore the pain. Thankful the beach was deserted at that early morning hour, I waded into the water, took off my top, and used it to wash off the dirt and blood. My shirt was dirty and stained, made even worse when I used it as a washcloth. I put my wet T-shirt back on and rolled up the legs of my sweats.

I walked slowly, forcing myself not to sit down every other step and rest. Finally, the walkway I used from my house to the beach was just up ahead. Home was so close and I was too exhausted and sore to jump up and down or cry.

Chapter Thirty-Eight

I cut through the neighbor's property, a rental, where no one had lived for a while.

"What are you doing lurking around?" a voice said from behind me.

I let out a scream and fell backward.

Mr. Wicker's bony hand shot out and grabbed my arm, pulling me upright. "Well?" He was my eighty-year-old neighbor, who lived on the other side. He always had a smile on his face, probably because he flirted with every woman on the block.

"I'm trying to sneak into my house. I want to find out if it's full of people."

"Your mother's there, that hottie friend of yours, the gangster-looking boyfriend, and some other man."

"How do you know all that?"

"Who needs television when you live next door? Besides, all of them use this side path and go in the back way. Don't they know where the front door is?"

"I used to wonder the same thing. Now I rarely think about it."

"You look like crap."

I glared at him. "It's been a very long night."

"You can't stand out here all day." He smiled. "If you don't want to go home, you can come to my house."

"Thanks for the offer, but I have to face them sometime." I started down the path.

"If you decide you want someone older and more stable, just let me know," he called.

A nosy neighbor could be a disaster, but I didn't have time to worry about Mr. Wicker knowing who came and went from my house. I took a deep breath and tried not to limp as I entered through the French doors.

"I'm home."

My mother, Fab, Zach, and Slice stood around the kitchen island, staring at me as if I were a ghost.

"Madison," Mother shrieked. "We thought you were dead." She crossed the room and hugged me. "Where have you been?" Tears in her eyes.

"Oww," I said. "It's been a long night."

"Glad to see you're okay," Zach said. The look on his face told me that was a big fat lie.

"Don't look so sad, Fabiana. I'm alive."

Fab ran around the island and threw her arms around me. "I would've never forgiven you if you'd died."

"What did you tell them?" I whispered.

"Stop whispering, you two," Zach said. "What the hell happened and where have you been?"

He looked as though he were about to explode.

I turned and gave him a weak smile. "I'm tired. Let's talk later." I wanted to run and hide.

"You…" Zach started.

Slice interrupted. "All of us thought you were dead."

Zach managed to calm down. "We know you were inside Byce's warehouse when it exploded."

I gave them the glossed-over version, not mentioning Creole. "I got trapped on the adjoining property by a couple of guard dogs. It turned into a long wait before they lost interest in me. I was so relieved when someone came to feed the dogs, or I'd still be sitting in a junky old boat. I would've called, but I lost my phone, and I had no money for the payphone. It's a long walk when you're sore."

"What about your promise to let me and my guys do our jobs?" Zach asked through clenched teeth.

"You were right. Is that what you wanted to hear? I'm sorry." My voice dripped with sarcasm. "Excuse me, I'm going to take a shower and a nap. You can let yourselves out." I didn't care how rude I sounded.

"Madison Westin, you stop right there," Mother demanded. "We were all worried about you."

"I'm very sorry that I worried you for a single second." I smiled at my mother. "I'm fine. Does anyone know why the warehouse blew up and if anyone was hurt?"

"Two people are dead. Tony Carlos and Juan Pablo, workers at the warehouse, set it to blow and didn't know what they were doing. They blew themselves up with their own handiwork," Fab said.

"What about Alex?" I asked.

"Sid Byce told the police his son was on a fishing trip in the Bahamas." Zach shook his head. "The explosion was ruled an accident."

"Two dead people and it's an accident? That's convenient," I said.

"Sid Byce found out he was being investigated for trafficking," Zach said. "He thought he had the situation under control, and when he realized he was out of time, he took matters into his own hands, shut down the drug operation, and exiled Alexander."

"What about Pavel's murder?" I asked.

"The shooter, Tony Carlos, died in the explosion," Zach said.

"You put your life on the line for someone you didn't even know," Mother said angrily.

"I didn't intentionally put my life on the line for anyone. Wrong place, very wrong time. Who knew Alex was as crazy as he turned out to be? Very convenient he had a boat waiting, and all the evidence was blown sky high."

"Did you think about Brad and me when you were risking your life?" Mother asked.

"There was a risk factor that I didn't take seriously. In the beginning, it was about our family and clearing Jax. Then, it became about Pavel. He didn't deserve to be shot to death by drug-dealing scum. No one gave a damn about who paid for Pavel's murder."

"How would your dying have helped Pavel?" Mother asked.

"Dying wasn't part of the plan. I was frustrated that no one seemed to be seriously investigating Pavel's murder. Jax was the designated scapegoat. I asked Zach for help, and all he did was make up lies because he felt compelled to protect me from myself. Which was more important than putting the real murderer in jail."

"I found out through a friend that the Feds were investigating, and I decided not to say anything," Zach said. "I couldn't take the chance you would tell anyone else. Local authorities weren't in the loop because of the influence of the Byce family. The quantities were huge, and Alex was reckless and looking at being charged with an assortment of felonies."

"If you had told me the Feds were investigating, tonight might've ended differently."

"I didn't trust you to keep your mouth shut. You'd never resist telling Fab." Zach glared at me.

I sucked in my breath at the insult. "Will Alex

ever get arrested?"

"He would've if the Feds had gotten to the warehouse before it blew," Zach said. "All the evidence was lost in the explosion. They knew Alex had taped everything that went on there. He had also received a shipment that he didn't have time to distribute. The plan was to arrest him, the warehouse workers, and all the salesmen that showed up for their product."

"Any chance of using the tape Fab gave to Kevin?" I asked Zach.

"It's handled," Zach said.

"What does that mean?" I asked. "At the very least, it shows that Alex Byce was an accessory after the fact to murder."

Zach stared me down. "Like I said."

I really disliked Zach at that moment and wondered if it was the end for us.

"I, for one, am very happy that you're alive," Fab said.

Zach wasn't about to be derailed. "Sid Byce might be ruthless in business, but he doesn't deal drugs and wants nothing to do with them. I respect the man. He doesn't deserve to have everything he worked for trashed by his worthless son."

"You respect him? Well, your good buddy threatened me," I said. "He didn't want any interference with his plan to frame an innocent person. If it weren't for Fab, he might've hurt me."

"Byce liked Pavel and wanted the case solved. He went about it in a heavy-handed way, but he knew about the plea bargain. In the end, he backed off the case because it was the right thing to do."

"At least we know what happened," I said.

"I need a break. I can't be on call to save you from yourself," Zach said.

I gave a sarcastic chuckle. "A break from what? We don't have a relationship; we have sex."

"Really, Madison, I don't want to know that," Mother said.

"It's an ungrateful job, especially when you can't be counted on to do what you're told," Zach said.

I stared at him for a long moment. "I'm sorry I worried all of you and that you thought for one moment I was dead. I promise not to take any silly chances in the future." I hugged my mother, went upstairs, and locked myself in the bathroom.

Chapter Thirty-Nine

My phone rang on the way to the courthouse in Miami.

"Can you afford for your husband to jump bail?" Joseph asked.

"No." I took a deep breath. "What's going on?"

"He's not showing up for court today. He's packed and ready to run to Mississippi with Apple."

I slapped the steering wheel. "You're out of your mind. He doesn't know anybody there."

"Apple has some family there. She called them last night, and they're fine with hiding a fugitive. There's a trailer out in the woods waiting for them. They're still here, waiting on their ride."

I hung a U-turn in the middle of the highway, almost skidding sideways off the road. "I owe you."

"Now that's what I wanted to hear. We'll negotiate after you deal with lover boy."

"I'm on my way. Do not let him leave. If you have to, throw yourself in front of the car and fake your death."

"You'll owe me big if I have to get on the ground," he grumbled.

I realized I should've made Jax spend the night at my house, but he'd said he wanted to party on his last night of freedom. If those people who thought I drove like an old woman could only see me now. I stomped on the accelerator, flew down the Overseas Highway, and careened off at my exit. I pulled into the driveway of The Cottages, slammed on the brakes, and tried not to run to Jax's door. My best bet was to feign ignorance of his flight plans.

I turned the doorknob and was frustrated to find it locked. I wanted to bang on the door as if there were six Feds waiting to drag his butt away, but I knocked politely.

Robert opened the door just enough to step outside, then closed it behind him. "What's up?"

"Get out of the way. I need to talk to Jax."

"He left for the courthouse about fifteen minutes ago."

"Take a look at my shoes." I motioned toward my feet. "These are my most pointy black pumps, and if you don't move, I'm going to kick you so hard you'll limp for a week."

He moved his hand downward and stepped away from the door. "He's just scared," he whispered.

The place was trashed and reeked of weed. Apple flicked her cigarette into a bowl of water on the table in front of her. Jax, dressed in a suit, sat in a chair, drinking that sweet liqueur he liked so much.

"Come on. I'm driving you to the courthouse," I told Jax.

"I'm not going to jail." He downed a second shot.

"You got a sweet deal, and you're going to throw it away and live on the run with Apple? That is the stupidest of your many stupid ideas," I said. "You'll get caught, and then what? Hardcore prison time, that's what."

"They're not going to come looking for me, now that the damn murder case has been closed."

I rolled my eyes. "Florida extradites for jaywalking."

"You don't understand," he whined.

"You're right. I don't." I took a breath to stay calm. "I arranged for your bail with a bondsman. Do you care if I lose The Cottages?"

"I'm sorry. This property can't be more important than my life."

The door opened, and a skinny, longhaired, twenty-something stoner stood in the entryway. "Hey, dude, your ride's here."

"Just let Jax go," Apple pleaded. "We'll be happy with my family."

"If you cared for him at all, you wouldn't be encouraging him to take off," I said, disgusted.

"You live around here?" I asked the skinny stoner.

He looked me over and smiled. "Yeah."

"Do you know Spoon?"

His eyes narrowed. "What's it to you?"

"I'll take that as a yes. You give a ride anywhere to this man here," I pointed at Jax, "I'll call Spoon and tell him. He'll be very unhappy."

The stoner looked at Jax. "Sorry, dude, I gotta go. Good luck." He ran out the door, not bothering to close it behind him.

"What the hell did you do that for?" Jax yelled.

"Get your jacket, and let's go. You don't want to be late for court."

"I'm not going."

"Leave your suitcases here and I'll come back for them and keep them until you get out," I said.

Jax poured himself another shot.

I threw my arm across the table, sending the bottle and the shot glass flying. "You either ride with me, or you can ride with Brick's two men who are sitting across the street."

Robert came back in. "What's going on?"

"Jax and I are leaving," I said.

"Can Robert ride with us?" Jax asked.

Robert answered, "Don't worry, I got Apple and me a ride. We'll see you there."

* * *

In the courtroom, I sat next to Jax and held his hand so he couldn't get away without a scene.

Finally, the bailiff called Jax's name, and he went before the judge with Tucker and pled guilty. The judge sentenced him to six months and a fine. The sheriff walked him into the jury box where Jax took off his jacket and his belt, handing them to me. He had given me his wallet and keys in the car.

"I don't have the right to ask, but would you come visit?" he whispered.

"I'll think about it," I said, overwhelmed with sadness.

The sheriff put Jax in cuffs and took him away. If he hadn't been led away into the holding cell at that moment, I'd have started crying.

Tucker came up beside me. "You have shit taste in husbands. I know it was you that bailed him out. I figured Jax would run. Too bad, I would've had a good laugh if he'd left you owing money or better yet forfeiting property."

I glared at him. "You have a nice day."

I walked into the hallway where Robert and Apple stood by the window. Apple was crying. I hadn't noticed before, but she was drunk. I should have reported her to the sheriff and watched while she got arrested. The thought made me smile.

Robert looked at me. "I know. I'll be out of the cottage by tonight."

"What's next for you?"

"I'm going to hang around, wait for Jax to get out of jail. I got a job at Lipstick at their

Homestead location. I hooked with up a dancer, and I'm moving in with her."

"What about Apple?"

"She and Jax only decided last night that they were running. She'd already met some old guy at the Croc who said he'd take her in as long as she cooked, kept his trailer clean, and blew him."

"Isn't that what every man wants?"

Robert looked at Apple. "No."

"Good luck," I said and walked away. With more luck, I'd never see Robert or Apple again.

I walked down to the first floor to the court clerk's office. I stood in line and filed the dismissal of Jax's lawsuit against me. I breathed a deep sigh of relief. I wouldn't want to be Ann, Tucker's assistant, the day the papers arrived in the mail. It would be her job to give them to him.

Watching a person you once loved go to jail was depressing. All the what-ifs made me incredibly sad. Jax was smart, had potential for three people, and when he got out, I hoped he would conquer his biggest demon, alcohol, and maybe life would start going his way.

Fab lay on my couch, watching a game show and yelling the answers at the screen. "Where have you been?"

"The courthouse. I honestly had my doubts I'd ever get Jax there, but it happened. Now he's a guest of the county for the next four months, and I won't have to worry what's next."

"Forget any promises you made and do what you want," Fab said.

"Life isn't that easy for some of us. I'm a woman of my word. When I give it, I honor it."

"Moron called. The boat's done; he and Jax finished late yesterday. He's taking it to storage for you. Harder signed the release as soon as the plea was in the works. Seems Harder was being super cooperative because he needed his jet ski fixed."

"I'm happy the boat got finished before Brad got back. Hopefully, it'll be a nice surprise, and we can put everything behind us."

"I'm surprised you're storing it in the same place," Fab said.

"We added a layer of security so that when Jax gets out of jail, he can't *borrow* it again."

"What happens when Jax does get out?" Fab asked.

"We talked about that, and he's going back home. He has a great family, and they love him. By then, Robert will have been fired for one stupid thing or another, and they'll both leave."

"I almost forgot. Moron said he'd drop off the keys and the final bill. He said he'd take you out for a ride any time you want."

"I don't think so. I won't be ready for that for a long while, if ever."

"Pavel didn't actually die on the boat," Fab said.

"It'll never be the same, though. So the

consensus is that Pavel jumped overboard as a big joke, or because he was mad at his girlfriend. He somehow managed to swim to shore, despite his blood alcohol level. Because he was in the wrong place at the wrong time, he got shot. That just sucks." I shook my head. "His murderer blowing himself up saves the state a few bucks on an execution. One guy kills another, and look at the ripple effect on the lives impacted."

"The only loose end is Alexander Byce," Fab said.

"Rich man's justice."

"He's under his father's control now, which could be a prison of sorts. I understand his exile is permanent."

I put my face in my hands. "Long day." I sighed.

Fab clicked off the television. "I brought my bathing suit. Let's go for a swim."

* * *

I pulled the rafts out of the storage box beside the pool and threw them into the water. "I'm sorry I bailed on you last night. I didn't want to deal with everyone, so I took the easy way out."

"I thought it was funny. Zach and your mother wanted to yell at you some more, and, of course, grill you with more questions. They were a frustrated bunch when you went upstairs." Fab laughed.

"You should've come upstairs after everyone left."

"I did, because I had questions of my own, but you were already asleep."

"So how mad was everyone?" I asked.

"I told them they were disgusting. They were grief-stricken when they thought you were dead, and when you weren't dead, they couldn't wait to gang up on you. I also told them you had a mind of your own, and none of them were going to keep you from using it."

"I bet that went over big."

"I want to apologize to you," Fab said. "I honestly thought you were behind me when I left the building. When I got out and turned around, you weren't there. I about had a heart attack. In the next second, the building blew up." Fab's eyes filled with tears. "I stood there in shock until I heard the sirens."

I splashed water on her. "I'm here now."

"I wouldn't have been able to live with the guilt if you had died. I wouldn't have had another friend in your memory."

"You're catching on to this friend thing." I smiled. "Thank you for always having my back and never once bailing on me."

"Back at you. How did you get out? I didn't know which way you went or how we got separated."

"I saw an exit sign and headed straight for it. Out of nowhere, a man grabbed my arm and pulled me down the long hallway to the door. He kicked the door open, and in the next instant, the building exploded."

"Who was the guy?" Fab asked.

"I didn't ask his name."

Fab narrowed her eyes. "Why do I think there's more to the story?"

"Do we tell each other everything?" I asked.

"I'll have to get back to you on that one."

Chapter Forty

No one knocked on the front door except my mother and brother. I wasn't in the mood, but the knocking was incessant.

I opened the front door, and Creole grinned down at me. "I hear you've been asking around about me."

"I, uh, no…" I stammered. His mere presence had me thinking indecent thoughts. His face was bruised and scratched from our dirt roll. Without thinking, I ran my finger across the largest bruise on his cheek.

"I'm here to collect this." He pushed me up against the wall and kicked the front door closed. Tracing a trail with the tip of his tongue down my chin, down my neck, nibbled lightly, sending shivers through my body. Taking me by surprise, he backed me against the front door, pushing my hands above my head, holding them in place while devouring my lips.

A red light went off in my head that what was happening might not be a good idea. "I can't do this. I have a boyfriend."

"Damn. I was looking forward to stripping you naked."

"I've already gone too far."

He put his arm around me and pulled me into the kitchen. "How about a cup of coffee?"

I knew Zach was mad at me, but I wasn't ready for us to be over. Making coffee gave me a moment to catch my breath and think before I crossed a line that would change our relationship forever.

Creole sat at the kitchen island with a mug of coffee in front of him. He grabbed my hand and pulled me around in front of him. "I hope this is not where I have to apologize for taking advantage of you."

I laughed, releasing the tension. "No, no apology."

"Good. I'm starving. Do you cook?"

"I can put a frozen waffle in the toaster."

"I'll stick with the coffee." He picked up his mug.

"You said I was asking around about you. I didn't tell anyone you pulled me out of the warehouse. I figured it was the least I could do, since you made sure I didn't blow up along with everything else."

"I didn't find out until late yesterday that you were missing and presumed dead. Then I heard you turned up alive. If I'd known you were missing, I would've gone looking for you immediately."

"Look what I found." He pulled my Glock and cell phone from his waistband.

"Where did you find them?"

"About a foot away from where we landed. Your gun works fine. I can't say the same for your cell phone."

"Thank you. I'm glad you found them. The explanation as to how they were found at the warehouse explosion would have been a huge problem."

He laughed. "Did you know I used to live here?"

"Here? When was that?" Elizabeth had owned the house a very long time. My guess was that he was around my age, in his early thirties.

"Lived might be misleading. I stayed here on and off during my childhood. The only real home I had. Maybe we should do this like normal people." He took my hand and kissed it, bringing back great sweaty memories. "I'm Luc Baptiste. I heard you've been asking questions."

I blinked my eyes in surprise. "I've been looking for you. And was close to giving up. And Creole is?"

"My street name."

"Street name?"

"Take a deep breath. I'll start from the beginning, and you'll see that you're safe with me."

I topped off his coffee. "That would be a good idea."

"I grew up several houses down with my mean drunk of a father. I learned at an early age if he couldn't find me when he got home, he'd get bored and pass out. I took to hiding out in your aunt's garden shed and spent many a night out there. Until Liz caught me."

"What did she do?" I knew without a doubt she'd have ridden over hot coals for an abused little boy or girl.

"She trapped me in the shed one day and forced me to listen to her. I'd never been that scared before or since. I knew I was headed straight to jail, and my father would find out."

"I bet neither of those things happened."

"She surprised me when she told me she'd been watching me for a couple weeks while I used her shed and swam in the pool so I'd be clean for school. She talked me into coming into the house, and she cooked me breakfast. She then informed me that there were rules for staying at her house, and they didn't include sleeping in the shed. I'll take one of your home-cooked waffles."

"Coming right up. I have the best raspberry jam." I popped the waffles in the toaster. "What about your father?"

"She kept my secret, and he never found out. When I got to be fifteen and could defend myself, he stopped beating on me. After that, I spent all my time here."

"I wish I'd known all about this from her."

"Liz protected me. Her finding me was the best day of my life. She hid a key on the back patio, and when I needed to escape, I came here and slept in the guest bedroom. I had a place to sleep, all the food I could eat, and she encouraged me to make something out of my life. She told me I was smart and could be whatever I wanted."

"She was good that way," I said, tears in my eyes. "Why didn't Brad and I ever meet you?"

"I was shipped to Grandma's every summer. There was work to be done, and I was the family workhorse. The food there sucked. Breakfast was the worst. It consisted of toast swimming in coffee with milk, and do you know why? Because the dog liked it that way."

I shook my head. "That's disgusting."

"After high school, I went into the Army. They paid for my college, and then I went into Special Forces. Your aunt encouraged me to dream big, and I did. When my third tour was up, I didn't reenlist."

"How does your living at The Cottages fit in?"

"I don't actually live there. I use it as cover for my current job. Liz rented it to me when I started working the Byce case. I'm a DEA agent out of the Miami office."

"Did my aunt know?"

"I didn't have any secrets from Liz. I loved her like a mother."

"I was trying to find you. I asked a few people. All of them said they'd never heard of you. I even asked a skip tracer to run a report, but I never heard back."

"What were you going to tell me?"

"My aunt left several envelopes to be delivered to special people in her life, and yours was the last. I felt guilty that I might never find you."

"Four days before she died, we had lunch down in Marathon Key at a seafood dive. She looked good to me. I replay that lunch over and over in my mind as though there were something I missed, and if I'd noticed, I could've saved her, and I wanted to save her."

I covered his hand with mine. "I didn't see you at the funeral."

"I was there. I watched from the back. No one noticed me because the funeral was such a circus. I thought she deserved better. I was angry at your family for a long time, until I heard Tucker was the one who had planned everything."

"Why haven't you introduced yourself?"

He put his mug in the dishwasher. "I've been on the Byce drug-running ring for more than a year now. I couldn't jeopardize my undercover status. In my line of work, you never take the chance that you can trust someone. It took me a while to figure out that you hold a lot of people's secrets close."

"Now a few of yours." I smiled. "After all that,

Alexander gets away, and your case blows up."

"Not quite. Late last night, Alexander was taken into custody. By now, Daddy Byce must know we have his progeny in jail, and that's where he'll stay for awhile anyway."

"That's great. How did that happen?" I asked.

"We had him under surveillance in the Caribbean, and for whatever reason, he came back on his own. Once he set foot on United States soil, we had him."

"I didn't think he was that stupid."

His eyes turned steely. "The rich think they can write the rules however they want."

"I heard all the evidence blew up."

"Right before the building blew, I lifted the surveillance DVD's from his office. When I came down the stairs, I saw you and your cohort take off in different directions. I tossed the back pack to one of my partners and went after you." He laughed. "Do you know how many times we showed up in the same place? At first it was funny, and then not so much."

"I was warned more than once to stay out of everything. People tell me I don't listen very well."

"That's a shock." He rolled his eyes.

"At first I wanted to clear my ex-husband for selfish reasons and to get rid of him. What about Pavel? No one mentioned his name after the novelty of his dead body being plucked from the water wore off."

"Byce carries a lot of weight around here and isn't bashful about working his connections. And he employs a lot of your neighbors."

"Do you think Sid Byce was totally oblivious?"

"For the most part. We believe he was tipped off that we were hours away from a raid. I'd bet hard cash Sid arranged for the warehouse to be blown up. Proving that is another matter since everyone died and he has an alibi."

"What about his spawn?"

"We tried to pressure Alexander into talking, but the first words out of his mouth were 'I want to call my lawyer.' His five-thousand-dollar-an-hour lawyer told him to keep his mouth shut, and he did."

"Will there be any charges related to Pavel?" I asked.

"He's the casualty in all of this. Shooter's dead and we have nothing that links Alexander to the murder."

"A disk was mailed to me, and it shows Tony Carlos confessing to Alexander that he killed Pavel. Pavel was peeing in the wrong place at the wrong time. Tony didn't ask any questions, he just shot him. The disk was turned over to local police."

"I'm going to get that disk. Tighten the screws on that smug punk."

"That's a nice thought."

"I was across the canal the night that bastard

Carlos took a swing that sent you into the water. I knew there was no way I could get to you before you drowned. I really felt like I'd let Liz down again, and then you surfaced and took cover until they stopped looking for you. Good job. Just to let you know, that guy would've disappeared, never to be found."

"Worm food?"

He laughed. "Who've you been hanging with?"

"I protect my sources. There's something you should be made aware of."

He leveled his gaze at me. "What?"

"Elizabeth left me all of her IOUs from you."

"No, she didn't."

"I have it in writing. And…"

"There's more? I'm going to need to see proof."

I laughed. "I'm happy that we've been officially introduced."

He stood up and wrapped his arms around me. "I'm leaving before I make another attempt to wiggle you out of your clothes." He lightly kissed my lips.

"Friends? You're welcome here anytime. I'd like to introduce you to Brad." I walked into the living room, lifted the lid on a wood box that a high school boyfriend had carved for Elizabeth and pulled out the envelope, handing it to him.

"One more thing." He opened the front door. "If you break up with the bf, I'm your first call."

I laughed. "You'd be just what the doctor would prescribe."

He leaned in, kissed me, and disappeared down the drive.

* ~ *

PARADISE SERIES NOVELS

Crazy in Paradise
Deception in Paradise
Trouble in Paradise
Murder in Paradise
Greed in Paradise
Revenge in Paradise
Kidnapped in Paradise
Swindled in Paradise
Executed in Paradise
Hurricane in Paradise
Lottery in Paradise
Ambushed in Paradise
Christmas in Paradise
Blownup in Paradise
Psycho in Paradise
Overdose in Paradise
Initiation in Paradise
Jealous in Paradise
Wronged in Paradise
Vanished in Paradise
Fraud in Paradise
Naïve in Paradise

Deborah's books are available on Amazon
amazon.com/Deborah-Brown/e/B0059MAIKQ

About the Author

Deborah Brown is an Amazon bestselling author of the Paradise series. She lives on the Gulf of Mexico, with her ungrateful animals, where Mother Nature takes out her bad attitude in the form of hurricanes.

For a free short story, sign up for my newsletter. It will also keep you up-to-date with new releases and special promotions: www.deborahbrownbooks.com

Follow on FaceBook: facebook.com/DeborahBrownAuthor

You can contact her at Wildcurls@hotmail.com

Deborah's books are available on Amazon

amazon.com/Deborah-Brown/e/B0059MAIKQ

Made in the USA
Coppell, TX
04 March 2021

51257506R00192